To my very special friend

# Margaret Annetts

"Oh, what a tangled web we weave...
when first we practice to deceive."
**— Walter Scott**

With my thanks as always to Paul Mellor corrections.

*1*

1984 – Nottingham

There was a new element in Doug Pedley's life and one that meant he didn't have to get up and piss three or four times a night: heroin delivered by a needle. It wasn't cheap, but neither was 11 or 12 pints every night. He had been wondering what might happen if he tried to bargain down the price as one of his mates had done, and got his answer in the report that the friend would be in hospital for some weeks following an unfortunate accident. So he learned not to mess with these boys.

Not long before, the Tories under Mrs Thatcher had come into power. There were rumours that her own party wanted rid of her already, but Doug thought she had stickability and therefore he feared for his job as a fitter in a copper factory in Beeston. A skilled man who had served an apprenticeship, but now even skilled men were being discarded in the process of what was called rationalisation – being chucked on the dole on a "last in, first out" basis. It couldn't be long before they reached him. And what would he do for money then?

The current woman he lived with, Beatty Epton, earned what little she brought in as a tart – he had no illusions about that. She had a 10-year-old daughter, Ella, who would probably follow her mother into the same profession. Doug's sexual fantasy was a threesome with mother and daughter – he couldn't give a toss that she was only 10 and anyway she looked older.

Once redundancy came, there was money from his pay-off, some of which he put straight into the pocket of the bookie by trying to invest it on the horses and failing as fast as the horses fell.. The rest went on a new motor of which he was very proud. But then he needed money for the heroin or brown sugar as he called it. He always laughed when he thought of how the Rolling Stones had a song of that name, and most people did not know what it was actually all about!

He dreaded not being able to score and had heard terrible stories of what happened to those coming off – known as cold turkey, something he knew he couldn't bear. And this was where the idea came to sell Ella. He was pretty sure there would be no end of takers for a young girl. Her mother was open to the idea, confirming in Doug that she too was needing money for whatever she was on, and when he mentioned it, she was not even against joining in as a threesome, provided the man paid up. Doug said he would make sure of that. And Doug had a further idea for increasing revenue in the form of a concealed camera in the room. Why had he not thought of this before? Ella's screams seemed to excite the punters, and some hit her to shut her up which seemed to stimulate them even more.

In the summer holidays, a woman further down the street, seeing how well-dressed and apparently grown-up she was, asked Ella if she could look after her two small children for a couple of hours while she went for a job interview? Ella was more than happy to help. They were a four-year-old boy, Peter, and his three-year-old sister, Anna.

'Let's play a game,' she had said as she removed their clothes. She then sought to insert various objects into the vagina and anus of the little girl, and the anus of the boy. What she could not do was stop them screaming and crying, and so ran a bath in which they were later found to be dead, drowned.

Ella was taken into custody, but so also her mother and Doug, and would be tried separately. Being 10 years old and so just over the age of legal responsibility, Ella was charged with murder. Detectives had seen nothing like this and though they knew of similar cases, such as that of Mary Bell in Newcastle, they found it extremely difficult to deal with. Those who spoke with Ella found it uncomfortable that she could speak with no remorse or sense that she might have done wrong. She was also totally open about what had been going on at home and the part she had played in making money for the three of them. She even seemed proud of her abilities. The police spoke of her as the "little monster".

She was seen by psychiatrists and doctors who noted the amount of bruising on her body which she reported without dissembling as caused by some of the men who had used her. The forensic psychiatrist who had come from London to see her, reported he had never encountered any child whose mind was as totally distorted by her experiences as Ella's. and thought it would take a very long time for her to recover, if ever.

The Press, locally and nationally, interviewed everyone who knew Ella and paid for any photos and did exposés on what had been happening in the "house of horrors", though despite financial inducements they could persuade none of the men who had visited to come forward even with the promise of anonymity.

The Police, however, were more hopeful about discovering the identity of some of these men in their conversations with Doug, who they believed when he said he had not engaged in sexual relations with Ella (as she had confirmed) and he hoped that by giving them some names, it might prove a bargaining tool. He still got 20 years, as did Ella's mother.

Ella was taken to a small village near Lancaster, where, unknown to the residents of the community, there was a well-concealed special house adapted for the maximum security of a young person. Quite what the neighbours would have thought or done if they had known that within yards of where they lived, the "little monster" was being held on remand, hardly bore thinking. The village police officer didn't even know, and the only ones going in or out were two people from the social services, a psychiatrist and two house mothers responsible for her daily welfare. She would be here eleven weeks and her trial would take place in Nottingham Crown Court before Mr Justice Fletcher.

Ella was sad to be leaving her village retreat, as she had enjoyed the house very much and had got to know the two house mothers well. The journey to Nottingham seemed endless. She was taken into the courtroom on the day before her trial to familiarise herself, an outing amidst maximum security, before she was returned to her cell. Many people to this day recall the local newspaper headline published on the day of the trial's beginning: "Let her hang".

Ella's barristers, who had travelled up to see her in the village near Lancaster, had agreed with her that when the moment came, she should plead guilty to manslaughter on the grounds of diminished responsibility. There was quite a stir in the court when she did so, but her chief barrister argued that what had happened was caused by the terrible abuse that her parents and some other men, many of whom had now been charged with sodomy and sexual intercourse with a child, were the real villains. At the time these terrible events took place, Ella did not know what was going on, and how could she?

The Prosecution wished to do away with excuses, and insisted that at ten years of age, any child knew it was wrong to kill. He said that the people of the country would not be satisfied with a verdict that seemed to imply nobody had done anything wrong, because the people of the country knew the truth full well.

Expert witnesses were all on the side of her defence, though each had to withstand the assaults of the prosecution that they were nothing more than mealy mouthed liberals who could not tell the difference between right and wrong themselves. The barrister prosecuting completed his summing up by saying that this case was a clear cut example of murder, and that if members of the jury swallowed the permissive nonsense of the defence, the consequences for our society were considerable because there could no longer be right and no longer be wrong.

The judge was more measured in his own summing up of the evidence presented. He explained at some length the difference between murder and manslaughter. He drew attention to the absence of Ella's parents in the court, the result of their abuse of Ella in such an appalling way. Eventually, he sent the jury out.

Ella had understood very little of what going on despite having been with a nice woman court official appointed to help her. She couldn't fathom where the jury and the judge had gone, and wondered when the trial was over what would happen to her. She hoped she might return to the house near Lancaster, though the lady with her did not know.

The jury did not return for almost three hours and when asked for their verdict, the foreman indicated they had found her guilty of manslaughter by diminished responsibility. There was immediate uproar from the family of the dead children and their supporters and the judge had the public gallery cleared, allowing him to comment and pass sentence. His main concern was that Ella should spend time in a context in which she could grow and develop and understand what she had done, the issues of right and wrong not yet grasped, for which he wished her to receive continuous psychiatric care and treatment, and only when those caring for her were clear that she could safely return to society, would her release be possible. The sentence therefore was that she be detained at her majesty's pleasure. She was taken that night to a Secure Unit in a Children's Home where her only visitors were the officials appointed to see her. The judge had granted her lifelong anonymity, and she was now Amy Lewis.

The details that emerged in court meant that there was a drop-off in the interest of the Press in her – the hounding of Mary Bell went on, not least because her repulsive mother earned money by leaking information to the Press. Any's mother was locked up and Amy had already decided that if her mother was released, she did not want her whereabouts to be given to her.

In the home, she worked quite hard and would almost certainly have done well in her GCSEs had the Home Office not moved her at fifteen to an adult women's prison. The thoughtlessness of this had a detrimental effect on her and in the prison she found herself in trouble several times, learning bad ways from her fellow inmates, who did not know who she was. At eighteen she was moved once again, this time to an open women's prison from where two years later she was released. There had been the normal pre-release course, but her needs were considerably greater, and no help was given regarding handling the press. She went to live in an ex-prisoner's hostel in Hull and got a job in a local library. One evening on her way from work to the hostel she was attacked, and an attempt made to tear her clothes off, but Amy's days in prison had not been wasted and she had learned some self-defence which, when applied with fury such as she now felt, left the man knocked out by a brick which had come to her hand as they fought. To her dismay, the police charged her with Actual Bodily Harm. In those days before computers, she carried with her always a document from the courts in Nottingham revealing her identity and the guarantee of anonymity.

'It's the Little Monster herself,' said one of the detectives interviewing her. 'Still seeking to kill. It's back to prison for you and this time I hope you rot there.'

This would undoubtedly have taken place on the following morning, but when she was arrested she was, as is the custom, allowed one phone call, and there was a number on her document which she had been told she must ring if ever she needed immediate help. There was a code she had to use and give the location of where she was being held.

It took only 90 minutes for something to happen. The Chief Constable unexpectedly appeared and said he wished to see Amy Lewis alone. At once he recognised from the state of her clothing that almost certainly she had been attacked, as she had claimed, and at once dropped all the charges against her. A taxi was summoned to take her back to the hostel, but now her time here was over. The police knew her identity and therefore soon everyone else would. The Little Monster was working in a public library and the police talking on every street corner.

The Home Office advisor found her a small flat in Lowestoft on the Suffolk coast which, with her savings and a job waitressing, she just about afforded. By this time she was Joan Stafford and it was as Joan that she became friends with one man with whom she worked, which in turn led to her moving in with him. He wanted marriage, but she had said nothing about her past and true identity, both of which would emerge in the legalities of a marriage. She was now pregnant and said she would change her surname to his to give the impression of being married, if he wished. But he did not wish and one day, whilst she was out, went through all her private papers and discovered the truth that he was living with the Little Monster. Immediately, he was fearful for the unborn child she was carrying. Would she kill this one too?

'I was ten,' she told him when he confronted her with his knowledge, 'and I had been subject to horrendous sexual abuse from adult men. I know I brought about the deaths of those children, but I did not know what I was doing. When I think about it, I am as sick and horrified as everyone else by what I did.'

'You should have told me.'

'How and when? Should I have mentioned it during our lunch break at work: "Oh, I forgot to mention, I killed two children, and did you see the football results?"'

'I think you should move out.'

'What, all of me, including the part that's getting bigger every day and for which you played a small part?'

'When it's born, I'm going to make sure it's not left in your care.'

'Our baby is not an it, and he or she will be loved in a way that I never was.'

'I'm going to a solicitor in the morning to find out my rights.'

'Fine. Tell him to look it up under "Little Monsters, How to deal with".

The solicitor was of little help other than advising a divorce before discovering they were not married, and then said the law would be on the side of the mother when the baby was born unless neglect could be proved.

By the time he arrived home from work that evening she had gone and had done so with a new name and no clue left behind as to her whereabouts. Alice Watts moved to a 2-roomed flat in Ipswich and prepared to give birth. Katia was born in Ipswich with no father named or present, but Alice didn't mind in the slightest. She would care for Katia by herself and she wouldn't want for anything, especially love. She had a job as a waitress in the Marks and Spencer café but spoke very little to her colleagues and they all thought her somewhat stuck up. Not that she minded that. What was more disturbing was an overheard conversation in the café one morning when a customer spoke to another about trying to track down the "little monster", the child killer. He had heard a rumour that she might be living in Ipswich.

As soon as she got home, she made contact with her control at the Home Office, and she set in motion the arrangements whereby she would move to a small house in Saxmundham. Nothing further was heard from whoever it was doing the tracking.

Katia continued to attend her school in Ipswich and again Alice got jobs waitressing and cleaning, and continued to keep herself to herself.

## 2

However well-laid, our schemes have a tendency to go awry, as was noted in the eighteenth century by the poet Robbie Burns. Jo had been expecting a new career as a psychotherapist and was devastated when her application was turned down. The interviewers thought she needed more time away from the police force so she could un-learn some of the ways of working with people she took for granted, but Jo thought they were also uneasy offering a place to anyone called *Dame* Joanne, an example of what she thought might be inverse snobbishness.

Then came a further bolt from the blue when she received a letter from the Home Office that she could not continue to do her job as Detective Chief Superintendent part-time. Either she returned to full-time duties or they would reluctantly accept her resignation, knowing full-well, that the house she shared with her son Ollie went with the job.

Then the plan for Dani to leave her job as Chief Constable and come to live with Jo, fell through when lawyers for Greater Manchester Police Combined Authority and the Mayor pointed out to her she had a contract which still had four years to run, and if she broke the contract, they would be obliged to sue. This information, which she received on the day she was planning to leave Manchester for Suffolk, halted her progress.

Finally, one evening there was a knock on the door and Jo opened it to find Marie standing there with Josie. They looked terrible and as Marie crossed the threshold, she collapsed in tears and held on to Jo for grim life.

'Are you here by yourself?' asked Marie in a broken voice.

'Just Ollie and me.'

'What about Dani?'

'Not unless she's hiding.'

'Oh Jo, my dearest, dearest darling, I have been so stupid. I turned my back on the most wonderful person in the world. Please forgive me and if you can, and I know I may be too late, please take me back.'

By now, both women were in tears and kissing with the passion each knew so well, and they had gathered to them two little people who both clung closely.

'Before anything else, I must make some supper for us all,' said Jo.

'I have some bags I should bring in,' said Marie, 'if that's alright with you.'

'I don't understand. This is your home. You forget we are married so you can bring in whatever you like.'

The children were overjoyed to be back together and played one of their familiar games. It had been less than two weeks but you could see the joy on their faces as sister and brother were reunited. Jo went out and helped Marie unload the car.

'Haven't told you yet, but we won't be able to live here much longer.'

'Why?'

'I've resigned from the police. They told me it was full-time or nothing.'

'But what about your counselling course? That was the whole point of working part-time.'

'They turned me down. Said I would be too stuck in the ways of police interrogation to be a counsellor and told me to try again in two years' time.'

'Darling, that's awful and ridiculous. Anyone who's ever worked with you knows how brilliant you would be because you already are. You must be so disappointed and appalled.'

'I should have arrested them all for wasting police time, but what about you? You said you were thinking of leaving the RAF and getting a job in commercial flying.'

'Ah, well. What I didn't know when I signed up as an officer was that I was signing a contract committing me to a minimum of five years' service, meaning I'm only halfway through though they would let me transfer to the USAF.'

'God, we are a daft pair.'

' O Jo, I'm so, so sorry for what I did. You are the epitome of love for me, so why did I need to go astray for a short while to realise just how much it is so?'

'I tell you what, Marie. Let's get all of this stuff inside and then get some food and when the children have gone to bed, then we can talk and tell our stories to one another, and then, in the morning, no more stories of the past couple of weeks, no more recriminations, just getting on with our life together as a family as we face a slightly uncertain future together in terms of where we live.'

'That makes my point,' said an exasperated Marie, 'you'd be brilliant as a counsellor. What kind of dickheads were they that turned you down?'

'O Marie, how I love you,' and in the garden with a gentle rain falling they hugged and kissed, and those who have not witnessed it should know that lesbian kissing is one of the wonders of the world!

Bath time and story time went on and on, and in the former, everyone got soaked and nobody minded. Eventually, and it was just after ten o'clock before Josie and Ollie fell asleep, Jo opened a bottle of wine. The time had come for grown-up story time.

'I suppose I had better begin,' said Marie, but I need to cuddle up to you as I do, perhaps to stop you laughing at me because I think that more than anything, that will be your response, and rightly so.'

'I'm intrigued.'

'Mike Tremlett is a good doctor and wouldn't be at the Papworth if he wasn't, and his care for Karen was exemplary. This is not an excuse but with Karen dying and being in a hospital in Cambridge, a stupid part of me was back with Nathan, and when Mike invited me to live with him, I stupidly accepted. But oh, what a shock I was in for, and not at all what I had anticipated. Mike is an evangelical Christian plus plus. He said his wife left him because she couldn't take living so near the Truth (by which I assume she must have meant the religious fruit cake she was married to), and boy is he ever? When he said grace before every meal, he prayed by name for each of his patients and staff, not to mention everyone who had helped produce the food, which was getting colder by the second. As bedtime approached, I wondered what might happen, and what did happen was that he showed me to my room and went off to his, clarifying that any sex outside marriage was deeply sinful, so my darling I return untouched by male hand.

'Each morning he left me a list of things to be done and said that I needed to set my heart beating to a different mode (his exact words and don't forget he was a cardiac specialist), putting behind me the terrible sin of homosexuality and a marriage that wasn't, because women cannot marry other women. Poor old Josie caught it too when she spoke of her two mummies. He also said that leaving the RAF was a necessity because I was taking up work opportunities that should be done by men. I told him that there was no man was as good as I was in flying as I did. He said that was sinful arrogance, and that there was so much about which I needed to repent. The bastard.

'On Sunday we all had to go to Church. They don't have real vicars, so yesterday morning Mike was the preacher. His sermon went on for nearly an hour and the whole event lasted 2½ horrendous hours. The congregations there seem to love doctors in their midst because in some strange way their presence legitimises the nonsense they seem to believe. They sang the most ridiculous songs imaginable and not only did they wave their arms in the air, but they danced and had healings with people behaving most oddly. From a sociological point of view it was fascinating but in every way I thought it juvenile crap.

'Because it was Sunday Mike wouldn't use his car and I wish I had taken mine, but I knew then that it was my fault, that he was not a source of blessing to me, as he insisted, but that he was my punishment for leaving you, so this morning I got up very early and prepared our bags for leaving after school. When he saw them he asked where I would be going, and I said I was returning, if you would have me, to you and my marriage and the authentic experience of love. He snorted. Yes, truly it was a snort, and said I was heading back into sin. And then I said something so very crude but I meant every word: "Better cunt than cant". He was clearly appalled, or at least I hope he was. He left at once and probably prayed for a religious cleansing firm to come and exorcise the house.'

By now Jo could could barely contain her laughter.

'Oh my darling, now I've left the police, don't you think we should have that framed and up on the wall, even if only in our room?'

'Well, I should be ashamed, but I'm not and I only wish I had said it in Church.'

'It was wonderful. Anyway, it's my turn to come clean, though it's not as funny as yours. As you know I invited Dani to come and take part in the interview we did with the Police and Crime Commissioner who had committed rape and thought it was an overrated crime (he got 10 overrated years by the way). We had to have a Chief Constable and I know her best. So she came and asked me to spend the night with her. I went to her room late at night and lay on the bed next to her and then promptly fell asleep, as I imagine she did. I woke at two o'clock to go to the loo. Dani and I were still fully clothed, and she was asleep. I left at once. On the following day we had a major piece of criminal law to fulfil. I could not have done that if we'd had sex together, but I was feeling lonely and you know that I love Dani, but when the time came she wasn't you and there was no way I could undress and get into bed with her.'

'How did she cope with that?'

'I made a joke of it by saying that at least we had slept together.'

'She did laugh, but on my way back I travelled with Bonnie and she asked me about being gay and a police officer. I said something I regret. I told her that my great fear was that you might leave me for a man, that some lesbians who once had been married, sometimes go back to that.'

'And then, when you got home, that's exactly what I told you, said Marie. 'They talked quite a lot about prophecy at the wretched church yesterday, so it must have been that mysterious fella "the Lord" they talk about all the time who was responsible. Well, my Dame can outdo him any time.'

'But why did I say that to Bonnie? Even now I can hardly believe that I did so. Perhaps it was a case of synchronicity which Jung wrote about, a certain barminess which overtook us at the same time. Whatever it was, I'm sorry I thought it and I'm sorry I said it to Bonnie. We are together and not just still in love, but even more so through this.'

'And yet, Jo, I was profoundly shocked that you didn't say grace before our supper.'

'Gosh, I'm so sorry and did I ever tell you that you are an idiot.'

'Once or twice, though usually once or twice a day!'

'Are you back to your normal time of leaving in the morning?'

'No, I'm on holiday and as you are no longer a police officer, we can have a proper holiday together, once that is, we've got the children off to school.'

What we may have to do on this holiday, is look for somewhere to live and of course it will have to be near enough to an aerodrome for you to get to work. It doesn't matter to me. I rather fancy being a waitress in a teashop.'

'I think I would rather fancy you in a waitress outfit, or even more so, without it. That reminds me, on my last night here we slept in separate rooms. That was my fault completely.'

'In which case, I think you ought to make up for it tonight.'

The children joined them in bed in the morning, a little surprised that neither mummy was wearing anything, but full of joy that they were together again. Jo said she would take Josie to school and Marie would go to playschool with Ollie.

Once the two school runs were done, Jo and Marie sat with coffee and toast at the dining table.

'Don't they say that absence makes the heart grow fonder?' said Jo.

'I believe so, my love, though if you don't mind me saying so, the heart is not the only part of us that grew fonder.'

'I really do not know what you're talking about,' replied Jo, now standing and walking around the table, pulling Marie to her breasts, holding her tightly and kissing her head.

'We should begin to consider where we want to live. I've sought out some options, places we can rent, near to schools.'

'Or places we can buy.' said Marie. 'So much has happened in the last 12 hours that I forgot to tell you that in her will the proceeds of the sale of Karen's house are split between you and me. We should be able to buy something nice for that.'

'Karen did that for me?'

'Karen loved the four of us, and although only Josie was her only actual blood relative, through Nathan, her love knew no bounds.'

'Has her funeral happened yet?'

'No, it's next Tuesday at Cambridge Crem.'

'Oh thank God, I haven't missed it.'

'I doubt whether it will be packed out.'

'That doesn't matter. It's quality that counts.'

'I've asked for no hymns and just the funeral service from the Book of Common Prayer, which I know Karen loved. The priest was ever so nice but persuaded me we might prefer the 1928 version to that of 1662, so she won me over.'

'I sometimes wish I knew more about an older form of Christianity than the modern junk with which we were presented at school. I suspect it contained great wisdom .Singing "Shine, Jesus, Shine, as we did at school did not, and immunised me against religion ever since.'

'I'm not sure those older forms would have been able to recognise lesbian marriage.'

'Well, more fool them. I love you Marie – wholly and holy.'

Marie nodded her head slowly, and Jo could see the tears flowing down her cheeks.

'Remember, my darling, we agreed no more recriminations after midnight last night. What matters now is our future life together.'

'Have you told your mum and dad?'

'I called them whilst you were in the shower and, typical of them, they took it calmly, as if to say "Of course, that's what we were expecting." It will be lost on you, but it was that total ability to remain calm that made my dad such a brilliant huntsman. Even if there was a fox afoot in a covert and some hounds were what's called "feathering" – knowing there was something they could smell but not certain, my dad would never interfere but let the hounds do the work in their own good time. Only when there was indication from someone that a fox had left the wood or covert, did he do his best to get the pack together.'

'I've never been hunting,' said Marie, 'and you make me almost wish I had. You make is sound like an art. Your dad must miss it.'

'I suppose he does in a way, but he's not bitter about it. It's time had run out in the world of woke, in which animals matter more than humans. Anyway they can't wait to see you and Josie even though it hasn't been long since they did.'

'So what have you got lined up for us?'

'We have to start again because renting differs greatly from buying. When will we know about how much we've got from the sale of the house?'

'We know now. Without telling us and perhaps with a premonition of her death, Karen put it on the market about two months ago, and unsurprisingly it sold within a week for £320,000, which sum has been with the solicitors ever since. We both have savings, having not lived extravagantly, meaning we could buy something outright with no mortgage. The question is where you want to live.'

'It needs to be close to an aerodrome, otherwise getting to Lakenheath by bus might take ages.'

'Oh, but Lakenheath is much nearer than my former bases in Lincolnshire, so extra time driving is not a problem.'

'Well, where I most fancy living is Saxmundham. It's a lovely small town and near Aldeburgh and the seaside there. Which Josie and Ollie would adore.'

'I would love that too, my darling, and the contrast between that and my work will be wonderful.'

'Ok, I'll have a look on the Estate Agents' website and see if there's anything.'

'On one condition.'

'Go on.'

'That when we get our new house, we buy a dishwasher.'

'Gosh, woman, you drive a hard bargain, but go on, I agree!'

There were two houses in their financial range and Jo telephoned to book a visit to each later in the day, emphasising that she was talking about a cash sale, though the assistant was puzzled at first how it could be there were two wives involved and even wondered if it was a Moslem seeking to purchase. Eventually the penny dropped.

The first house was in Framingham and though ideal, they at once preferred the house in Saxmundham, though were unsure whether to call it a village or a small town, and when they asked the assistant who had met them, she didn't know either. She was, however, very intrigued by Jo and Marie, who held hands and kissed from time to time.

'May I ask you something personal?' the young woman said, and Jo and Marie looked at one another and smiled. This was not the first time.

'How did you discover that, you know, it was women who attracted you rather than men?'

'I knew nothing other,' said Jo, and when I was five or six my mum and dad knew and were perfectly happy about it.'

'Mine was more of a tortuous route,' said Marie. 'As I grew up, there was no thought other than getting married and having children. I married a doctor which was regarded as more or less hitting the bulls-eye but it was a big mistake, and then I met Jo and I realised what love and joy could be as well as the most glorious sex life imaginable which could never be offered by a man.'

'Oh! Is that really true?'

'Yes, I can assure you. I have known both and there's no comparison. And whilst we're discussing things that are glorious, we wish to put in an offer on this house.'

'Yes, well, please come back to the office. You mentioned it being a cash sale.'

'Yes, and no chain behind us. We shall want to be here as soon as possible.'

'That will be great.'

They walked down the road to the office where they met the manager Ms Brownlow who, when she heard of the offer, the cash sale and the absence of a chain, was all over them.'

'I hope Cathy could answer all your questions.'

'Certainly, and we tried to answer all hers – all of them,' said Jo with a mischievous glance at Cathy, who blushed.

Marie did the negotiating, dropping £20,000 from the asking price for a quick cash sale. Ms Brownlow left them to call the vendor.

'When we arrive, Cathy, do come and have a coffee with us. We have two children you can meet as well, who would love to meet you, I'm sure. I will leave it until then to let you work out how, but we've given birth to one each.

Cathy's face was a picture of total puzzlement.

Ms Brownlow returned with a broad smile.

'Your offer has been accepted – congratulations, and welcome to Saxmundham. There were forms to complete, and this threw the two estate agents into total stupefaction as they were signed: Dame Joanne Enright and Flying Officer Marie Enright, RAF.

To call Karen's funeral low-key would be completely to over-state as there were only five in the congregation, but the priest, Judith, caught their mood perfectly and the read the funeral office so very well, that any kind of sermon or address would have been superfluous.

Marie had a word with the other three people present whilst Jo speak to the priest. She reminded Jo so much of the former Olympic athlete Kelly Holmes, another DBE like herself, a woman Jo always lusted after when she saw her on tv. Judith too was mixed-race and Jo smiled to herself that is was the first time she had been to a funeral and found herself fancying the vicar!

Marie returned to Jo with a broad smile.

'There were really only four of us present. The lady with the red hat admitted she had come at the wrong time and missed the one she was meant to be at so thought she'd join ours instead.'

'In which case, she had a treat. I know nothing about Judith, but she was very good.'

*3*

Dianne had to leave Alexandria in a hurry. Archaeologists are normally left alone in Egypt, they just get on with their work. A public lecture in UCLA, repeated in Toronto and in Edinburgh, had been reported back to the Egyptian government and she had been summoned to the Ministry of the Interior to account for the many criticisms she had made of the government and told that if she ever attempted to repeat them here, she would be arrested and deported.

Dianne was quite pleased with this response because it showed that news of her lectures had spread. She hated the political situation in Egypt but the much more revolutionary fruit of her research into the almost total non-historicity of those parts of the Jewish/Christian Bible set in Egypt, notably in the books of Genesis and Exodus were the things the government should fear, she thought. The Egyptian government were short-sighted enough only to concern themselves with contemporary politics, which meant that she had thought she had got away with it until her words were picked up in a monastery in the desert between Alexandria and Cairo. At once they recognised that wide publication of such abhorrent views would undermine not only their own Coptic Christians, already under constant attack from Islamic extremists, but the stream of visitors from America and Europe, coming to see the realms of Abraham, Joseph, Moses and the Exodus, which this wretched woman now threatened by claiming that none of this happened. When potential loss of income was concerned, the government took notice.

With no notice, either to herself or the Canadian Embassy, a group of soldiers arrived one morning, shortly before she set off for the university, told her to gather her things and by noon she was on a Lufthansa flight to Munich. She was highly amused to be told that being American she would be deported because they did not wish to offend the Americans. Otherwise she might have spent years rotting in a prison cell. Handing her Canadian passport to the official airport before boarding made her glad Egyptian soldiers could not read English!

In important ways, her work in Egypt was complete and although there was much about the country she loved, it had not been easy to find friends. Most of the other archaeologists were white, something she most definitely was not, and she had thought it possible that hostility to her findings from those of a strong religious persuasion was allied to racism She knew too, that the religious ferment in Egypt was always liable to break out into seriously unpleasant hostility towards the Coptic Christians. So perhaps what had happened today was timely.

She had kept her laptop with her, though everything she had worked on and would need again was safe, not just in one cloud, but three. A scholar of her experience took no chances with technological breakdown, political interference or the malice of opponents, and there was no shortage of all three.

Late in the evening she finally got through to Toronto and the head of department, Shirley Gleeson, who was in fact two or three levels below her in the university hierarchy.

'What are you wanting to do, Dianne? We can always send you an e-ticket overnight from Munich back to Toronto or have you other hopes?'

'Well, wherever I go I'm wanting to recover from the hurly burly of my lecture trip, the hostility of those who hate my findings and now hate me and, of course, from the perpetual lunacy of Islam.'

'Are you really wanting to come back to Canada then? The country has gone woke mad, and you can be arrested for not using the correct pronouns, and if you think I'm kidding, trust me I'm not.'

'Yeah, people told me about it when I came to give my lecture.'

'But I have another thought. You know my partner Hugh comes from England. He still owns a house in a very quiet part of England, the county called Suffolk. He keeps trying to decide whether to sell it – it's fully furnished, but for now it could be yours if you could use it. Even there they have Wifi and you'll be able to take as much or as little time as you need to do your work.'

'It sounds idyllic. What's the name of the place?'

'Saxmundham, and there's been a fair amount of archaeological work done in the area, mainly Anglo-Saxon, including the Sutton Hoo boat. It would be ideal for you.'

'Yes, Shirley!'

She was instructed how to get the key, and told that the airport she needed to aim for was Stansted. When she finally turned out the light her mind had shifted from Alexandria to Saxmundham, and already was in love with the name. What could be better than a quiet English village where she just might bump into Miss Marple – her favourite sleuth on television?

The first available flight with free seats to London Stansted was not for two days and whilst she could get to Heathrow today, it was on the wrong side of London, but more especially some German beer would go down a treat, both in Marienplatz and the English Gardens. After a dry Egypt for so long, some Hefewiezen or Erdinger Kirstall would be wonderful. She might also pop into the archaeological department at the university where she was known, though, on the other hand, she might just have more beer instead!

Her stay over in Munich provided her with a complete break from thinking of or attending to work. Her laptop was never opened, nor any of the books she had rescued as she was deported. It was a kind of liberation, analgesia from the pain of daily duty, and in the end she really preferred beer to meeting up with Egyptologists in the university The only thing she focused her mind on was whether she was being followed, whether anyone or more, from the Mukhabarat, the Egyptian Intelligence Agency, was trailing her to see where she was going or even, to assassinate her, as it was always better to do such a thing in a third country. She had acquired some skill at checking behind her whilst in Cairo and throughout the city now, remained vigilant.

The flight from Munich to Stanstead was brief compared with many she made on her lecture tours which had criss-crossed the world, and not always given to welcoming and appreciative audiences who wanted their presuppositions, or prejudices, confirmed rather than challenged by evidence. Leaving the airport concourse at Stanstead she smiled broadly: it was raining! Of course it was. This was England, and it was something she had hardly experienced in Egypt, so was doubly welcome. A taxi had been booked for her in advance by the estate agent she had spoken to on the previous day to make the necessary arrangements to collect the key to the house. The driver held up a card with her name on as she came through the Arrivals gate, though he was a little taken aback by the amount of luggage she had.

'How far is it,' she asked.

'Just over 70 miles,' the driver said., 'an hour and a half and we'll be there. Have you come far?'

'Just from Munich today, but I've spent more than a few years working as an archaeologist in Egypt.'

'And from your accent I would hazard a guess that you're not from Liverpool.'

Dianne smiled.

'No, I'm a Canadian.'

'So how long are you intending to come and live in Saxmundham?'

'It will depend totally on how long it will take me, first of all, to get all my papers and records in order, and then to turn them into a book. In that respect it will probably take me at least a year and probably more.'

'Egypt must be a wonderful country for archaeologists. My old granddad was there during the war, serving under General Montgomery.'

'Is he still alive?'

'No, he died some 20 years ago. He was quite a character and told me many stories which I couldn't repeat about nights spent in the houses of sin in Alexandria.'

'Has the thought ever occurred to you that somewhere in Egypt you might have a half-uncle or aunt? There are several people now in their seventies who never knew who their fathers were. I don't think contraception was advanced.'

'I know that sexually transmitted diseases were rife among many British soldiers who served there.'

'Are you a Saxmundham resident?'

'No, I'm from Aldeburgh and I rely on the musical world for a lot of my work, especially during the Festival every year.'

'And dare I ask you if you knew Britten and Pears?'

'Britten died in 1976 when I was too young to know who he was, but I saw Peter Pears around the place, together with many of the greats with whom they worked. It has been a real privilege.'

Dianne was dropped at the house and her friend, the driver, Bobby Hollis, helped her unload the car, having obtained the key before he set off for the airport. She was very pleased with the place and spent the first hour getting the central heating and the internet up and flowing. That done, she emailed Toronto confirming her arrival with delight at what she had found. Saxmundham was going to be an ideal place to live and work and eventually determine her future.

A knock on the door was followed by a young woman from the estate agent, called Cathy, who arrived with some basic foodstuffs to get her through 'til morning. She was bright and cheery and full of information about the community. There were two ladies with two children two houses down who had moved in on Tuesday. They're really unusual, and more or less your age. I hope you get to know them, but please ask if there's anything you want to know. We exist not just to sell houses but to be of continuing assistance.'

'Thank you, Cathy, and thank you for the food. What they gave us on the flight from Germany didn't really count as food.'

'There's a Tesco Superstore down the road but the Ipswich supermarkets deliver here if you order on-line. There's only one pub, and if you wanted an exciting nightlife, you've come to the wrong place.'

'Dianne laughed.'

'I might just want to miss out on the nightlife, but what do you do about it?'

I get all the drugs I need from the Pharmacy – mainly paracetamol, but my genuine excitement comes from living so close to the sea. On my days off that's where I head. I don't know if you've ever heard *Peter Grimes*, Britten's second and greatest opera which is all about a fishing community in the 19th century. It could only have been written by someone who knew the moods of the sea, and the moods of people. I can sit on the pebbly beach and look at it for hours, and I often do. I can take you if you like.'

'Oh, Cathy, I'd love that. I've been living in the sands of the desert for too many years, so pebbles and sea would be wonderful. Just tell me when you're going next and I'll come.'

'We might have quite a load. Jo and Marie also want to see the sea.'

'Jo and Marie?'

The two ladies next door but one. Josie is starting at the primary school on Monday, and Oliver is still too young for school.'

'No men, no fathers?'

'I haven't asked yet but I will, as I'm intrigued, but they are married to each other, so probably not.'

'How will Saxmundham cope with that?'

'Even here we're in the 21st century and apart from the self-righteous lot frequenting the Church in Kelsale I can't think there'll be the slightest problem, except for some women seeing how happy they are, wondering if they might change for the better.'

'There was nothing like that in Egypt.'

'All Moslem?'

'Almost all, but some Christians known as Copts who are having a pretty awful time – killings, churches bombed, so there wasn't a lot of time for lesbians.'

'Do you disapprove?'

'Not in the slightest and I'm already looking forward to meeting them.'

Across the road Alice had seen the new arrivals, the two women with their small children two days back and, today, the striking looking black woman arriving in a taxi. No doubt they all had a story, but if they ever came to know hers, they wouldn't want to know her – that was for certain. And she wondered just how much longer she could survive like that. At the moment she had Katia. But after she had gone, what then? There would be no point in life.

## 4

On her first morning back at Lakenheath, Marie first went and looked over her plane, an outside inspection especially important after not having flown during her three weeks' absence. All seemed well, but she was a little surprised to receive a radio call from the head of the base.

'Good morning, Flight Officer Enright. I hope you've had a good holiday and thank you for letting us know your new address etc.'

'And good morning to you, too, sir. What have you got lined up for me?'

'I'm sorry, Marie, but you've got a day of psychological assessment.'

'But I had one just about three months ago.'

'I know you did, but we've had a letter from a consultant in Cambridge, at the Papworth, who maintains you are severely mentally unbalanced and shouldn't be flying.'

Marie laughed.

'There's a surprise. I take it you are talking about Dr Tremlett, who is such an expert on things psychological that he is a cardiac consultant. Ok, sir. Of course I will.'

'I have no choice, Marie, when a senior doctor writes as he has.'

"It's not a problem, sir, and it will give me time to plan my work over the week ahead.'

'Ok, Marie, when you've done, come and have a cup of tea. I've missed you.'

'Yes, sir. I'll look forward to that.'

The nurse doing the psychological assessment was already known to Marie.

'It's always good to see you Marie, but you were done only a couple of months back.'

'I'm sure you would never speak ill of a doctor, Ruth ...'

'Don't be so sure,' she interrupted.

Marie grinned.

'My mother-in-law died in the Papworth and it threw me more than I had anticipated. He was so good and caring that I lost my way completely. Jo had been away for over two weeks and Karen's death had been such a shock, and when he asked me to move in with him, I did. There were two things I hadn't reckoned with. The first was that he was an utter and absolute religious nutcase, more so than I have ever come across, and in case you wondered, we never shared a bed. Finally I fled, because of the second thing, which was my realisation that I loved Jo and could never love anyone else.'

'Are you back together?'

'We were, straight away.'

'Have you recovered?'

'Yes, and I'd like to think I'm wiser.'

Unsurprisingly, Marie sailed through the psychological tests, which gave her time to look over her schedule for the week: two days instructing, one day visit to Estonia and another to the Cape Verde Islands, a long outing there and back.

'Where are the Cape Verde Islands?' asked the CO over a cup of tea.

'I've no idea,' said Marie, 'I'm hoping the First Officer will have a suggestion.'

They laughed.

'Look Marie, there's something about which I need to warn you.'

'Oh?'

'I've heard a rumour in the form of an email from RAF Cranwell that you're going to be promoted to Flight Lieutenant at the next postings.'

'Jesus!'

'No, just Flight Lieutenant, but keep progressing and you might get there eventually. It's great news, Marie. Congratulations.'

After she landed and parked up at Crowfield, Marie began the drive back to Saxmundham, her mind divided between the excitement of her promotion mingled with possible schemes for getting her own back on the nutty doctor.

Jo and the children welcomed her warmly, her first day away from their new house, and Josie's first day in her new school, and Jo and Ollie had made a new friend.

'You'll never guess what.'

'Ok, tell me.'

'I'm going to be promoted to Flight Lieutenant when the next promotions are gazetted.'

'Oh Marie, that's simply wonderful. Wow. What a start to our own new home. Flight Lieutenant! Imagine that, and how proud Karen would be. I'm so sorry she's missed it. But no one could be more proud than me. You are my wonder woman.'

'*You've* been called that in the past and now we are in here, Jo, you know you are going to have to give thought to what you want to do.'

'I was asked that today by our next door but one new neighbour, Dianne, she's Canadian but has spent years as an archaeologist in Egypt and has just been deported by the Egyptian government. She's here to get her volumes of notes in order and to turn them into books.'

'She sounds most interesting, but did she have any ideas for your future employment prospects?'

'Being her assistant.'

'And did you tell her what you were doing until just a few weeks ago?'

'No way. Anyway we should open a special bottle tonight to celebrate your good news, and also the good news that Josie loved her first day at school, and that Ollie starts at the Playschool in the Church Hall in Kelsale in the morning.'

The children heard the return of Marie and rushed through to tell her everything. Marie pressed on with making the supper which they only got round to eating after bath and story times.

'Did you say Dianne was deported from Egypt?'

'Yes. Frogmarched to the airport and put on a plane to Munich. She managed to take some papers with her but fortunately most are in the cloud or, in fact, three clouds for their protection.'

'So what was so precious and dangerous to the government? Usually people like her just disappear.'

'She assumes she was saved by her international reputation, but it was all to do with her archaeological work which she maintains shows unquestionably the events written about in the Bible, and the persons named there, never happened and never existed. She admits she's not the first person to suggest these things, but she has done more archaeological research than others. As a result, she's hated by Jews and Christians alike, and the Egyptian government fear a substantial loss of tourist income on which they rely so heavily.'

'Don't you just love religion?'


Jo had wondered if she might have to wait as Ollie settled in to a new new playgroup, but as soon as the door was opened he was off and never looked back.

'No problems there, Mrs Enright,' said the leader.

'Jo, please.'

'Just one thing, and it concerns the form you completed yesterday. You seem to have put down two mothers, instead of putting Flight Officer Enright in the father's column.'

'Ah, that would be because Ollie has two mums. Using IVF an egg was removed from my wife, Marie, fertilised in the lab by sperm from an anonymous donor, and then placed into my womb. It doesn't always work, especially first time, but it did for us, and so Ollie has two mums. Genetically he will receive from Marie as the donor, but I brought him to birth.'

'So what does he call you both?'

'He calls us both mummy and clearly isn't confused. He's a miracle of our age, and more lesbian couples are being enabled to do the same.'

'I've never heard of that before, but it's quite wonderful.'

'Ruth Davidson, the Tory politician in Scotland, and her partner Jen, did the same. They also got a boy.'

'Would you have preferred a girl?'

'No way. Boys are much more naughty and incredible fun.'

The woman laughed.

'Gosh, I have learned so much this morning and it isn't even half-past nine!'

'You never know when it might come in useful,' said Jo with a slight suggestive raise of her eyebrows.'

Jo was not at all sure what the face before her was doing with this comment.

It was not a chilly day, and she enjoyed the walk back into the village and gazing at her watch as she approached, she continued down the hill where she bought a newspaper and then opted for a coffee in the small tea and coffee shop. It turned out she was the first customer of the day and chose a window seat. When the waitress approached she recognised her as the person living across the road.

'Hello there. I'm Jo and live across the road from you. I've seen you coming and going to work. We've just moved in.'

'Of course, I recognise you now. Welcome to Saxmundham. I hope you'll be very happy living here.'

'Is there any chance of a black coffee and a toasted teacake with just butter, no preserve?'

'I'll fetch them.'

Jo, being sensitive to such things, felt there was an unease about the woman and wondered why. Soon the coffee and teacake arrived, the latter enormous.

'There's only one of me, you know,' she said, pointing to the plate.

The waitress smiled.

'I bet you'll finish it off all the same.'

'You might just win your bet. May I know your name? If I was to see you in the road I can hardly shout out "Good morning, waitress".'

'Alice Watts and I have a daughter Katia who's 16 and goes to school in Ipswich.'

'And very bonny she is too, though it's a difficult age, if I remember rightly and hope I don't.'

'You know very little about the influences they're under at school, what with drugs and sex, but all you can do is to go on loving them no matter what.'

The door opened and two new customers entered, and Alice left Jo to concentrate on her teacake.

When she called Alice over for the bill, she asked, 'What time do you finish, Alice?'

'It's early closing on a Tuesday so I'm away by 12-30. Why?

'I want to visit Aldeburgh and the seaside and wondered if you'd come and be my guide, and we can have some lunch there and see how bad the waitressing is.'

'You're not a journalist?'

'No, Alice, I promise you I'm not, but before we go come into our house for a moment, I will assure you I'm not.'

'Ok.

Walking back to the house, Jo pondered Alice's words. It struck her that the only person anxious about the presence of a journalist would be someone with something they wished to conceal.

Alice called just before 1-00.

'Sorry to be late we had a lot of annoying customers today, she said a grin.

'Tell them to go away,' said Jo. 'Anyway, come in and let me show that I am not and never have been and would never be a journalist.'

She handed her a photograph.

'That was my team on the day I left just a few weeks ago. They were handpicked by me and mostly called me boss. This other picture is of Marie and I at Buckingham Palace and that thing I am holding is a DBE for services to the country which I'm not allowed to take about, which is a great pity or I could go around the country talking about them.'

'Why can't you?'

'The Official Secrets Act.'

'Were you a soldier?'

'Good heavens, no – far too dangerous. No, I was a Detective Chief Superintendent, and then I ran a special team called the Sensitive Crime Unit and before that I was head of Norfolk CID.'

'And honestly, please Jo, do you not know who I am?'

'Of course, I do. You told me this morning you're Alice Watts with a lovely daughter, Katia. I know nothing more, but should I?'

'Oh Jo, I'm surprised my neck's not permanently twisted over my shoulder to see if journalists might be coming, and for years I've not been able to speak about it. Katia knows of course and now just takes it for granted.'

'Alice, can I make a suggestion? Sometimes it helps a great deal when you're telling a story, especially if it's a painful one which I suspect this one might be, to do so without seeing the eyes of the other person which you fear might be judgemental, by which I mean let's go into the car for a drive.'

'I know you could find all the details on the police computers even though it was now a long time ago, 36 years ago in fact, and I don't think there were computers back then. My name, as you would find on all my documents, is Alice Watts, but before that I was Joan Stafford, and prior to that, Amy Lewis, but for the first ten years of my life I was Ella Epton. But as far as most people are concerned, my name was given to me by the police: the "little monster" and the newspapers have continued to use it.

'I was granted lifelong anonymity, but not lifelong freedom from being hounded by the press and unprotected by the police. The thing is, Jo, when I was ten, I drowned two small children in the bath in their home. I really didn't mean to kill them. I just couldn't get them to stop crying.'

'Was their mother prosecuted for leaving them in the care of a child?'

'I don't know, but I heard nothing about it. Perhaps they thought she'd suffered enough.'

'Well, my darling, I think you've suffered enough and now I live across the road from you, I will do all in my power to protect you from the press and police alike.'

'Why would you want to do that?'

'Because you have suffered an appalling abuse or misuse of justice. If you had lived in Sweden, Denmark, Norway or Finland, you would have been well below the age of criminal responsibility, which is 15 and placed under under the care of social welfare. You would not under any circumstances have been placed in prison. Attempts would have been made to understand what had happened. The Press would not bother you and you wouldn't have had to change your name. What we do is simply barbaric. I'm wholly on your side and you can rely on me.'

Jo was aware that Alice was crying.

'You mean it, don't you?'

'Yes, Alice, I do.'

'Why? I've not met anything other than sheer hostility from the police. It was they who gave me the name "little monster" and every other one has been glad to use it. Ironically, it was only in prison that I was free of it.'

'I'm truly sorry for all that and although it will mean nothing, I wish to apologise on behalf of the police service. I have been the most senior ranking office short of being part of the executive, and I want you to know that I am on your side.'

'And what about those two children I killed?'

'Tell me more?'

They were Peter, aged three, and Anna, two. I had things done to me by men and my mother, objects inserted painfully front and back. When I was looking after them, I was told that I said let's play a game and I tried to do to them what had been done to me. One of them started crying, and it set off the other, and I didn't know how to stop them, so apparently I ran the bath and drowned them.'

Jo allowed her words a few moments of silence.

'My darling, you were the victim of a terrible crime and our ridiculous legal system declared you to be the guilty one. You were not because at ten years of age you cannot have known what you were doing, and yet I'm not wholly convinced if the same thing was to happen now that the same outcome would not follow. The Press continues to chase after Robert Thompson and and Jon Venables, and of course whilst they continue to do so, at least it means they are considerably less interested in you and Mary Bell. Now, we are here and isn't it wonderful. Do you know where we can get a sandwich?'

'A hundred yards further on there's a café where we can get something.'

'Great. And it's my turn to pay.'

Alice laughed.

'Tell me, are you the only lesbian fairy godmother in the world? Oh, my God, have I said the wrong thing?'

Jo laughed.

'Not at all. It's a new title I think I should start using. Detective Lesbian Fairy Godmother. I think the villains would give up as soon as they heard it.'

By now, they were both laughing.

In the café, Jo laughed when Alice ordered a bacon sandwich.

'What's funny about a bacon sandwich?'

'Detective Chief Inspector Ed Secker was given the advice that after every post mortem he attended he needed to have a bacon sandwich to get the smell of the mortuary out of his system. He so enjoyed this that he would always volunteer to attend any and every post mortem just so he could get his bacon sandwich.'

'Do the police have to attend every post-mortem?'

Only when it is suspected that foul play has played a part in the death'.

'Isn't it horrible?'

'The first two or three can feel gruesome but once you get used to the smell and make sure you carry a clean set of clothes in the car, then it's much like any other job and a great deal depends on the forensic pathologist and the extent to which they communicate what they are doing. In so many respects they're the real detectives. Now, my lovely Alice, my sausage bap is getting cold.'

After lunch, they walked on the beach and Jo decided that they'd had enough conversation on death.

'I bet it's cold here on a winter's day when the wind is coming from the East.'

'It's not exactly warm today,' replied Alice.'

'You're right, but I'm so enjoying being out here with you, so thank you for coming.'

'No, thank you for suggesting it.'

'And we must do it again. But tell me something about your wife.'

'Flight Lieutenant Marie Enright, you mean. I arrested her once upon a time and locked her up in a police cell.'

'You're kidding?'

'No, it's true. Overnight I discovered that I'd made a major error and had to release her. In fact, I offered to drive her home. A short time after that I moved in with her and having realised the extent to which I was in love with her, we got married. She had been married to a man and was now divorced. She was and is aeroplane mad, and her own was left to her by her pilot father. The RAF recognised her talent, and she now pilots some of the largest transport planes in existence, and trains others. She travels literally all over the world and loves every minute of it.'

'Are your two children from her first marriage?'

'Josie, the elder is, but Ollie is ours, and I can see you're puzzled, but it's straightforward. Ollie is an IVF child. Doctors removed an egg from Marie which was fertilised by sperm from an anonymous donor, and then, amazingly, implanted in my womb. I had the pregnancy, and I gave birth.'

'Jesus.'

'Not quite, but nearly.'

'That is wonderful, Jo, more wonderful than anything I've ever heard.'

'So is Ollie, and we must be getting back so I can collect him and Josie.'

## 5

Marie landed back from the Cape Verde Islands, having found them after all and received a message to call in on the CO.

'Marie, if you are unhappy with what I am asking, then please say so. I might still have to ask you to do it because you are best, but at least I will know you're not happy.'

'That's really great to know, sir,' she said with a grin.

'On Tuesday I want you to fly to the brand new Berenice Military base in southern Egypt, on the Red Sea coast. The payload is a prototype of a new form of tank which the government is hoping to sell to the Egyptian government and you can have the details for flight preparation on Monday morning.'

'Why might I be unhappy about that, sir?'

'It's proximity to Saudi Arabia, first of all, and the possibility that the Saudis have asked the Egyptians to look out for you and their wish to hold you and hand you over.'

'Isn't that a little unlikely, sir.'

'You, a woman, made a fool of them. I don't need to tell you of all people, but you won't want to be descending and making your approach from the Red Sea. And whilst you must do the flying and landing, it might be wise to have a male First Officer doing the talking.'

'I shall be quite a way from Akrotiri, sir, so I presume there will be no backup.'

'The Israeli Airforce has been asked and will provide that if need be. You will carry four tank personnel, Royal Engineers, but they will stay behind. Otherwise it will be you and the First Officer, plus an Arabic speaker which might come in handy.

We're still trying to find someone appropriate. But Jo, there is something else I must remind you of because I know you have never had need of it. Immediately to your left in your pilot's seat is a green button which when pressed will open a small compartment. You are a member of Her Majesty's Armed Forces and as a Flight Lieutenant you may use what it contains.'

'Yes, sir.'

As Marie flew her own tiny plane back to Crowfield she smiled at the contrast between what she had been flying during the day to the mid-Atlantic and back, and the short distance she needed to fly from the base to where her car was. But Marie was diligent about her flying and would not leave the hangar at Crowfield without having done a full external check, even though her flight had been short.

Once in the car en route for home she had completely forgotten about Egypt and could only think of Josie, Ollie and Jo, and how excited they would be to see her, and she them. When everyone was there, the place was a mass of laughter and total silliness, good for them all.

Over supper they shared their day. Jo said nothing about what she had learned from Alice and never would do so – and for a long time Marie had been used to that, but it worked the other way too. Marie was bound by the Official Secrets Act and although she was happy to let Jo know where she was flying to, mostly the reasons she was flying here and there, she had to say nothing. The exception had been her experience in Saudi, but because of the potential link with that she mentioned she was flying to Egypt.'

'Call Dianne, and let her know.'

'I'm not allowed to do that.'

'She's an Arabic speaker.'

'Yes, well, having lived in Egypt for ten years I would imagine she would be.'

'Think about it, darling.'

'I will, but don't forget, she's just been deported from the country. Landing in a military aircraft in a new military base with a military pilot wanted by the Saudi government may not be the wisest career move.'

'I take your point,' said Jo, 'but Dianne will only do what she wants to, but she might have useful background. She lives next door but one, and unless our next-door neighbour is an expert on the River Nile, Dianne is likely to be the nearest source of information for you.'

'Well, now we have a dishwasher I will leave you with it and see if I can suggest Dianne and I meet before I leave on Tuesday.'

Marie phoned before she went to see Dianne, not simply to find if she was in, but to let her know who her late visitor was.

'Hi Marie, it's good to see you and thank for the call. You could of course be a clever Egyptian spy pretending to be you but I took the risk.'

'Well, I'm not, but I wanted to mention Egypt, but first I must tell you about my flying visit to Saudi Arabia.'

She recounted the experience, and the feeling generated in Whitehall that the Saudis don't like being made fools of, and especially by a woman.

'Yes, that will have been received as a humiliation, but what surprises me is that having sent up two fighters after you they did nothing more than escort you and not force you to land. I assume they can fly faster than you.'

'Oh yes. But I think I was safe because we all belong to the pilot's union and they had a reluctant but real respect for what I had done. They also knew, because I made sure they heard, that I had two RAF Typhoon fighters from Cyprus on their way. Anyway, with their air-to-ground radios off, as we reached the end of Saudi airspace, in excellent English they wished me a safe flight home and hoped to see me again! I flew on to Akrotiri and stayed the night there and refuelled. But now something else has arisen, on the Red sea opposite Saudi.

'Are you talking about Berenice?'

'I have to deliver equipment and four instructors. Because we don't want Saudi ATC picking up my voice, my First Officer will do all the radio work though I will fly the plane and already I have decided to come in from the West over Libyan and Northern Sudanese airspace. That should avoid any risk of having to make my approach over the Red Sea where Saudi jets operate.

'Once I have unloaded machines and men, I shall look to get airborne as soon as possible. I will refuel there but if for any reason they don't let me, I will have more than enough to get me to Hatzerim Air Base on the edge of the Negev Desert, plus if I need protection the Israelis will scramble two jets.'

'Doesn't it scare you?'

'Far from it. I adore flying and the more tested I am, the better I feel about myself. If I hadn't been in the RAF, I would have missed so very much in the aviation world. My transporters are just about the biggest aeroplanes in the sky and every time I get to the base and see the one I'm flying that day, my heart skips a beat, and another beat that within the RAF I'm the only woman licensed to fly them, and teach one or two men to do likewise. My regular First Officer, David, is the product of my training and the only one so far I could allow to sit in my seat and take command.'

'Marie, that's wonderful to hear, but I'm not sure I could add anything to your preparations, which are wholly beyond my experience.'

'Ah, that might be because I missed something out.'

'Go on,' said Dianne suspiciously.

'My CO wants me to carry an interpreter. Neither David nor I have any Arabic, and if by any chance there is a holdup by those controlling traffic movement on the ground, he thoughy it might be a good idea to have someone up front with us talking to them in Arabic.'

'And you just happened to remember that in the same road is an Arabic speaker who knows Egyptian accents and who might sweet talk the in letting us leave.'

'Something like that.'

'Let's be clear. Someone from North America who has just been deported and threatened by the Egyptians should risk life and liberty by flying with someone who is clearly a madwoman, however beautiful, back into the leading military base in the country where, if I was to set foot on the soil would be at once arrested, subjected to a kangaroo court and either be imprisoned for a long time or simply disappear for being present in a military aeroplane when not a military person. That's what you're asking?'

'Yes, you sum it up well.'

Dianne thought for a moment or two.

'I'm trying really hard to find reasons for saying no, but I can't find any, so I guess the answer is yes.'

Marie stood and crossed the room and gave Dianne a warm embrace and kiss full on the lips.

'What time were you planning to get up in the morning?' said Marie.

'About 7, I suppose.'

'Make it 6, and we'll set off at half past. We'll drive to Crowfield and then fly into Lakenheath. The mess there does a good breakfast. The CO has to give his approval but unless he has managed to get Cleopatra, he will love you. I can then show you one of my big toys. How does that sound?'

'When I found Saxmundham I stayed because it was remote and quiet and I knew I would get work done and books written. Little did I know I would live alongside a former police chief detective and a madwoman who is surely related to Amelia Earhart.'

'One of my heroes, a true wonder woman. I always get back however.'

'May I remind you of that on Tuesday? But I'll tell you the real reason I'm happy to come. It's not adventure, of which I've had more than enough. It's because in meeting you and Jo, for the first time in many years I've found friends and with friends you'll do anything.'


Once Marie had left for Lakenheath with Dianne, Jo picked up the phone and called Alice. She had already seen Katia leave for school.'

'Hello?' said Alice cautiously.

'Alice, my darling, it's Jo, across the road and it occurs to me we could open our windows and shout at one another.'

Alice laughed.

'Alice, this is a terrible impertinence I know, given that we've hardly known one another long, but do you think that before you spend your day serving coffee, you could do me a great favour and take Ollie to his playgroup in the church hall. One of my former colleagues is pretending she'd she can't do without me and wants me to meet her.'

Of course, I can and will. Do you think he knows me well enough?'

'Oh Alice. He's a boy, so any woman entrances him. And he does like you.'

'What time?

'A quarter to nine.'

'I'll collect him.'

Once they had set off, Jo set off for her former station at Stowmarket. Bonnie had called her the previous evening saying there was something important needing to be discussed. Jo loved the Suffolk countryside and on the way she had a call from her mum and dad. Could they come today for the weekend? Jo was over the moon with as she adored them.

It was good to be back in Stowmarket and she recognised the cars of some of the team. She parked and went upstairs, and the first person she saw was Kelly, an ex-prisoner of whom Jo thought extremely highly of and sent her to MI5 to further the already extensive technological knowledge and skill she has acquired behind bars. The opportunity Jo had provided had been the making of her, and she in turn adored her former boss.

'Kelly, my darling (everyone was Jo's darling, but everyone also knew she meant it) I've been summoned by the boss. Do you know why?'

'When you sent me to MI5, they taught me never to lie, but to answer a different question as politicians do, so I should answer you by saying something like "She's very much looking forward to seeing you" which is the truth but skirts your question. On the other hand, you are Detective Chief Superintendent Jo Enright, so I will say that I do indeed know why, and I am delighted about it, but that I'm not allowed to tell you.'

'Kelly, your answers have got longer and longer.'

'Thank you, Jo. That's kind of you to say so.'

'I didn't mean it as a compliment.'

Kelly pointed towards the briefing room and to Jo's embarrassment, as they should, everyone stood as she entered, including Bonnie.

'Sit down, idiots,' said Jo, to everyone's laughter.

'We're just doing a briefing on a new case,' said Bonnie.

Jo sat down and listened.

'We don't need everyone and they wouldn't want us all to be there cluttering up the castle anyway. So, those taking the high road to Scotland with me are Ed, Esther, Tom and Steph. Darcey and Belinda will work from here with whatever comes up, and you'll have the benefit of Kelly.

The door opened again and everyone stood once again, even Jo, when she saw that the new arrival was the Suffolk Chief Constable, Alan Roberts.

'As you were,' said the Chief.

Immediately Jo knew that this was a set up.

'Jo, how good to see you,' said the Chief.'

'Good, but not a surprise, Alan.'

The Chief laughed.

'Ok, everyone but the Chief, Jo and me, get some coffee across the road, and ask Kelly to join us,' said Bonnie.

Kelly came in.

Bonnie turned to the Chief.

'Kelly is the one member of the team who has to know everything, sir, and if she doesn't know she is unbelievably capable of finding out, so it's best we tell her everything from the beginning.'

'You did time, I believe.'

'Sadly the only thing I'm not good at is fraud when in a good cause, but I learned so much inside about computers and technology, and even more about caring for those whom society dumps. I have no regrets about it, sir, none, and the greatest thing of all was that Chief Superintendent Enright saw the best and gave me a wonderful chance. I can tell you this, sir, there is not a single member of the team that has just left the room who wouldn't give their eye-teeth for Jo.'

'This is all very embarrassing, but could one of you three give me some idea as to what's going on?'

'Well, it will have to be me as I'm the one guilty of the crime of deception,' said the Chief.

'Alan,' said Jo, probably the only police officer short of the executive to call him by name, 'what have you done.'

'It's a bit like what Kelly has just said – doing the wrong thing for the right reason. When you retired, Jo, I'm afraid to say I didn't forward the papers you completed but placed them in my safe and instead I completed papers authorising a sabbatical, which means that you are still Detective Chief Superintendent in charge of SCU. Now that most of the team are heading for a case involving the Royal Family in Scotland, it means that I have to recall you to active duty here though day-to-day responsibilities will be handled by DI Bussell and DS Gorham, but both will answer to you. Good, well I'm glad that's sorted. I must be on my way to a meeting in Cambridge and will inform the other Chiefs that you're back in charge.'

He stood, and the three of them did likewise as he left the room.

'Could someone explain to me what has just happened?' said Jo, looking puzzled.

'It's quite simple,' said Kelly, 'you've been had, boss.'


The three women crossed the road to the coffee shop and Bonnie did the honours regarding coffee and toasted teacakes.'

'It's good to have you back, Jo,' said Ed, 'even though we're leaving you tomorrow and heading north. Bonnie is good, in fact very good, but we all know she's not Jo.'

'You will understand, Ed, that until about 20 minutes ago I was simply Jo Enright, a former police officer and now ...'

'No boss,' said Darcey, 'you were Dame Joanne Enright. Never forget that because we don't.'

'As I was saying, 20 minutes have gone by and apparently I

never left the force after all.'

The unit laughed.

'And where are you heading tomorrow, Bonnie?'

'Glamis Castle, owned by Lord Glamis, Simon Bowes-Lyon.'

'And therefore related to the late Queen Mother.'

'Yes, indeed. There's a ghost but we're going to investigate some very earthly goings on.'

'Bonnie, my darling, if I'm to mind the shop in your absence, is there anything current I need to know about?'

'Darcey and Belinda can fill you in with what they're up to. It isn't much. They work well together, which includes an ability to argue forcefully about aspects of work and then get over it immediately. But since you left, the head of the team is not me, but Kelly. Of all those you've recruited, she was the least likely to be drawn into a special police unit, and yet she's so good. She's not as experienced as Aisling, who after all worked for MI5 in Belfast, but in terms of what she can do with computers and technology, since she returned from a month with Major Atwood in London, she's phenomenal.'

Jo smiled.

'You don't need her in Scotland?'

'She says transmission and wifi are not good from there.'

'Ok. I'll take her, Darcey and Belinda with me back over the road and have a chat. Is that ok?'

'Er, boss, you're the boss.'


'Until I can come to terms with what has just happened, I'll work from home and leave to you, Kelly, the processes of linking me up with everything here.'

'That's not a problem, boss. Perhaps we can have a girlies' outing to the Suffolk seaside, and I can fiddle with your equipment.'

They laughed.

'In which case I'd better make sure Marie is present! But in fact I was thinking the exact opposite – next Tuesday, when she is flying to Africa for the day. Come in time for coffee and then we'll have a walk on the beach – bikinis not recommended – and lunch in a café that DCI Secker would think ideal after a post-mortem. How would that be?'

They nodded their approval.

'I have some things for you, boss, before you go: 'your warrant card, a new police mobile and your firearms certification. You haven't changed your car but if you will trust me with your keys, I'll tinker with the radio.'

Jo took out her keys and handed them over.

Her "normal" mobile rang.

'Hi Alice.'

'I notice you're not back yet, so to save you having to rush, would you like me to collect both Ollie and Josie and bring them here?'

'That would be brilliant, my darling. I won't be too long but I'm with a bunch of total idiots I have to take care of for a few days but as soon as I can escape from their clutches, I'll set off.'

'If we knew you didn't love us, boss, we'd walk out on strike.'

'You know you're not allowed to, Darcey.'

'Yes, ma'am.'

'I've just time for a cup of tea, Darcey. You know how I like it.'

Darcey smiled, recognising that Jo never drew attention to a meeting with one of the team but found opportunity in the almost ordinary of encounters.

'I gather you and Darcey are living where Chris, Andrew and Aisling lived. Is that working out ok?' said Jo to Belinda.

'When we first met her, I knew Darcey and I were meant to be together. She is the most irritating person I know because she thinks ahead further than I do and she is usually right, but I love her so much.'

'And returning to the force? Was I right to encourage you? Is it good to be back?'

'You are the reason I returned, and now I have the chance to work with you. What's not to like?

Darcey returned with drinks for four on a tray.

'I have known Janice, as she was then, since she was a recruit, and whilst I know how much you love her, Belinda, nobody in this world loves her more than me and nobody knows more than me how superb she is at her job. Isn't that right, my darling?'

'Whatever you say, ma'am,' she replied, and then stuck out her tongue at her boss.

'Hey, you can't do that to the boss,' said Kelly walking back into the room.'

'You're quite right, Kelly, but I make an exception for Darcey.'

'Teacher's pet,' said Belinda, gently punching her partner.'

## 6

'If I'm going to be able to do this job properly, Kelly, it will only because you will be my ears and eyes. You know what I need to know and don't, so you are the filter, and even if Darcey and Belinda think something not worth bothering me but you do, I want you to send it through. I've read the MI5 report on your time with them and I trust you as they discovered they could do too. My one dread is that they will want to take you as they did Aisling.'

'I won't deny it would be great working full-time with Major Atwood but she is more mechanically-minded than me – all those astonishing inventions she develops – I prefer electronics and computers and the sort of things I've just done to your car. Another drink, boss?'

They were in the café before Jo set off for home.

'No, I'm fine, thanks. Tell me about the team and how they're working together.'

'Bonnie's clearly a very good detective but she doesn't enjoy the same  regard as team leader that you did.'

'Anyone in particular?'

'Tom and Steph can be disruptive at briefings and, in your words, both have a tendency to fly solo without speaking to Bonnie. I would say they both need their wings clipping but having just taken over, Bonnie seems reluctant to do so.'

'Thank you, Kelly. I can't remember who told me this, but I'm pretty sure it wasn't you.'

'Nor me.'

Outside the station, members of the team were loading the cars with equipment.

Jo saw Esther and went to her.

'Is this working out, Esther? You're further away from Paul.'

'Yes, but we make sure we meet when we can.'

'And what about the team. Everything ok?'

'They miss you, Jo, and a couple are a bit disruptive.'

'So I hear. I'll have a little word.'

Steph and Tom were also loading a car, as Jo approached.

'Having you both in the team was important because you bring experience and ability, and Steph even brings a former Catholic priest along with her which I hope is working well.'

'It is, Jo, and we're wanting to get married in the Spring.'

'That's brilliant. My great hope for you both is that you're still working for the team then, and to make sure that is the case you will travel to Scotland in separate cars – I'll arrange it – and from this moment you will both stop pissing about, and give your support, 100%, to Bonnie. You won't be working together again. If, when you get back from Scotland, Bonnie tells me your nonsense has continued, it will be the end of the line and you will be transferred. And the merest hint of a racial element in this and you go. But I know it won't continue, because I've put my trust in you two in the past and know how capable you are. Don't let Bonnie down and don't let me down either. Am I making myself clear?'

'Yes, ma'am,' they said together.

Jo turned and entered the building to catch a word with Bonnie about the new travelling arrangements, and to wish her well.

'I've had reason to give a warning to Tom and Steph, Bonnie, as I gather they've been less than helpful. They know that if when they return you tell me that things haven't changed they'll be out – as simple as that. No half measures in a team this size. I've said you will make some changes to travelling arrangements and that they will not travel together nor work together again. I'm sorry I'm treading on your toes like this and we don't want to lose them but this crap has to stop and I sincerely hope  there is not a racist element to it.'

'All those who think you're wonderful in every way, sometimes think you're also a great softie but they don't know you as I do. First and foremost you are a tough police officer and detective who will always do the best for justice and truth, and that includes what you've just done. I was running out of patience with them, so thanks, Jo.'

'Seize your authority and use it, Bonnie. That's what you're a Super for. I don't think you'll get more nonsense from them, but come down hard on them if you do, and my threat to transfer them if you report it, is not idle. They will go.'

Jo should have been thinking about having been forced back into her work, as she drove home, or even thinking about Marie's imminent journey to Egypt with Dianne, and if you had asked her what her mind was occupied with she wouldn't have been able to say, but there was something troubling her, something eating away inside that was preventing thought about these other important things. And as she neared Saxmundham, she had to turn once again into a mummy.

Alice, Josie and Ollie knocked on the window and waved. Jo crossed the road, and Alice opened the door to her.

'We're just having some home-coming drinks and biscuits. I'll put the kettle on if you'd like to join us.'

'The nicest thing said to me all day. I'd love to come in.'

The children quickly got over the hugging-mummy stage and returned to their play, and Jo and Alice sat in the kitchen.

'Good day?' asked Alice.

'Not at all what I expected. I met up with my old team who are about to set off for Northern Scotland to work on a sensitive case, when all of a sudden who should enter the room but the Chief Constable. He then gave me the news that my retirement documents had become lost in his safe and that therefore I am still on active service as Detective Chief Superintendent and head of the Sensitive Case Unit, which was, to say the least, one hell of a shock.'

'Does that mean you'll have to move house?'

'No, and that's definite.'

Jo was aware of Alice's sigh of relief.

'And what about your day, my darling?'

'I was terrified, Jo. But Josie and Ollie didn't notice, and we enjoyed ourselves so much just walking and up and down the road. I can't thank you enough for trusting me so much.'

'Why should I not?'

'Well, I'm sure some would not do. I could hardly get accepted to become a childminder as I wouldn't even get past the first hurdle of the DBS check. And come to think of it, am I technically allowed to bring Josie and Ollie in after school?'

'Alice, sitting next to you is not only a Detective Chief Superintendent of the Suffolk Police Force but also a Dame of the British Empire for exceptional service to the state, and if I say it's ok, then believe me, it's ok.

'Tell me, how do you get on with your team?'

'We are totally relaxed and when not in public, use our first names. We go out for curries together and laugh a great deal, and that's because I have mostly handpicked them and know I can rely on them to tell the truth at all times and to work hard. Sometimes, if they let themselves down, or let the team down, they all know I'm capable of being hard and I really can be, even to the extent of transferring them. But they know I love them and that it would take something very serious to stop me from doing so. I miss Chris however. We were more or less contemporaries and we've worked closely together, She was once my personal protection officer and saved my life by facing head on someone waiting to shoot me, but she is also a former British Taekwondo champion and utterly fearless when confronted by thugs – she prefers them two at a time, and I'm not exaggerating. In Norfolk criminals dreaded her coming to the door.'

What's she doing now?'

'Tragically, Chris fell in love, and she did with so with Dr Claud Athington, who was an outstanding forensic pathologist, 30 years her senior. It was wonderful for them and for the rest of us. Then he fell ill with cancer of the pancreas and was clearly going to die. I was bridesmaid for the wedding in their bedroom. A week later he died, but he left her with a wonderful gift in her tummy, who is called Andrew Claud. On one of our last big cases she fell hopelessly for an officer from Armed Response, and although she felt guilty, I told her to seize the opportunity as I knew Claud well enough to be sure he would agree. She is now back at work, head of CID there, and technically his boss.'

'I've met no one like you, Jo.'

'In which case, Alice, please look closely in the mirror tonight, because when I look at you, I'm not sure I've ever met anyone with more courage, and a great deal of sheer beauty. I count it a privilege to know you, Alice. Now I'd better gather these lost sheep of mine. They would probably already prefer to stay here and wait for Katia coming, whom they adore.'

They both stood, and Alice reached out to Jo and took her hand, and smiled.

Convincing the CO that Dianne was the ideal person to accompany Marie, David and the tank to Egypt was straightforward as he had done done nothing about it himself.

'The rules are simple, Marie, as you know. None of the flight deck crew, which will include Dianne, must leave the flight deck and the door to the hold, containing the soldiers with you and the tank, must remain locked and not be opened in any circumstances.

'Yes, sir.'

'I briefly glanced at the flight plan you forwarded. You will be high enough over Libya not to excite any interest.'

'North Sudan may not be so keen, sir, so I thought I'd keep my height until we're close to the Egyptian air space and then descend rapidly, not quite as used to be the case for landing in Baghdad but perhaps enough to make Dianne's ears pop.'

The CO laughed.

'I did some of those flights into Baghdad. They were a tight corkscrew descent and truly frightening.'

'And you had passengers too.'

'Yes, and in planes not designed for what we were asking of them. I think you should find your trip easier. And don't forget the Israeli Air Force will come to escort you if you need them to and be ready to refuel there. I'm told that they are hoping you might need them as they have no women capable of what you're flying and they're wanting to see you in action.'

'I can always train them, sir.'

'Dianne, please take this impossible Flight Lieutenant away from me.

'Gladly.'


They walked across towards the plane they would be flying.

'Here she is.'

'She? Are you sure it's a she?'

'I have no doubts. I have no wish to be inside a man or have a man inside me.'

Dianne laughed.

'I've seen nothing so large, and you fly this by yourself?'

'I have a First Officer who takes over when I need a wee, but mostly when we're in the air, the automatic pilot will follow exactly the flight plan I produce. As we leave Libya and go over Sudan, I'll take charge again for the landing, though David will do the talking with ATC so they don't think it's me.'

'Well, I'm really looking forward to it and though the CO says we are not to leave the flight deck, it will be odd being so near Egyptian soil and unable to touch it.'

'One other thing, Dianne. You will have to wear the basic RAF flying track suit. If we had to come down anywhere, it would be necessary to have you as a bona fide member of the RAF. You will receive some papers on Monday when we travel here We have to stay overnight as we're flying at 5:00 am, which means being in the plane by 4:00.'

'What sort of papers?'

'Just flying orders. Nothing more. It would be suspicious if on landing somewhere you didn't have them.'

'In the plane by 4:00, did you say?'

'Were you not out early on digs in the desert?'

'I suppose so.'

'Anyway, it's a five and a half hour flight so you'll be able to catch up en route, though if all goes well and if they let us refuel, the return flight will be quicker because we won't be carrying the tank. Between you and me, my plan is to refuel before I open up and let them have the tank, which they want more than they want us.. In that way we can go once it's done.'

'You're really happy doing this, Marie, aren't you?

'I love it. My dad taught me to fly when I was well below the minimum age, but it's been Jo who has encouraged me every bit of the way. I'm deeply ashamed to say that recently I behaved so badly towards her, and I mean extremely badly, and when she opened the door when I came back it was as if nothing had happened at all and she welcomed me with open arms and lots of kisses. Perhaps you don't know, but lesbians are the world's champion kissers, and we broke the world record that evening.'

'I envy you loving and being loved.'

'It hasn't all been plain sailing, I'm afraid. I was once married to a gynaecologist, and Josie is the fruit of that relationship. We divorced, and I went to live with a police sergeant. He was a nice man and then, one fine day, his superior officer called to see him, and I fell in love at once with her, which didn't help because Jo arrested me and locked me up for a serious crime. After 24 hours she released me and confessed her own love for me.'

'Have you sold the film rights?'

'We married and between us had Ollie, via IVF. I gave the egg, some nice anonymous man provided the sperm and Jo became pregnant. Simply magic. But then a few weeks ago, I completely fucked up and nearly lost everything and anything worth having. When I knocked on her door, anyone less than Jo would, rightly, have told me to piss off. But her love for me had not failed, nor mine for her.'

'I'm afraid I've been married to Egypt's past, and she has been a demanding mistress.'

'I was about to say that I could take you clubbing in Cambridge but then I remembered I only know the gay clubs, like the AAA, though I'm getting a bit old for there.'

Dianne laughed, but the sort of laugh that made Marie wonder if it was covering up an embarrassment of some sort.

Arriving back in Saxmundham, Marie invited Dianne for some supper, and they found the house if total chaos, with the two children and the two adults on their knees playing some game or other and screeching with laughter. In charge was Katia who was enjoying herself as much as the others. Marie and Dianne only seemed to enhance the noise and laughter.

'How about if I go down to the Golden Fish Bar and bring back loads for us all to eat?' said Marie.

A roar of support went up from all. Alice went with her and by the time they returned there had been a transformation taken place. The two children sat at the table with Jo, Katia and Dianne.

'Fish and chips never caught on in Canada which is a great pity, but as you can imagine there were not many chip shops in the Egyptian desert though there were some good tasty fish in the Nile.'

'I'd love to go to Egypt,' said Katia, 'and see the Pyramids and have a ride on a camel.'

'Believe it or not, Katia, but there are many more pyramids in Sudan and even in Mexico. Not so large, maybe, nor with their fascination linked to the Pharaohs but when you've been to Egypt, see the others.'

'It must exciting to be an archaeologist.'

'Well, like most things in life, it's 95% routine, digging, digging, sifting and trying to work out what you might have found which puzzles you for an hour and then you turn it over and you see it at once and feel a total fool and fraud. And perhaps I mean 99% is like that, and then one day and quite unexpectedly you find something that makes sense of other things you've found and it's all worthwhile. But it's mostly not like Indiana Jones or at least I've not met Harrison Ford anywhere in the field.'

'But what a village this is,' continued Katia. 'Across the road we have an international archaeologist, a Flight Lieutenant in the Royal Air Force and Detective Chief Superintendent of Police, and all women. It's a perfect Careers Lesson every time I look out of the window. It would be so good to get you to school and talk to the girls there.'

'I would gladly do so, Katia,' said Jo.

'Me too,' added Marie.

'Include me in,' said Dianne.

'In which case I shall have a word with Mrs Charlton first thing in the morning.'

'What about you Alice?' asked Marie. 'I believe all women have a story to tell and that the young should be able to hear them.'

Alice looked to Jo, who smiled back.

'Alice will eventually have the most important story of all to tell one day, but it's not quite complete, so Mrs Charlton will have to wait a while longer, but I'm convinced it will be worth waiting for.'

They all stared at Jo and pondered her enigmatic words, though none more so than Alice and Katia, both of whom had puzzled looks upon their faces, though even after a short time, Alice had a sense that she could trust Jo completely.

## 7

Marie knew Jo well enough not to ask her anything about her words as they had eaten their fish and chips, just as Jo would not dream of asking Marie about her flights plans, payload or attending dangers of her work for the RAF. The essence of their love lay in the recognition that what was confidential remained so, even from one another. Both were bound by the terms of the Official Secrets Act and knew the consequences of falling foul of it.

Alice worked in the café both days at the weekend and Katia crossed the road to look after the children whilst Marie did the shopping and Jo had gone into work to catch up with some paperwork and find out what she had missed during her period of "retirement". No one was there, but she knew Kelly was constantly accessible. Although she had brought some first-class people into the unit and before that in Norfolk, she was most proud of Kelly. She too ought to go to speak to the girls in Katia's school, a perfect example of someone who had done something stupid and illegal and then in prison used the place for what it was intended to be used for and and emerged truly as a swan. Kelly had the fastest mind she had even known, and this had also been reported back from her month training with MI5, but from her time in prison where she had seen broken women, she had also developed a remarkable compassion, so much so that Jo was sure that if a woman serial killer had been arrested, Kelly would surely say, "Go on, boss, let her off, poor thing"!'

The genuine test of Kelly's compassion was soon to come, just as Darcey and Belinda were about to be tested in ways they could never have imagined. But that was in the week ahead.

Katia identified closely with Marie because she was the most glamorous and gorgeous woman around, and also the most amazing – a woman who could fly massive aeroplanes. It was almost as if Marie could read Katia's mind for when she arrived back with her shopping bags, she said to the two children and babysitter, 'Who wants to go for a fly and see some old aeroplanes?'

Katia did not join in the "Me, me, me" chorus, but she certainly did so silently. She had never flown, unlike most of the girls at her school, and this was an amazing adventure. They drove to the aerodrome and waited patiently as Marie went through all the pre-flight preparation. Ollie and Josie knew the form and clambered into the seats and attached their seat belts. Katia was last in and found herself given a headset enabling her to hear ATC and to speak to Marie. She watched intently as Marie completed a final list of checks and then spoke to Air Traffic Control using permission to line up and then take off. Katia's heart was in her mouth as Marie accelerated along the runway and then her heart rose even higher as the ground disappeared from under them. All the time Marie was talking to some invisible persson about wind, height and weather. By now Katia was loving it and loving how the land beneath them looked. Cars were tiny and there were no people.

As they passed over Stowmarket Marie indicated that Jo was down there at this moment.

'We have two mummies,' said Ollie. 'One up here and one down there.'

'That's clever,' said Katia, turning to the children who were clearly so used to this. That turn round, however, was a mistake against which Marie should have warned her, for often on a first flight in a small aircraft, it can bring on immediate sickness – and it did.

Marie looked across at Katia and saw she had gone white. She produced a bag and gave it to her.

'Not long now. You'll be fine. Keep looking forwards and it'll go. It's my fault for not telling you in advance. Don't worry,

Katia, it's perfectly normal for first-flyers. It won't happen again,' and by the time Marie was making her final approach to Duxford, Katia was feeling ok and caught up in the communications between Marie and the Air Traffic Control on the ground. She was a little taken taken aback by how low they flew over the M11 and then they were on the ground.

Marie explained that everyone landing had to pay a fee, and much to her delight this task was assigned to Josie, who clearly knew exactly what to do and where. Then they went inside the Aircraft Museum and first all all had some lunch.

Katia thought this might be the happiest day of her life and when Marie showed them amazing aeroplanes, including Concorde, she could barely take her eyes off Marie and the thought of another flight. Marie, who knew nothing from Jo about the background of Katia and Alice, sensed that there might be something dark in the past of mother and daughter, but had no intention of asking anything about it. If there was something and Jo knew about it, then that knowledge was safe.

There was no sickness on the way back and Marie extended the journey so Katia could see her school in Ipswich from above, and the floodlights at Portman Road where the once great Ipswich Town play football.

Katia was still a little uneasy when the time came for landing but marvelled at what Marie could do and was sorry to have to leave the plane and return to a boring car. Inevitably it was all she could talk about throughout the evening to the extent that Alice envied her and was determined to drop some sort of a subtle hint that she too had never flown and would love to do so.

'Marie is flying to and from Egypt on Tuesday,' said Katia.

'I guess that's what happens in the RAF. Jo told me she trained for the sort of plane she flies at work for 6 weeks in America,' said Alice.

'Mum, are Jo and Marie what are called lesbians?'

'Yes, and they are married. But ask them about it, because I know they will be happy to tell you. Marie was once married to a man, and Josie is her daughter from that marriage, but Ollie was born almost, but not quite, magically by IVF. Jo became pregnant and gave birth but the fertilised egg came from Marie.'

'They both say they have two mums, but there must have been a man involved to have sex with one or the other?'

'Some men donate sperm to clinics for this sort of thing. They do so anonymously.'

'That's interesting. In the Bible it says Mary was a virgin and yet had a baby. That could happen now if a fertilised egg was placed inside a virgin then it would be a virgin birth.'

'You're correct but I can't think there's all that many virgins in Ipswich!'

'Mother, I'm shocked at such cynicism, and I'll have you know that your beloved daughter is still a virgin.'

'Katia, I will always love you whatever sign of the zodiac you wish to be.'

'I worry about you sometimes, mum!'

'What do you mean "sometimes"?

They dissolved in laughter and hugged one another, both with tears in their eyes.


On Monday morning, before she left for work, Jo walked up the road to Dianne's.

'I just wanted to wish you a safe journey under the command of my wife, and to say that it has been nice getting to know you and that whilst I hear Egyptian prisons are not fun, I'm sure you'll survive.'

'Jo, you must be such a rich source of consolation to those you arrest!'

'Thank you. No, enjoy the trip and enjoy seeing Marie doing what she's brilliant at. I've never flown with her in one of those monsters, but she takes it completely in her stride. My only word of advice is that if she tells you to do something, she will mean it, so take it as an absolute order and do it.'

'I intend doing so.'

They gave each other a hug and kiss. Jo came away somewhat disturbed. Although Bonnie was black and she regularly kissed and hugged her, this black woman was different and for the first time since her death, she was reminded of Ellie.

Marie took the children to school and play school and then invited Alice in for a coffee, as she didn't work on Mondays and soon wouldn't be working at all as the café closed for the two darkest months of the year.

'Thank you so much for taking Katia up in your aeroplane on Saturday. I must confess I've never flown, and she said it was the best day of her life despite feeling suddenly very sick at one moment.

'That was my fault. I should have told her not to turn round as on a first flight it confuses the inner ears so much that they want to throw up but she didn't and most don't, but it's a horrible feeling. But I'd love to take you up sometime and soon. My dad was a commercial pilot in America and he taught me to fly when I was far too young officially. Now I fly the sort of planes he would hardly have believed could get off the ground. I'd like to think he'd be proud.'

'I'm sure he would, and do you have to wear RAF uniform when you are flying?'

'Not dress uniform as when you're on parade, but flight pilot suits, a bit like track suits, but clearly recognisable as military wear just in case we have to land in hostile land.'

'Good heavens, I never thought of that.'

'It doesn't happen very often, I'm pleased to say, but just in case. If we're in uniform, there's usually an attempt made to repatriate us before some sort of awful incident – there would be in Iran, for example – but without uniform we might well be taken as spies and put on trial, so we wear it.'

'Do you have food with you?'

'No air hostesses I'm afraid, but we have rations and water, plus the facility for making tea and coffee. It's a tight fit on the flight deck, but happily my First Officer, David and I get on really well. I taught him to fly this particular plane and I have every confidence that he could take over at a moment's notice, and of course I get him to take over quite a lot anyway so each can have a break from concentration. He has twins much the same age as Ollie so we share stories all the time about the children. For most of the time being up there is just normal and for much of the time the plane is being directed by the automatic pilot who follows the flight path I have set for it.'

'Well, my automatic pilot is set to collect Josie and Ollie this afternoon but had determined before then I must do some washing and cleaning. Thanks for the coffee and all that fascinating information about your life work, and thanks again for giving Katia such a wonderful time.'

'It was my joy to do so, Alice, and you're next. I must give some thought as to where we might go, though only if on your first flight you promise not to turn round and be sick on my back seat.'

Alice laughed.

'Oh I promise, Marie.'

It was just after 2:00 when Dianne made her way to Marie's home.

'Is Jo not to see you off.'

'She did that before leaving for work. She's used to it. She goes to Stowmarket and I go to Africa, Finland or wherever.'

'Is she enjoying being back working?'

'If you ask her, she will say it was never her plan to do so and look grumpy about it, but actually she's delighted to be doing it again.'

'Does she talk about her cases to you?'

'Never until perhaps afterwards.'

'Isn't that frustrating in a marriage?'

'Neither of us may discuss our work with anyone, including marital partners, because we're both bound by the Official Secrets Act. It happens of course, and occasionally with serious consequences, but in this house it doesn't I'm pleased to say because inevitably we both live with a measure of risk and the less we know the better. Now, let's get going. David will join us for the briefing and will do external checks on the plane, then the four soldiers will come and be with the three of us for some food, probably in the local Italian.'

'Am I allowed to come to all this?' asked Dianne.

'Yes. If only to scare the wits out of you.'
'Oh, well, that's alright then.'

Jo had forgotten just how much paperwork accumulated each day on her desk though with Kelly empowered as chief filter person it was considerably less than it might otherwise be. Kelly always noted what she had filed under WPB so Jo could check it but never needed to do so. With Belinda and Darcey out investigating some trouble and damage in St John's College, Cambridge (clearly much too sensitive for the Cambridge Police or even the University authorities – the two Proctors), Jo and Kelly went to Bury St Edmunds for a Thai meal at the *Giggling Squad.*

As they ate, Jo spoke.

'Kelly, as we both know, our work is of the most sensitive kind, even more than most police work, which is why we are in business..'

'I hope, boss you never find me lacking in that department.'

'I always thought Aisling was 100% secure, and she was and has to be when working for our friends in London, but you are no less so, which is why what I am about to tell you will be made known to no one else in the team and when you hear what I about to tell you, I think you will fully understand why.

'A long time ago, before you were born, and I was just one-year-old, there were two murders of tiny children, for which another child, aged just ten, was blamed, put on trial in an adult court, found guilty and sentenced to Her Majesty's Pleasure, which kept her locked up for many years before releasing her with a so-called guarantee of anonymity, which is a joke as the Press have continued to hound her.'

'I've heard of Mary Bell. Is that who you mean?'

'No, and for now, the name is not important. I'm going to take a colossal risk which may really bring about the end of of my career. For reasons almost wholly due to my intuition I think that this person did not do it. I think further that the person who did, has spent 36 years getting away with it and and inflicting untold misery and unhappiness on another person.'

'Has this person told you this is the case?'

'No, quite the opposite. She, and it is a she, maintains that she did the killing.'

'Then I don't understand ...'

'The thing is that I have a very strong feeling that at the age of ten she was told she had done it so often and given a formula of confession that the little girl who had suffered horrendous abuse up to that time came to think that the adults must be right. Even now when she tells the story, I can hear the formula being repeated.'

'Because I trust you completely and know something of your detective mind, I can understand what you are saying, but I have several questions, the first of which is to ask why you have told me and no one else. Surely you need Bonnie and Esther to be working on this with you. The second is to ask how on earth you intend to proceed on what is not just a cold case, but one that's been in the freezer for years?'

'The answer to your first question is that I want someone I respect and trust 100% but who will not be internally hampered by police procedure. You and I are going to deal with this because we're not hampered in that way despite my rank, which suggests that I will always observe police procedure when of course I won't. I might add that being a Dame might also come in useful. Having you to work with is the very best I can think of.

'And how we are going to do it is, first of all, to check out my hunch about the formula, for which I need you to come to stay the night in Saxmundham and meet this person.'

'When?'

'Tonight. Marie is flying before dawn tomorrow and staying at the Base overnight. She mustn't, and indeed everyone mustn't learn about this so it's an ideal time for you to come. I'll even cook for you and if that doesn't turn you off working with me, nothing will!'

'Of course I will, boss. What time will you want me?'

'7:00 will be fine. I'll let Darcey know that I'm giving you the night off and that she can do the on-call. She won't mind, especially if I tell her she won't mind!'

Kelly laughed.

'One other thing, Kelly, you must learn to call me Jo.'

'Pity. I was hoping to call you Your Damehood!'

Darcey and Belinda arrived back with little to report other than naughty students drinking too much, though their presence there enabled the College to make an Insurance Claim. They had to confess, however, that they had spent 20 minutes or so in Heffer's Bookshop just a few yards down Trinity St.

'20?'

'Well, maybe 30,' said Belinda.'

'H'm, I had a feeling DI Bussell was not telling me the complete story. The most important thing is, did you buy anything worth reading?'

'It sounds pretentious, I know,' said Belinda, 'but I did Latin at school and I like to keep it up as best I can. After all, you never know when I might get the chance to use it in the course of my work.'

'O definitely. Most days I imagine, even if only to say *Eheu*. And on that subject, my darling Darcey, I want you to do call tonight. Kelly has to be elsewhere.'

'Of course I will, and if I get called, it will at least liberate me from the strange but lovely lady in my bed who will be reading Latin.'

Jo made her way home, arriving just after Alice would have collected the children from school. She parked the car and crossed the road and even from outside could hear the children laughing as they played. Alice responded to her knock.

'Hello, mum, the children are in fine fettle as you can hear. Come in and have a cup of tea.'

'Gladly. Hello Ollie, hello Josie.'

They both waved but were in the middle of a game and wished no interruption. Jo and Alice retreated to the kitchen.

'Is there any chance you and Katia could come and have some supper across the road about 7:00. There's someone I want you both to meet. She's called Kelly and of all those I work with I would trust her utterly with my life even though she's a civilian and not a police officer, but she has been trained by MI5 (or as we call them "our friends in London")' I want you and Katia to know that Kelly can be trusted in every way.'

'It all sounds mysterious.'

'I ought to add though, she's not above teasing her boss, i.e. me and you will love her.'

'Ok. Katia and I trust you completely, and if you say we should do the same with Kelly, then I will.'

With the children in bed and asleep by 7:30, the four of them could sit down to eat in good time. Katia kept them entertained them in the main by an account of her recent flight with Marie to the Duxford Air Museum and Jo repeated her own excursions with her wife, though also recounted the story of Marie's emergency landing in a field of cows of which she was terrified and then being hijacked on her way to work. The others were astounded by both stories.

With the tables cleared they all sat down in the sitting room, with Alice and Katia wondering what was coming next.

'Ok, down to business,' said Jo, 'which is why I've gathered you here. Alice, you have told me the story of what happened all those years ago, and you, Katia know it well. I'm a senior detective because I seem to have a peculiar capacity for hearing when things don't ring true. I believe Kelly would bear that out.'

'I would and it's most odd, not something I've met in others.'

'The bottom line of what I am saying, Alice and Katia, is that I believe Alice, you were lied to, that you were given lines to repeat as in a play, because you did not kill those two children, but have had your mind so twisted when you just ten, that even now you will find find what I have said difficult to accept. There were two children murdered, but I am convinced they were not killed by you but by someone else and that person has put you through years of unhappiness.'

'But I remember doing it.'

'Of course you do, because when you are so young your mind accepts what is told you, by the police, your wretched mother and Doug Pedley, living with her, and the actual murderer. I knew this at once when you told me your story when we were in Aldeburgh. I listened and I could tell, and furthermore, Kelly and I are going to prove it. I am not prepared that you should feel guilty after all this time when you are not guilty. After all Alice, if I felt you were guilty, would I be placing my children in your hands day after day with no worries on my part?

'And I want to free you, Katia, but first I want to try an experiment. Katia, will you and Kelly go back into the dining room, and I want you to tell Kelly the story of your mother's so-called crime. Kelly will record it to play it back in here, and we'll destroy the tape. Yes?'

Katia looked at her mum, who nodded, and then she and Kelly went back to the dining room.

'Why Jo, why after all this time?'

'Because I know you are not guilty. If I screw up then that will be me permanently finished but (forgive my next words, Alice) you're worth it.'

'Isn't it going to take ages?'

'I have no idea, Alice, but I am determined to do this, not for me, but for you and Katia. It will not bring you publicity or the newspapers and my aim is that no one here, and that includes my Marie and Dianne, will know anything about this until it's over.'

'But where do you start?

'Leave that to me and wonder woman in there, but I do have some advantages. In the first place I have a superior rank and no will object to my exploring archives especially as there were no computer records at the time and no one will know what I'm looking at. The second is that sometimes my honour as a Dame of the British Empire van be useful, especially as I'm permanently prevented from telling anyone how I got it. That mystery might well win us some time.'

Katia and Kelly returned, and the tape was played through.

'Exactly as I thought. Almost word-for-word of what you said to me, Alice. This is what you were taught to think and say when you were ten, and Katia repeats the story. I am even more confident now we are heading in the right direction. But I will stop this instant and never raise it again, if you and Katia want me to stop. I promise that will be the end, if you wish it.'

'Mum, we must go on. It would make such a difference to discover the truth to you, of course, but no less to me because I'm a person with no past. I can't ever talk about my life so far as other girls do, because I have no life so far I can talk about.'

'I know that, my love, and I would want to do it for no reason other than that were it not because I can't bear the thought that the Press would be involved again and that once again we would have to move and change identity. I really couldn't stand that.'

'You would have no part in the investigation, Alice, at any stage. We would deal only with those who were involved with the original events in Nottingham.'

Alice reached into her bag and produced a letter, which she opened and handed to Jo. It was on Channel 4 headed notepaper and had been sent by none other than Andie Bolam, someone well known to Jo, and to whom she had once offered a job as an undercover research detective knowing just how able she was at discovering many things, including as it now seemed, the whereabouts of Alice. The letter said she wanted to make a sympathetic film about her and that she would come and see her on the following Monday morning.

'Andie Bolam is as poisonous as the most toxic of all snakes, but she is very clever. She lies with impunity in her own interests and twice had a go at trapping me into serious sexual indiscretion, from which I am pleased to say I escaped. She is also very beautiful, all of which makes her almost a perfect model of the devil.'

'You see my dilemma?'

'Yes, I do. Kelly, you've seen her in action. What thoughts have you got?'

'As you say, she is very attractive and will tell you always what she thinks you want to hear in order to get more than you might want to give. But she is highly talented and always looking out with her astonishing antennae for major stories missed by others, and she's not beyond trying to turn nothing into something. How she found out where you are, I just can't understand, but she will have left traces behind and I will find them. If she has hacked into the Home Office computer she will go to prison for a long time.'

'In the meantime, I already have a plan in my mind for Monday,' said Jo with a smile. 'Alice moved away, apparently to Wales some 18 months ago, and the person at the door will most definitely not be you, though you can watch from my window where I would like you and Katia to spend the night. Is that a deal?'

'Deal,' said Katia and her mum in unison.

## 8

Dianne was convinced that she would freeze to death as she walked out to the Globemaster C17 with the others. As she stood waiting to clamber in, it was raining hard and very windy, though she had earlier been with Marie as she had enquired about the weather on their flightpath. The C17 was usually based at Brize Norton and flew from there, but her teaching was done at Lakenheath. David's first task as First Officer was to ensure the four Royal Engineers accompanying the tank were seated and told not to leave their seats until the Captain informed them. He then came to Dianne who was seated just behind him and Marie and given the same instruction. Dianne had brought a book but at this stage was much more interested, if not fascinated by all that had to be done by Marie and David before even thinking of starting the engines. They worked steadily and systematically through their extensive checklists. Dianne had respected Marie from their first meeting and that rose even higher watching her at work and she could tell how much she loved what she doing.

Their route would take take them over France, the Alps and then down the length of Italy, across the Mediterranean, and then over Libya before swinging East and beginning their approach over the North of Sudan into the new Berenice airbase on the coast of the Red Sea. The route had been communicated to the Egyptians and they were perfectly happy with it, as were the Sudanese. For most of the of the time over Libya they would cruising at above 40,000 ft which should cause no problems. The flight deck was not exactly warm, and Marie had warned Dianne to wear warm clothes under the flying suit.

Dianne heard Marie inform the tower that she was ready to start the engines, and then, after yet another checklist, Marie asked permission to roll to the end of the runway, where there was another checklist (and there would be another after they were airborne). Then they were on their way. The C17 has a short run before lift-off and she wondered what the people of Cambridgeshire were thinking as they were woken by the engine noise. Soon the plane banked sharply to port, and Dianne heard Marie say to David that she was switching to the Flight Plan by AP, and he confirmed it back to her. They rose to 40,000 ft, and more or less that was it. Marie swung her seat and chatted with her, leaving David on watch.

Once they were drawing close to the North African coast, Marie suggested to David that they go up by 3,000 ft and he agreed. Dianne asked why, and was horrified to learn that what remained of the Libyan Airforce had nothing with a ceiling that high and that they would have to shoot them down if they wanted them to stop.

'That's ok then,' said Dianne.

Marie and David laughed.

'Don't worry,' said David. 'They hate each other much more than they hate us.'

Dianne had already noticed that David was now doing all the conversation with ATC, just in case the Saudis were monitoring the flight and waiting to hear the dulcet tones of Enemy Number One: Marie, which might cause them to intercept, and unlike the Libyans, they really had planes that could get that high, which Marie and David knew, because they had been supplied by the UK!

The plane banked sharply to port as it made its way towards North Sudan and began to lose height. Dianne could tell from their posture and frequent short sentences to one another that this part of the flight was demanding their fullest attention. Still David did the ATC conversations, apart from one to alert the Israeli Air Force that they were just 15 minutes from landing. It was on a pre-arranged frequency and Marie knew there would be no reply, nor had she indicated who she was calling.

David received permission to make a final approach from the South and Marie brought about a perfect landing, and then David announced they would refuel before unloading, which clearly was not what ground control wanted but could not stop as they wanted what was inside the aeroplane. After refueling, Marie rolled the plane to where David was told to stop. Marie began enabling the rear doors to open and the four Royal Engineers took their leave, preparing for an Egyptian holiday, teaching those unable to speak English how to use a tank that was already suspect back home - the report was that all those in the tank were made to feel sick because of excessive vibrations. Three of the soldiers got the tank out of the rear of the plane and the fourth, seeing the rear doors close, approached the flight deck door which David opened, to offer thanks for their lift. The flight deck had heated up, given that the outside temperature was well over 110° and Marie was keen to get back into the air. David began the door closure, but the British soldier had been pulled away from the door and steps by some Egyptian soldiers and suddenly there appeared a soldier on the flight deck carrying the sort of machine gun that most definitely could not be used in such a confined space. He spoke in very broken English.

'Captain Enright and Dr Dianne Walter, you will both come with me now. Captain, we have a request for your extradition from the Kingdom of Saudi Arabia, you Dr Walter, are a spy, and you are both under arrest.'

Dianne spoke to him in Arabic and he replied abruptly.

'I shouldn't trust his sense of humour, Marie.'

'Let's see if he laughs at what's coming. Tell him I'm reaching for my Flight Bag and that I may not leave without it.'

She did, and he grunted.

Marie sat down and spoke into the radio still set to the Israeli frequency, 'Urgent departure.'

She reached down to her left and pressed the green button, releasing the compartment, in which there was a Glock 17, loaded and armed, and a yellow Taser. She put both into her Flight Bag and stood.

'Engines, David.'

Marie now made her way to the back and pointed to the pilot's door.

'Tell him to open the door, Dianne, and argue like mad.'

As she did, the plane shook, and the man panicked and turned angrily towards Marie, who pointed again to the door. He looked around, and she brought out the taser and pulled the trigger. He screamed and went down.

Marie removed his gun and pulled him down the steps to the outer pilot's door. She opened the door and pushed him into the arms of a small group of soldiers who had been expecting two women prisoners, and not an unconscious one of their own thrown to the ground by a woman wielding a Glock pistol she clearly intended to use. They withdrew and pulled their colleague away as Marie smiled and slammed close the door.

'Get rolling, David.'

Afterwards, Dianne could recall more than anything else how Marie had been completely calm throughout, almost as if she did this every day of her life.

She had taken over immediately and spoken to ground control, calmly fulfilling the strictures and demands of ground etiquette, before obtaining clearance to take off.

'This is an extremely smooth runway,' said Marie, though in seconds the plane had left it and was heading North alongside the Red Sea. At this stage, she was still flying on manual.

'How did they know the two of us were on board?' asked Dianne.

'That will be for Intelligence to discover and I truly apologise, Dianne, for putting you to such risk.'

'Hey, Marie, that's the most interesting and exciting thing that's happened to me since I lost my virginity.'

David and Marie laughed.

'That must have been some encounter,' said Marie.

Marie handed over to David the manual control whilst she contacted Lakenheath via Akrotiri to give an interim report, including that the Egyptians knew about the presence of her and Dianne on board. There was no time to wait for a reply as David summoned her attention to the radar screen.

'We have company, two MiG 29s. Just so you know, guys, we're not stopping or landing for them. At the moment they're staying behind us so one of them could be intent on shooting us down, though I doubt it. They are much more likely to want us to land at the Cairo West military airport, or at least I hope so, as by then our friends from Israel will have arrived and also from Akrotiri whom I will call now.'

The message to Akrotiri was the military equivalent of "Mayday" and the airmen would have scrambled and received orders once they were in the air.

To Dianne, the person least fazed by all that was going on was Marie, who communicated with the MiGs and give them the exact position of the two Israeli jets on their way to wish them well! She then informed them of the two Typhoons hastening from Akrotiri, and warned them that she had given orders that if any attempt was made to hinder her flight, the support aircraft would be free to engage in armed conflict.

'It's possible they think I'm bluffing but they will soon see I'm not, as the Israeli jets are now just 50 miles away and will be on their radar soon. They also know that any military action would end for a long time the possibility of further trade, and they probably will want more tanks, so let's not worry too much. I am getting fed up flying on manual however so once we spot our friends from the Negev I shall turn hard to Port and pick up our flight plan over Libya.'

Moments later came a radio message.

'Hi there, Marie. You love fun and games with Arabs. Thank you for your explicit instructions. You have two MiG-29s on your tail. What are you suggesting?'

'Shalom. Just get of rid them for us, and we'll bank to Port and pick up our line home.'

'We'd love you to come to the Negev. You're one of our heroes for what you did to the Saudis and we're dying to hear what you did at Berenice.'

'Nothing special. I just shot a man with a taser and threw him off the plane and then my First Officer set us rolling.'

'I bet your husband is terrified of you.'

'Actually, I have a wife and she adores me.'

'I've got a visual on the MiGs. Bring your wife sometime. We'd love to see you both.' He now lapsed into Hebrew to speak to his oppo. Marie watched the radar screen.

'Impressive', she said, as the MiGs decided lunch was waiting for them back at Berenice.

'Ok, David. 'Let's head 345 degrees please.'


It was another four hours before they made their approach to Lakenheath though Marie invited Dianne up front to show how they lined up on the wonderful Ely Cathedral, the ship of the Fens as it was called, at this time of the day lit up by artificial light but still a joy to see.

David landed the plane.

'Well, that was something else,' said Dianne. 'Thank you so much for what I thoroughly enjoyed and do you know, when things things looked somewhat bleak, I never lost confidence in you, Marie. You were so calm and amazing.'

'Having my hand on a taser and Glock 17 helped. I just keep thinking he was going to be the loser, not one of us three. In the end, it was easy. There is still the question to be resolved as to how they knew about our presence. Don't be offended or surprised if someone from Intelligence comes and knocks on your door.'

'Really?'

'Yes, it's vital we find out how this happened. Neither of us were on the manifest. The Israelis knew about me, but not about you. Anyway, now David and I have to go through the post-flight checklist, inside and out, and it's my turn to do the latter, but you can come and watch if you like.

'Gee, you give me all the cushy numbers.'

By the time they approached home Marie was feeling exhausted and ready for bed so was dismayed as she parked the car to see another vehicle which she recognised: the official car of the Chief Constable of Greater Manchester and would-be thief of Jo, Dani Thomas. She received warm greetings as she opened the front door from both Jo and Dani and entering the sitting room, found them at the table with lots of papers, and not as she had feared, bound in each other's arms.

'You made the ten o'clock news,' said Jo.

'You're kidding.'

'Not at all. It said that following an incident at the new military airport in Egypt in which an attempt was made to take an RAF officer and a passenger who was wanted by the authorities, the female pilot had used a taser against an Egyptian soldier and evicted him from the plane before leaving. The Ministry of Defence said the pilot had been both courageous and determined. Fame at last. But is it correct?'

'Completely so. But more worrying is how they knew I was flying the plane and the fact of Dianne being with me. That is much more worrying and suggests someone at Lakenheath has it in for me. The man I tasered said the Saudis wished me to be extradited, and that Dianne was a spy. It could have been unpleasant.'

'Are tasers normally carried?' asked Dani.

'If you are of the rank of Flight Lieutenant you have access to a compartment and authority to use what you find there. I was expecting to find a Glock 17, and I would have used it, but the taser seemed more humane, so I gave him 100,000 volts to remember me by. He was still away with the fairies when I dropped him into the hands of his astonished colleagues. I slammed and locked the door and shouted to David to get rolling. After take off they sent up to MiGs but I had already sought help from the Israeli Airforce and two Typhoons from Akrotiri. The MiGs were obviously told to come home. And what sort of day have you two had?'

'I drove here from London,' said Dani, 'to persuade your wife to come and do some detective training days in Manchester.'

'Any luck?'

'She knows she owes me, so I think I might be successful.'

'And I spent most of the day in the office with Kelly, going through some old cases we might consider,' said Jo.

'Successfully?'

'Oh yes, we had a wonderful lunch, together with Darcey and

Belinda.'

'Do they behave on duty?'

'They're brilliant, and you would never believe they were partners. Belinda never fails to speak of Darcey as "ma'am" when they are working.'

'Well, ladies, I must go to bed. It's been quite a day. I have been chased by jets before but this was the first time I've shot someone.'

'He'll live,' said Dani. 'I experienced one when they first came out. I went down, and it hurt like hell, but I survived.'

Pity, thought Marie, who trusted Dani with Jo as far as she could pick her up and throw her.

'So I see. Anyway, I'm not leaving early so I'll see you at breakfast. Sleep well.'

'We recognise how dangerous it can be in the police force, but perhaps it's not anywhere as dangerous as being in the military. After all, being shot down by a MiG would hurt a great deal. Marie's a very brave lass, Jo.'

'And she makes so little of it, unlike when she went off with that crazy evangelical doctor. That was much more dangerous.'

'Now back to cold case files. Are you sure you don't want to tell me what you want to do?'

'I would love to tell you, Dani, for of all people I'd like to work on this with you, but I can't do that without the person involved letting me do so and for reasons you of all people would understand, to break her trust at this stage would be the end.'

'I understand, Jo, of course I do, but I am willing at any stage to throw in my lot with you. If you are doing something this important, you may need a friend in high places, and you know you can rely totally on me.'

'Dani, my love for you knows no bounds – you know that.'

'I do. And I feel the same, although I should warn you that there is another woman in my affections. She is called Alecia Beth Moore and I went to her concert in Manchester last week. Most people know her as "Pink" and Oh God, is she stunning? I tell you I almost orgasmed when I saw her in the white dress she was wearing which revealed just about everything. When she sang Linda Perry's song "What's Up" there must have been some in the audience die.'

'Dani, you are funny. I hope you were there in your uniform.'

'Not quite. It was wonderful.'

'So when I come to do your detective training days I can feel its right to suggest to them they adapt their technique from your example of neo-orgasmic evenings in the Manchester Arena?'

'Er, perhaps not.'

## 9

Marie was not expected at Lakenheath until noon and sat with Jo after Dani had set off back to Manchester.

'What did she really want, apart from looking at you?' asked Marie.

'I'm no longer number one in her eyes. She has fallen in love with Pink.'

'The singer from America? That's far-fetched even for Dani, though I will admit that she's incredibly attractive.'

'How have you seen her?'

'On YouTube. Have a look. But she didn't just come to talk over some talks you might give her team, did she?'

'I'm doing some work on not just a cold case, but a freezing one, and I need to know what might be and what might not be possible. Dani has been an ACC and now is a Chief Constable. I had to run my ideas past her police nose.'

'And what did she say?'

'I couldn't give her any details but she thinks, as I hope, my rank and title should be able to work wonders especially if I'm devious, but from what you said last night, a taser might come in useful too.'

'I watched her last night, and every time she looks at you I can see her thinking that you are rightly hers and that I've just borrowed you like a book from a library for a little while.'

'And what you told me of your trip to Egypt makes me wonder whether there isn't a better way of earning your living in the air without such danger. It could have gone badly wrong and this morning you might even have been waking up in a Saudi jail.'

'We have to begin finding out today how that nearly happened. Either someone doesn't like me (quite likely), or someone is being paid to betray the RAF – a spy in other words. Either way, it's not good news.'

'Will you be late back?'

'No. All I have is the debriefing with David. Intelligence will do their work – your friends in the RAF police. I'll cook, my darling, but I'll let Alice collect Josie and Ollie. I do like Alice and Katia though Alice doesn't say much about herself.'

'Yes, I've noticed. I suspect there may have been some sadness in the past, perhaps to do with the breakup with Katia's father. But if she wants to talk, we're here.'

'What are you doing today?'

'I have to hear from Bonnie about their investigation in Scotland and decide about whether, and if so, how long, they should remain so far from home, as well as finding out if the naughty ones have been behaving.'

'*Your* officers?'

'Two of them, anyway. In my absence they were giving Bonnie a hard time, not I hope because of a modicum of racism because if I were to find that was the case, they would be out straight away. They're on their final warning.'

'Has it upset Bonnie?'

'Knocked her confidence a little, but I've told her to take hold of her authority as a Super and use it, like someone I know used a taser. And though you said last night you would have been willing to use the Glock 17, would you have been prepared to kill the Egyptian soldier?'

'I'm a soldier too, Jo, and like you I am invested with considerable authority, and in the face of an enemy soldier threatening me with a sub-machine gun in his hands, I would have regarded myself under military obligation to defend Her Majesty's soldiers, by killing him. And until I saw the taser I was expecting to have to do it. I would have not have felt any other obligation.'

'Were you frightened?'

'No, I'm only frightened of cows, and the cows that once lived in ancient Egypt have all gone now. Did you know they were not farmed for their milk, as in ancient times everyone would have been lactose intolerant, but they were kept for their blood for the thickening of stews and the like? It was quite useful having an archaeologist with us.'

'Did she enjoy the trip?'

'I think she was terrified by what happened and for the rest of the flight she read her book.'

Kelly had sent through some encrypted papers knowing that Jo had the knowledge she had been taught enabling her how to de-encrypt them. There were lists of files pertaining to cases not included on computers since 1995, which was late in time. Most forces, after the Yorkshire Ripper failures, had begun more extensive use of computers. It didn't take long for Jo to discover the references to the files of the 10-year-old Ella Epton. Whether they were all present was not recorded, but the small numbers recorded suggested that possibility.

Jo was already on her way into the office when she received a call from Darcey.

'Ma'am, DS Gorham and I were called an hour and a half ago from the Chief Constable of Cambridge's office to attend an unexplained death in Linton. It's someone called Professor Penny Babworth from the University where she taught mathematics, aged in her mid-40s, and it was immediately clear that this was not a natural death. We have called the Forensic Pathologist, and she is on her way. We haven't touched her but have done a full search of the house and grounds.'

'It sounds to me as if you've done everything right.'

'All but one thing, ma'am.'

'And that is?'

'The Chief Constable specified he wanted you involved because of something the victim was involved in and which wouldn't disclose to us.'

'He's just ruined my day. Tell Sheila I'll meet her at the mortuary. Poor Ed, he'll be devastated to miss out on a bacon sandwich. Have you found anything significant, by the way?'

'It's difficult to know what may be significant at this stage.'

'In which case please wait until Sheila arrives and then follow her to the mortuary and afterwards we can all have a bacon sandwich in honour of Ed and do some thinking together.'

'Received.'

'The name of Penny Babworth was familiar to Jo, though she couldn't quite recall how or where she had heard it. It would take a while for Sheila to get to Linton and then into Cambridge so Jo had plenty of time to call in and see Kelly who was rapidly turning from a colleague into a friend, someone she no longer just admired but enjoyed being with. Kelly had those wonderful but rare qualities of being able to make you feel good about yourself even when you made errors. Kelly made very few errors, and she worked hard. The one chink in her armour was her sexuality. She had once in a rare, unguarded moment said something about being undecided. Jo had not wished to follow this up, for it had nothing to do with her work and was entirely private but she was intrigued all the same and knew that Kelly must have some some sort of feelings about the fact that with the others were away in Scotland, here she was working with three detectives, all of whom were lesbians. Jo thought back too he earliest years in the force as a constable in Boston and smiled as she considered what her boss there, now departed this life, would have made of it all. Knowing what a miserable old misogynist he was, she thought she could guess.

Kelly had been at work, already rooting out essential information about the late mathematician.

'Professor Penny Babworth was at the top of her tree and on the move to the Massachusetts Institute of Technology after Christmas. Technically, she finished at Trinity College in the summer, staying on to complete supervision of three PhDs.'

'Lucky researchers. Trinity has always been known for its cleverest mathematical and philosophical geniuses, so she must have been a bright lass. Anything else?'

'That's just the beginning. She's been running the government's Zenith Project for the past three years.'

'What's that?'

'It's a major new encryption I heard about in London, aiming above all at decryption of just about everything. Our friend Major Atwell has been a member of her group.'

'That doesn't surprise me.'

'Nor me. I imagine you will need to speak to her, so I've booked a call for you with her at 11-00.

'Kelly you are a wonder.'

'There are other things Professor Babworth was also involved in and I will provide you with a full list, but this one seems a good place to begin.'

'You might just be right, my darling.'

At 11:00 Kelly called her friend Aisling, her predecessor in Stowmarket, before putting Jo through to Aisling.

'Oh, Aisling, it's lovely to hear you and I hope the country is safe.'

'We're trying our best, Jo. Major Atwell is here for you.'

'Hi, Jo.'

'Kim, my darling. It's bad news, I'm afraid. Your colleague from the Zenith Project, Penny Babworth, has been found dead in her home this morning, under suspicious circumstances. I'm going to the PM, and Kelly sent a DI and DS earlier. Might you be able to tell me something, not now, which might help me understand who her death advantages,'

'Are you going to need me to come?'

'I thought you would never ask. Come when you can.'

'I should be with you about 5:00. And I hope to hear the entire story I saw on the news about Marie in Egypt.'

'Typically, she's very matter-of-fact about it, but the courage involved was considerable.'

'That doesn't surprise me.'

'Are you bringing mother and child?'

'What, and risk letting you loose on Sharon? Of course I am. See you later.'

Kim and Sharon were Jo's role models and she adored them both, but especially Sharon, and who wouldn't? She decided there and then that she needed to ask Darcey and Belinda along too, and over coffee, before she set off for Cambridge, added

Kelly to the party, though six lesbians might be an overkill and she asked Kelly about this.'

'Are they human beings, boss?'

'I believe so.'

'Then as dear Terence wrote: "*Homo sum, humani nihil a me alienum puto*", "I am human, and I think nothing human alien to me."'

The traffic was heavy driving into Cambridge, but Forensic Pathology was still using the mortuary at Addenbrookes and parking there straightforward. The marked car which Darcey and Belinda were using was near the doorway as was Sheila's so they must already be at work as Jo entered the building and put on the over-suit she needed to wear.

'Good afternoon, Chief Superintendent,' said Sheila, as Jo entered the room to the sight of the body of a youngish woman open before her, with Darcey standing back a little, and Belinda even further back.

'You both need to come closer, ladies, or there are no bacon sandwiches for you,' said Jo. 'You have to see what the doctor shows you. It's very important and I need you both to be skilled at this.'

'Yes, ma'am,' they mumbled and came forward.

'You will get used to it,' said Sheila gently, but as Jo has said, criminal law demands you understand and have witnessed what I say.'

'Yes, ma'am,' said the pair together.'

'Though there is precious little to see. Her internal organs are all in good condition, but her muscles are wasting She may have been in the early stages of MS or even motor neurone disease, though I need to examine her brain to be certain.'

'But she didn't die of that?'

'My conclusion is most likely to be death by suicide, though Darcey and Belinda reported no syringes or ampoules, which, judging from the puncture mark in the cubital fossa, or the inner elbow, must be somewhere. I don't suppose she would have had too much difficulty getting whatever drug she used. However,

you are the detectives and if I were you I would want to know
how she got what she needed to kill herself and who it was who
assisted her, because you can be sure there was someone with her
and she didn't do this alone.'

'When will you know what she used?'

'I'll send the blood to toxicology and let you know when I
know, but if I were to hazard a guess, though one that is well-
informed, I would suggest a significant dose of insulin
administered intravenously leading to a rapid onset coma with
hypoglycaemia. Ask the GP about diabetes, but expect the
answer "no". This is possibly suicide by someone who knew
what lay before her in terms of a seriously debilitating illness. I
understand it and maybe would do the same.'

The use of the cranial saw and removal of the brain was too
much for Belinda, and she left the room.

'See if you can't persuade a neurologist-surgeon to let her
watch an operation. It will make her feel a lot better about what I
do,' said Sheila.

'You made me do that in Norwich, ma'am,' said Darcey to Jo.
'It was quite extraordinary. I hadn't realised that there are no
nerves in the brain.'

'Ironic, isn't it. The one place all the nerves in the body relate
to and you can do anything to it and it feels no pain.'

The post-mortem was more or less complete apart from some
work Sheila would do on the brain and Jo and Darcey left to get
changed. Belinda was still in her post-mortem outfit but looking
recovered.

'Sorry, ma'am. I've never seen that before and it was just too
much.'

Darcey approached her and kissed her full on the lips.

'Thank you, ma'am,' said Belinda.

'Quite right too,' said Jo, through her laughter, 'but I forbid you
to call her that in bed.'

In the hospital refectory, Jo insisted Belinda had to pay for the
bacon sandwiches as her forfeit, which she thought hilarious and
said she didn't know the police service worked in this way.

'Oh we do here,' said Darcey, 'I'm pleased to say. This is not a criticism, ma'am, just an observation, but Tom and Steph started larking about under Bonnie, not because she isn't a first class detective, (which we all know she is) but because she needs somehow to learn some of the fun and enjoyment you bring with you to all we do. I don't know if that can be learned but you are considerably less intense than she is even when we are dealing with something ghastly as we have just done and I think Tom and Steph are really missing you. Please excuse me if I'm speaking out of turn.'

'Excused. Ok, back to Linton, please. Every nook and cranny, every bin, and call Forensics, Darcey, and urge a fine tooth comb. Belinda, go and see the doctor and get her medical records, including a check in the local pharmacies on who might have unexpectedly wanted that amount of insulin. How did she get the syringe? Then check the neighbours and follow up on anything. Then I want the pair of you in Saxmundham no later than 6:00, not smelling of corpses, but not over the top either. Major Atwood from MI5 and Mrs Atwood, one of the world's most glamorous and able ladies will eat with us. Ok?'

'Where will you be, ma'am?'

'Paying a visit to Trinity College, though much good may it do me, and the Department of Applied Mathematics and Theoretical Physics, which will do me even less good.'

In both Trinity and the Mathematics department, Jo was more than happy to make use of her double title when necessary. Secretarial staff almost fell in a corporate swoon when she announced herself as Dame Joanne Enright, but those apparently lost in equations halted only when they heard the words "Detective Chief Superintendent".

In both places senior and junior members were stunned by the news brought by Jo, that their colleague had been found dead in circumstances requiring investigation, and that at least one other person was being sought in relation to the death. As she was speaking however, she was giving most of her energy to her eyes and what she could see on the faces of those in front of her. This time there was a definite facial response on one don at Trinity and as soon as the group listening broke up, Jo made a beeline for him.

'Please tell me who you are and how you knew Professor Babworth?'

'Why are you asking me and no one else?'

Jo said nothing.

'Penny was my colleague here for ten years as a Fellow. Your news is so very sad and I hope you can get to the bottom of it all as soon as possible.'

'When did you last see her?'

'On Monday, when she came into college dinner.'

'And how did she seem?'

'Thoughtful and quiet, as she always was.'

'And you are?'

'Am I obliged to tell you?

'Is there a reason you would not wish to do so, sir? Your refusal to tell me could be taken as being of significance, and I would have to ask you to accompany me to the police station. So I will ask again who you are.'

'Dr Melvyn Hogg, astrophysicist.'

'And did you have reason to work with Professor Babworth?'

'Very little, as our disciplines were not much related.'

'Was any of this on the Zenith Project?'

'I have not heard of that before, which didn't mean she spoke of it without giving it a name.'

'Did you ever visit her at home in Linton?'

'She hadn't lived there long, and I never saw her there, though I saw more of when she lived in Great Shelford.'

'How long has she been in Linton?'

'Her mum died in August and she moved in then?'

'And how did she seem in terms of her health?'

'Much as ever.'

'You liked her, I can tell, but was it ever more than that, Dr Hogg?'

'You perhaps have not yet found this out about her, Superintendent, but for reasons I could not share, Penny was (to use a rather old-fashioned term) a devout Anglican, who often attended Evensong here in the College Chapel. Yes, I liked her very much and might even have thought I loved her, but I am married and as far as Penny was concerned, anything more than liking was not possible.'

'That marks her out these days.'

'In a university it does,' said Hogg.

'Thank you so much for all your help, Dr Hogg. You have provided me with important background though something of what you have said conflicts in my mind with what may have happened to her, in that we are considering the possibility that she may have taken her own life.'

Jo looked closely at him as he took this in.'

He shook his head.

'No. That's not Penny.'


Jo had some shopping to do on her way home for those coming to eat, but driving along she called Marie to find out how the debriefing had gone. There were two people she hadn't recognised at the meeting, possibly from the Security Services, neither of whom showed the slightest interest in the details of either the flight or what happened when they had landed, other than the use of her name and that of Dianne.

'Yes, I suppose that they they want to discover is how it was known you were both flying,' said Jo.'

'The CO commended David and me, but it's not over yet. I warned Dianne that they would come to see her and I'm certain they will, and perhaps me and you.'

'Not tonight, darling. I've got Kim, Sharon and Emily, Darcey and Belinda and Kelly, you and me, coming to dinner. It has to do with a suspicious death this morning and a secret project she was working on with Kim.'

'Are you cooking, or me,' asked Marie.

'I am.'

'In which case I'll come, but I forgot to tell you, you know we have a compulsory drug test when we land, well David failed his last night. He's grounded and in the hands of the force police.'

'Were you aware of anything in the flight?'

'No, but I suspect they were uppers, to keep him bright and

sharp.'

'Amphetamines or coke would be the most obvious. Was he searched after landing?'

'I imagine so, but I wasn't told.'

'No. Oh dear, I'm sorry about tonight.'

'I'm looking forward to seeing them. Poor Kelly, she'll be like a fish out of water.'

## 10

'That was very brave of you, saying what you did to the boss about Bonnie. After all she's Jo's own appointment to lead the team,' said Belinda.

'I don't think the boss is capable of holding grudges – she always says life is too short for that.'

'And of course you are in love with her.'

'Of course I am, but my love for you exceeds any possible alternative, and tonight you'll meet Sharon who we all know Jo adores, and then there's Dani who won't be there tonight, but who's Chief Constable of Greater Manchester. Jo does seem to love older women though she and Marie are about the same age.'

'Well if you admit to being in love with her, I can dare admit that I always find her very attractive, especially when she's in uniform.'

'You're just kinky!'

'I haven't heard you complain before!'

They laughed together as once again they approached the house in Linton, where already they could see the van of the Forensics team, who had set up a white tent outside the front door. They both put on their own suits, identified themselves to the officer on duty and entered the house again where they had earlier encountered the dead body of Penny Babworth.

The senior scientific officer was just beginning work with his team, so Belinda said to Darcey, 'I'll go and see the doctor, ma'am, and call in at the pharmacy, and leave the rubbish bins to you and these gallant people.'

'Thank you, sergeant.'

Belinda adored Darcey, but she also greatly enjoyed working on her own, and as a detective sergeant she was expected to show initiative. After her rape, when she had resigned from the force and thought of spending the rest of her life stacking supermarket shelves, she knew that this life was what she was cut out for, and it was Jo who recognised this in her and had brought her back in and promoting her. It was little wonder that she too loved Jo.

The receptionist at the Surgery was far from helpful.

'The doctor has appointments all afternoon, I'm afraid.'

Belinda smiled a somewhat menacing smile.

'So have I, and I'm trying solve an unexplained death, possibly a murder in the village and that takes precedence over someone with a painful big toe or whatever, so please now call the doctor and tell her I shall be in next to see her.'

What is your name again?'

'Detective Sergeant Gorham.'

A voice behind her spoke: 'You had better come with me, officer.'

Belinda turned.

A woman of about the same age as Belinda stood there.

'I'm Dr Ventner. Let's go into my room.'

Belinda followed her down a corridor and into a room.

'Did you know, doctor, that in the late 1960s there was a dreadful case of paedophilia here in Linton, in the vicarage and organised by the vicar. It was done for the benefit of clergy from London and involved junior members of the choir. We know one of those involved – he became a bishop and is now retired and in his 80s, and at least one of his victims has reported this to the Cambridge Police, but with so many of the principals now deceased it would be nearly impossible to establish a case for the prosecution, and after Stuart Hall, Rolf Harris and others the public has lost its appetite for jailing men in their 80s, added to which we have a heavy enough burden to carry in the present without going back 50 years or so. We are reliably informed that the Archbishop of Canterbury, Justin Welby knows about this, but has done nothing to call the retired bishop to account.

'I want to talk about Professor Penny Babworth, a patient of yours I believe, whom you may have heard was found dead this morning in circumstances we need to understand if we are to rule out foul play.'

'Penny came to see me six weeks ago complaining of unusual muscle weakness, slight clumsiness and occasional slurring of her speech. She went as a private patient to a neurologist who diagnosed what I feared, for she had reported classic symptoms of early motor neurone disease. Penny was an extremely brilliant mathematician, but also wise and the diagnosis was familiar enough to her not to need telling that it was inevitably going to result in a worsening of her condition and death. I don't think she minded death, for she was a committed Christian, but the thought of that she had to face was simply too much for her. She wasn't a Stephen Hawking; she wanted to be as fully alive as she always had been.'

'Do you think therefore she might have committed suicide?'

'I don't know because she did not say that was what she intended to do, but it wouldn't surprise me if that is what she did, and if she did, it would have been a perfectly logical decision which I would have supported.'

'I'm glad you said that, but please accept that I have to ask you the following questions: Did you assist her suicide, if it was suicide?'

'Penny was not someone who needed assistance in anything.'

'But did you assist her suicide, if it was suicide?'

There was a pause whilst the doctor thought.

'Assisted suicide remains on the statute book as a crime. Is that right?'

'I very much regret to say that it is.'

'And if I was to say that I assisted the suicide of a patient, am I right in thinking that you would arrest me?'

'Not only that, but the effect in a small community of a GP admitting that would make such a doctor a mini-Shipman, and probably labelled Dr Death. If you were to tell me you did not assist her suicide because she of all people needed no assistances and that the last thing she would have done would have wished was to lay open her GP and friend to the possibility of such a charge, I would say that such thoughts make absolute sense, and that whilst accepting a coroner's verdict of suicide given that motor neurone disease had been diagnosed, we may have to acknowledge that she was very clever and would have been able to get what she wished to bring her death about.

'But there is one problem with that and it concerns the absence of any implements she might have used. My Inspector and I were first on the scene after her cleaner found her and there was no sign of any drug or syringe. We're still waiting for a toxicology report.'

'Well, that should tell you.'

'Whilst I am extremely sympathetic to any doctor who might find him or herself in a difficult position regarding matters relating to end-of-life issues, I am but a detective sergeant and because you have been unable to answer my question about whether you assisted your patient, I need to call my Inspector, who is at Penny's house at the moment and ask her to come and see you. I'm not asking you to stop work, and believe me, you will not find my Inspector any less sympathetic, but she has the authority to decide what next.

'I suspect I have no choice. I will try to see several patients with painful big toes, as you so eloquently described it to the receptionist, though I should tell you gout is no joke, and a source of considerable pain.'

'So is being a police officer sometimes, doctor.'

Outside Belinda called Darcey who was doing precious little and pleased to hear from Belinda, who brought her up to speed.

'What's your own feeling?' asked Darcey.

'That she did little more than answer Penny's question about the best way for her to take her life. I think it possible that the doctor visited the house early this morning or late last night, to clear up anything that needed to be cleared up, but after Penny's death.'

'In your opinion, did she assist Penny's suicide in any way?'

'There is no evidence that she did.'

'In which case, until there is further evidence, we can go no further with her. After the toxicology report arrives it might be different, but until then you've done everything the boss asked of you, apart from calling at the Pharmacy, which I'll do now. I'll meet you back here. Socos have nearly finished and come up with nothing. It seems to me a tragic case of someone knowing what she faced and doing what she knew she needed to do.'

'There is one other call, I think we should make, and that is on the Vicar of Great Shelford, where she used to live and still worshipped.'

'Ok, my beloved Sergeant.'

They laughed together.

Darcey drew a blank at the Chemist and they drove on to Great Shelford. It was the vicar's day off and they found him in the garden digging. They introduced themselves, and he gave every indication that he was expecting them.

'Come on in. I need a cup of tea and perhaps you do, though I could offer you something stronger if you wish.'

'I've been waiting to say this,' said Belinda, 'not while I'm on duty, sir.'

The vicar laughed.

'I get "more tea vicar?". My wife works full time in Addenbrookes as a sister on the Children's Ward, so I try to fit in the cooking around my work.'

'You both have demanding jobs,' said Darcey.

'That really is a case of the pot calling the kettle black!'

When he returned with the tea, he said, 'I thought I might see you today. You have come about Penny, I'm sure. Well, let me say at once what a wonderful person she was. I know she was a brilliant mathematician, but she had another life, a life of regular prayer and service, above all, of those who like herself, lived alone. Many people tonight will be pretty devastated..'

'You mentioned her regular prayer. Would that be contradicted by what we are having to consider, that she took her own life?' asked Darcey.

'I'm sure she would certainly not see that as any kind of contradiction. When she received her diagnosis she came to weekday Evensong, just her and me, as was often the case. She was as peaceful as she always was and afterwards told me. We have been good friends for a long time and when she spoke to me of her realisation of what Motor Neurone would do to her, there was no way I would ever have tried to talk her out of it. In fact, I gave her a copy of Biathanatos, by the 17th century poet and Dean of St Paul's, John Donne, which is a work commending suicide where it is appropriate. Penny thought the time had come and found the work very helpful indeed for a Christian in her position.'

'You don't feel that by giving her that book, you encouraged her to kill herself?' said Belinda.

'No one could make up Penny's mind but herself. It certainly wasn't assisted suicide if that's what you mean and before you ask as you may have to, I did not assist her suicide, though I would be less than honest if I didn't say that my friendship with her was sufficiently close that if she had asked, I would have been willing to do so, and pray with her as she died.'

'When did you last see her?'

'After Sung Evensong on Sunday night. As she came out of Church, she said to me, 'Richard what a friend and spiritual guide you have been. It will be this week,' and she kissed me.

Darcey and Belinda needed to change and get to Saxmundham, and made their report to Jo from the car.

'You've done thoroughly good job. Thank you and well done. Drive safely and I'm looking forward to seeing you.'

'She's so good at giving praise and seems to know about RIP and PIP.'

'What on earth are they?' asked Belinda.

'Reprimand in Private, Praise in Public.'

'I like that, though it wasn't like that where I was before.'

'Nor at school, I can tell you, where most of my teachers adopted SET.'

'What was that?'

'Shout every time,' replied Darcey.

Emily came through into the sitting room, where Sharon was sitting.

'Guess what, mum? Josie and Ollie have two mums as well. It's not just me.'

'Of course it's not, but it makes you all special.'

'I think I should have a baby brother, so there are two of us.'

'This mum is getting a bit old for that.'

'No, you're not. Do you remember that man from your old newspaper who came for supper last week? He said you looked pretty good for your age.'

'I'm not sure that was a compliment.'

In the study room, Emily's other mum, Major Kim Atwood, together with Darcey, Belinda and Jo, were hearing some details of the work in which Penny was engaged.

'It's all to do with a means of decrypting the attempts of criminal and political groups to communicate and establish empires of various kinds. At its heart lie four key holders: one in Paris, one in Washington, Penny in Manchester and me at MI5. There could be no communication of material without all four key holders using numeric keys at the same time. Without all four, there can be no sharing of work and silence will operate.'

'Is there not a backup in case what has happened today happens?' asked Kelly.

'Why? What has happened today?' asked Kim.

Jo, Darcey and Belinda looked at one another with blank looks.

'Surely I told you, Kim,' said Jo.

'Of course you did, but I'm sure this evening that you didn't. You may have noticed that your Forensic Pathologist, Dr Sheila Colville has not been in touch to report on the toxicology testing, and when you all left the mortuary she was beginning work on the brain. Up 'til that moment all the signs were clear – this was suicide in the face of the onset of MS Motor Neurone Disease, of which Penny Babworth was herself convinced, backed up by her GP and her consultant – but as soon as Dr Colville examined the brain, she realised there were no signs of neither disease. She immediately called a neurologist in Addenbrookes who was in complete agreement.

'Dr Colville called us and we immediately brought the senior Irish Forensic Pathologist over by helicopter and confirmed all that Dr Colville discovered. What this implies is that over a period of weeks or months, someone or more than one person gave Penny drugs that made her experience the symptoms of MND and in effect either pushed her to suicide, or, and this has to be considered, in fact murdered her during her last evening in such a way as to make suicide the obvious conclusion.'

'Have we to start again, ma'am?' Darcey asked Kim.

'No, we have to take over now, since it's clear that what we are dealing with is a person or persons unknown determined to stop the Project. For the time being, they have succeeded. However, I think you, Jo, along with Belinda as you interviewed her today, should pay another visit to Penny's GP. Whoever has been doing this is extremely clever and knows enough about MND to make it see that was that Penny had, knowing that for her suicide would seem the logical and inevitable thing to do, and also convince her doctors. Dr Colville informed me that there was a significant mark of an injection in Penny's arm and implied that this may well have been done by someone Penny knew because there is no sign of a struggle or any distress. Toxicology has shown that significant amounts of Etorphine were in her blood and would have been the immediate cause of the death. Perhaps your doctor thought it a mercy killing, and you Belinda were clearly not unsympathetic to her, but maybe she is guilty of manslaughter through what we might call "induced negligence". What do you think, Jo?'

'I've heard of that sort of thing and I think Agatha Christie had a story based on it, but motor neurone is a very sophisticated form of it, and bears witness to a very sophisticated person seeking to bring it about, knowing that she would be logical enough to commit suicide. With a consultant agreeing with the GP on diagnosis, I can see little scope in pushing for murder – after all she presumably only treated her as the diagnosis demanded. Whether she gave the final injection we shall need to see.'

"Ma'am,' said Belinda, 'should I have seen this when I saw the doctor?'

'No', said Kim. 'At that stage you only had what seemed to be a relatively straightforward suicide. From your report I am more than convinced you did your job well.'

"I agree,' said Jo, but let's see how the doctor copes with both of us tomorrow. Darcey, my darling, a call from an Inspector might be taken more seriously by the doctor than a Sergeant. Could you phone her now and ask her to present herself at the Cambridge Police Station at 8:00 in the morning, no matter what?'

'Yes, ma'am.'

Darcey left.

'You said that most of your team are away.'

Yes, they're having a holiday in the far north of Scotland chasing art thieves around the various castles, but Bonnie tells me they're nearly done so the peace of the office will soon be destroyed.'

'How is Kelly? It was very hard sending her back to you and I fear that one day we shall come for her.'

'Not yet, please. You'll see her later as she's joining us for dinner. She's just popped out to see one of our neighbours whom she knows. Much more important, Kim, is the question asked by your daughter of your wife. She wanted to know she can't have a brother or a sister, as Ollie and Josie have, and is enjoying the fact that like her they too have two mummies?'

'I'm sure Jo could tell you all that's involved in preparing for IVF pregnancy, let alone the glories of morning sickness and going to the loo seventy times at night, painful breasts, varicose veins and the horrendous sight of your body in the bathroom mirror. No doubt at your age, you would sail through it, but no more at my age.'

'I've been told you are a great mother,' said Belinda.

'The really great mother is Sharon; I'm often the absent mother.'

'But would you still recommend being a mother?'

'Undoubtedly. It's simply wonderful.'

'Belinda, my darling. Please don't expect consistency from

Kim. She would echo Oscar Wilde and insist that "Consistency is the last refuge of the unimaginative" and if there is one thing I know about Major Atwood, it is that she has a rich imagination.'

They all laughed.

Across the road, Alice and Kelly were chatting together in the kitchen whilst Katia did her homework.

'Is it some sort of police get-together?' asked Alice.

No. Much more like a lesbian outing. Yes, there are three police officers, an senior army officer, an RAF officer, and a very glamorous lady who was a head teacher of a posh school, once married to the Moslem Portsmouth bomber, who was shot dead by police as he tried to stab her. Oh, and me.'

'And is everyone a lesbian?'

'Yes, I think so.'

'Including you?'

'I don't know. If all women were like Jo or looked like Marie, then who knows, but I honestly don't have the time to find out, especially as I love my work so much, and in prison I met some really horrible women, though I guess the men I might meet in prison would be even worse.'

'Were you working in prison?'

'No, I was in there for attempted fraud.'

'For how long?'

'Over three years before I got parole.'

But how on earth did you get a job working for the police and doing such highly confidential things as I know you do?'

There is just one word with which to answer: Jo. She has what I might call "second sight". It's why she has such a reputation as a detective, because she can see deeper than anyone I know. It's why I believe you and Katia can trust her completely, as long as we are patient. But she has several things on her side. First is her mind, then her job title at the top of the police tree, and then she is a Dame of the British Empire, which is not bad considering she's just 16.'

'That's how old Katia is.'

'It's what men who don't have the skills that Jo does, and

haven't had her promotion say disparagingly about her, but she takes no notice. Now I must now go to the lesbian tea party.'

'I saw Marie on the television. It said she was extremely brave in Egypt and threw an armed Egyptian soldier off the plane and took off followed by two Egyptian jets trying to make her land. She seemed so calm about it all,' said Alice.

'Perhaps she'll tell us over supper, but both she and Jo say very little about what is important. However, Jo asked me to ask you and Katia whether you would like to sleep across the road on Sunday night. Her mum will take your place and when this journalist comes on Monday, she will be told you moved away 18 months ago to somewhere in Wales.'

Alice smiled.

'Why have I only met Jo and you now?'

## 11

As they drove in early into Cambridge to meet with Dr Carol Ventner, Belinda could ot resist making observations on the previous evening dinner.

'I was awestruck by Major and Dr Atwood. I've not known many women like them – unbelievably accomplished and yet so totally ordinary. Only you and Marie are up there with them.'

'Belinda, the first time I met you I knew that you were someone with great ability and I was pained to think some horrible man had taken that from you as well as the rest. I was determined that you should have the chance to do what I know you are more than capable of. There is no reason on this earth that you shouldn't be in the upper ranks before too long, so never do yourself down. And don't overlook the fact that Sharon, Marie and myself have all had to spend time in the darkest shit imaginable on our way to what you call "up there".'

'I shan't ever forget what you have enabled for me.'

'Well try this. You will do the interview this morning and I'll be there alongside you. It won't be recorded as there is no need at this stage. Ok?'

'Oh! Well I'm glad you didn't tell me this last night. I would never have slept.'

The doctor and someone from the Medical Defence Union were sitting in the waiting room as Belinda and Jo entered.

'Good morning Dr Ventner. Thank you for coming in so early but it might give chance to get back to the surgery in good time. This is Detective Chief Superintendent Enright, and you are?'

The man with the doctor replied, 'I'm Dr Tim Bullock from the Medical Defence Union.'

'This is a voluntary interview and you are not under caution nor will the interview be recorded but it will be more private in one of the interview rooms. No one will be watching or listening to anything we say in the Audio Visual Rooms. I can however arrange for tea or coffee to be brought.'

They shook their heads and followed Belinda into an interview room.

'First, can you remind me when you first diagnosed motor neurone disease in Penny Babworth?'

'It was on September 26th when she came to see me, complaining of muscular weakness, slurring of speech and constant tiredness.'

'And you referred her to a consultant neurologist, Dr Aberdeen, at Addenbrookes?'

'She wanted an urgent appointed and could afford a private appointment.'

'Passing over what he said to her, what did he report to you?'

'He said that his opinion was the same as mine, that she was in the early stages of MND, that he could not of course know what her life expectancy would be, but that the stage she had already reached, suggested it would not be long. He made the familiar recommendations of care.'

'Any recommendations with regard to medication?'

'Only Riluzone, which may slow down the development of the condition. He also thought she should have a MRI brain scan to rule out other possibilities but he was clear in his own mind what we were dealing with.'

'Did you begin that course of treatment?'

'No, Penny did not wish to do so.'

'Being a doctor must be a little like being a detective. You are looking for evidence from what might be complex circumstances, as we have to. Sometimes for you, this will be a matter of life and death, whereas quite often for us it is after a death.'

'Yes, though I hadn't thought about that coincidence.'

'So, you will be surprised to know that on the basis of a post-mortem examination by two senior Forensic Pathologists, Dr Penny Babworth did not have motor neurone disease and that in terms of her organs including the brain, she was perfectly healthy.'

'You can't be serious; that's just not possible. Everything pointed to MND.'

'As I said, everything may have done, but the postmortem examination of the brain was clear, she did not have MND. But she thought she did and you cared for her as if she did, and I think it would be most surprising if you did not discuss with her the end of life options she faced including suicide. I must remind you that you are not under oath but I have to repeat what I asked yesterday and which you chose not to answer. Did you give practical advice about suicidal options?'

'Trust me when I say that Penny needed no advice from anyone about almost anything. She never asked about the practicalities of suicide because she could discover such information for herself without burdening her doctor with guilt.'

'Two doctors who must have thought about such things in med school if not subsequently: how would you choose to commit suicide, and it's something doctors do with a frightening regularity? Dr Bullock.'

'Barbiturates and vodka, and lots of both, in the hope that I wasn't sick.'

'Dr Ventner?'

'Etorphine.'

'Well, that was the way Penny departed this life, as toxicology has made clear.'

'Does that make me a suspect?'

Jo spoke: 'No Dr Ventner, it does not. It just makes you the victim of a terrible crime in which Penny, you and Dr Aberdeen, were tricked into thinking something quite sensible which was deliberately done to encourage her to take her own life. It is an extremely serious crime and one which is being attended to by the Security Services because it has major security implications which needless to say you don't need to know about. It is my belief that what was done to Penny over a prolonged period was wicked, even evil. You doctor, I have no doubt did your very best but all those involved have been up against something quite awful.

'But now I have to inform you that what you have been told this morning is bound by the Official Secrets Act. It's not something you need to sign any more. It is enough to have heard what I have said, and, please forgive me, I have to tell you that speaking of this to anyone at all, is a serious crime. Thank you for coming.'

The doctors rose and shook hands with Jo and Belinda and left.

'Thanks, boss for doing the ending. I wasn't sure what to say at that point and almost certainly I would have omitted the Official Secrets Act.'

'Well done you, for doing such a first-class interview. And I know we've not attended a post-mortem, but I could murder a bacon sandwich.'

'I might have to arrest you if you do!'

As they sat enjoying their well-earned breakfast, Belinda looked up at Jo and asked: 'So that means we are totally out of it now, does it?'

'Belinda, my darling, what on earth makes you think that?'

'But I thought Kim said they would be taking over.'

'Certainly there are forces at work which will have wished one of the four keys to be stopped, thereby halting the work for a considerable time. They could be criminal forces or political forces. These are the things which Kim and her friends must be working on. But someone in Cambridge has been doing things to Penny, bringing about the symptoms of MND. Finding that person remains our concern and when the team returns from Scotland in the next couple of days, I want us to find that person.'

'You used a word that made me shudder. You said that what was done to her was evil.'

'I am addicted to the works and thinking of Freud, and understand something of the processes of the human mind, and yet sometimes only that word can do justice to what is done. This is one occasion when I think only *evil* will do.'

'Would you wish to have capital punishment restored?'

'Absolutely not. There are too many mistakes made by us, by the courts, to allow the one punishment that cannot be rescinded and corrected, though I won't deny that sometimes when I consider certain crimes such as this one, I understand the emotion that longs for revenge and destruction, but happily that decision is not mine. You and I have a job to do to the best of our ability, so that is what we do.'

Arriving back in Stowmarket, Jo wanted a chat with Kelly, and leaving Belinda to write up their earlier meeting, they crossed the road for a coffee.

'How did Alice and Katia take the idea of moving her out on Sunday night and Monday morning?'

'Perfectly happy.'

'My mum's delighted too. It's her first experience of involvement in my work and she can't wait.'

'I take it she'll be perfectly safe?'

'They're journalists and a tv crew, not assassins, though they're not interested in her well-being but a shameless story.

## 12

Jo's mum was not called upon. At 2:45 am Jo's phone rang. It was Kelly.

'Sorry, boss, but you need to respond to this. I've already sent Darcey and Belinda. It's a body behind Waterbeach Railway Station, and I'm sorry to have to tell you that it's the body of Andie Bolam. Darcey recognised her straight away.'

'Have you rung Sheila?'

'I am about to do so after calling you.'

'Thank you. And then call forensics.'

'I've done that already.'

'I thought you might. I'll call you later. Try and get some sleep.'

'Serious?' asked Marie, alongside Jo.

'Yes, someone has murdered Andie Bolam.'

'Oh my God. Where?'

'Waterbeach, behind the station.'

'What a beautiful girl.'

'Not quite so beautiful now, I imagine. I'll see you later.'

Once she was out of the village Jo drove with blue lights giving due warning to anything that might be on the road. She picked up the A14 just outside Stowmarket and was then able to increase her speed up to 90mph before turning at the big roundabout on to the A10 around Milton and then into Waterbeach. Belinda and Darcey had done their work together with some uniformed officers and secured the sight, and lighting was being installed. As yet there was no sign of Sheila. Having shown her warrant card, Jo, put on her white overall and approached the tent that had already been erected around the body.

'Any word from Sheila, Darcey?'

'Yes, ma'am. She should be here soon. DCI Molyneux has been in charge and is over there, smoking a cigarette.'

Jo crossed over to where Molyneux stood.

'I haven't been muscling in where I shouldn't, ma'am,'

'It wouldn't matter if you had, but out of interest how did you get put on to us.'

'It was you personally, ma'am. I found her name in her bag which I left where I found it, and when I called it through, her name rang bells with yours. Apparently you once locked her up and then got her released.'

'I did, and how I wish now I had never released her. She was a journalist with Channel 4 News and always flying too near the sun. Now it appears her wings have come off. Thank you, Chief Inspector, for what you've done here. The Forensic Pathologist should be here soon. You're welcome to stay.'

'Thank you, ma'am. You have a reputation for being easy going with an amazing detective nose.'

'Oh dear, I shall spend all day wondering whether that was a compliment.'

Molyneux laughed..

I'll leave her to you, ma'am, if I may.'

'Of course. I hope we meet again.'

'Indeed, ma'am.'


Jo could see that Sheila had arrived, and not having yet seen the victim, walked to the tent and in. She wasn't easily shocked by the sight of death, but this was different. Andie had been one of the most beautiful and desirable of women. A knife had literally defaced her: a long deep slash over each side , across a slit throat and several slashes on her exposed breasts, and blood everywhere. Jo wanted to cry. Such beauty had been torn apart and destroyed, and such talent seeping into the ground with her blood. It was, she thought, what serious churchmen might call "blasphemy". And now she had to discover why and by whom.

Sheila joined her.

'I've seen her on the News and someone has gone to a lot of trouble to devastate her astonishing beauty.'

'I got to know her well, Sheila, but what I know about her is that she had a fearful capacity to work on stories that many people wouldn't wish her to. This beautiful girl, as was, made a lot of enemies.'

'Whoever did this was left-handed, Jo. All these cuts run from right to left. Anyway, let me have a good look and then I'm afraid it's back to Addenbrookes in the morning. By the way, I don't think I shall get the cause of death wrong this time.'

'You didn't, Sheila. Once you worked with the brain you got it right and there were two of you making that diagnosis together.'

'Do you know Jonty McGuigan? He's as lovely a man as he is a brilliant Forensic Pathologist. It was good to have him alongside me.'

Jo left the tent and summoned Belinda who had been drawing together the reports uniformed officers had been receiving from those living near.

'I'm sorry about this, Belinda, because it will be boring but look all around the place and even before daylight look and look and try to see what might be there.

Jo and Darcey would have to return in the daytime. In the meantime, she encouraged the uniformed officers to keep well off the land. She then sent most of them back to the base, leaving three to ensure no one intruded. Socos were present but needed the daylight to function properly.

Jo then gave Kelly a ring.

'Hello Kelly. Andie was almost certainly staying in a hotel in or near Cambridge. I need to get into her room as soon as possible. You know what I'm asking.'

'Yes, boss.'

'Whoever it was doing this to her has done everything possible to destroy her beauty.'

'Oh Jo, I'm so sorry, both for her but also for you. I know you had ambivalent feelings about her but you always wanted the best for her and recognised her incredible beauty.'

'Kelly, my beloved, you know too much. Do shut up or I shall be in tears. Darcey will be with me, and as soon as you identify the hotel, let us know.'

'Received.'

Astonishingly, it was just five minutes later that Kelly called back.

'Cambridge Country Cottages and very nice too, just up the road from where you. She was in number 2 with a colleague called Maureen Watson, the Producer, and the Sound and Camera pair are in number 7.'

'I've got a big smile on the face meant for you, Kelly. Well done.'

She relayed the information to Darcey and said that as there was nothing to be done until daylight, they would go up to the Country Cottages and talk to those there. A man, possibly the manager, was awaiting their arrival outside. Darcey parked the car but kept the blue lights on at Jo's instruction.

Jo and Darcey approached the man.

'I was told the head detective would be here. Wouldn't it be best to wait for him? He's Superintendent Enright.'

'What a strange coincidence,' said Jo, not much amused. 'I'm Detective Chief Superintendent Joanne Enright. Take us to the room which Miss Bolam was occupying.'

The man was more than happy to do so rather than face up to his own prejudice and error. He knocked on a door and then entered.

'Wasn't this cottage being shared with a Maureen Watson? Where is she?'

'I've no idea. When I came earlier, the room was empty. It does happen, especially on Saturday nights, that not every resident returns to their rooms until morning. I'm no one's moral guardian so as long as they pay before they leave they can do what they wish.'

'Darcey, see what those in number 7 are up to.'

'Yes, ma'am.'

'Please remain outside the room,' said Jo to the manager, as she put on her blue gloves and entered. It was clear at once that neither bed had been slept in, meaning that the priority had to be finding Maureen Watson. She assumed at this juncture they had been been clubbing in the city though couldn't speculate on the nature of club. Andie had once once told Jo that she was 100% lesbian but Jo was unconvinced as the only person she knew who was 100% lesbian was herself.

Andie's overnight bag was on a table at the other end of the room, but revealed no evidence that anyone had gone through it searching for anything. There were files beside the bag. Jo opened the first and amazed to see the name of Dr Penelope Babworth inside and papers relating to her work and death. This was serious. How on earth did a Channel 4 reporter get hold of this, and this would have to go back to MI5 immediately, though perhaps after she could present them with more information of what Andie had been doing.

The other file was less surprising. It was a file on Alice Watts, and included her full history from the age of 10. To Jo, this was dynamite.

Completing her examination, Jo was rejoined by Darcey, who had woken both the sound and camera men who knew nothing as to the whereabouts of either Andie or Maureen, only that they had said they were going clubbing in Cambridge. Jo told Darcey not to let them leave their room and that she would need to talk with them.

'Oh Andie, you poor, poor thing,' said Jo aloud to herself. 'You deserved so much better than this.'

She called Belinda.

'I need you here at the cottage complex, just up the road from the railway station. Something massive has emerged.'

Jo then rang Bonnie in Scotland.

'Jo, do you know what time it is, even in Scotland?'

'Sorry Bonnie, I need you and Ed back today. Enough said. There's a flight at 7:00 from Inverness, Logan Air direct to Birmingham. Change there to Air Marie, "Scourge of the Egyptians", who will bring you to Cambridge. I wouldn't ask this but...well, you know.'

'Yes, Jo. The only difficulty will be waking Ed, but I'll do so now.'

Jo now had the difficult task of calling Marie at such an unearthly hour and asking her to fly to Birmingham, though Marie never turned down an opportunity to fly into a new airport and she would ask Alice if she could take the children over to her. The news of Andie's death shocked her deeply and was a little puzzled why Jo should insist no mention of this should be made to Alice, but she was a person who knew what is to obey orders and these had come not just from her wife, but from the Detective Chief Superintendent of Police. Hers was not to reason why, though in fact since Jo had first responded to the call from Kelly, Marie had been sleeping only fitfully, occasioned by her anxieties over the intelligence investigation into the difficulties over the Egyptian flight.

There was first the matter of David using drugs, but that morning she had received a call from the Intelligence Team that David had been arrested. Apparently his bank account showed considerable amounts he wouldn't account for, and which MI5 said originated from a bank in Switzerland known to be used by the government of Egypt for illicit purposes. An extensive search of his house had revealed beneath a floorboard a mobile phone containing nothing until subjected to examination by a technological wizard who revealed extensive communication with the Egyptian Embassy in London, and specifically mentioning the flight, the flight plan, deception over voices on approach, and the presence not only of Marie but also Dianne.

Marie felt no sympathy for David, who would not be seeing the light of day for a long time to come. He had been willing to put at risk the existence of both Dianne and herself for little more than a mess of pottage. The great sadness she felt, however, was that unlike doing an emergency landing in a field of cows and being hijacked, she could not the include the story in her eventual book of "My Life as a Pilot". It would be for covered by the Official Secrets Act, and now she had to train up a new First Officer. Compared to this, a flight to Birmingham was nothing.

It was getting light and before she met with the lighting and camera men, she excused herself from Darcey, made a much needed visit to the loo, and her period had chosen an especially bad moment for a regular appearance, though most of all she wanted to get outside for a few moments and shed the tears she needed to for Andie, who was a total pain the in the neck, too clever for her own good but exceptionally talented with it, and so incredibly beautiful, a beauty now for ever defaced by some barbaric bastard of a man, she assumed, just as once the Puritans had taken such delight in defacing the beauties of English cathedral and churches.

As she walked back to the hotel, Belinda arrived from the railway station.

'Belinda, before we go in, you need to know about a file I found in Andie's room.'

She went through the file and its contents.

'What does this mean, 'ma'am?' Other than reporting it to the Security Service, I mean?'

'It means there's a security leak somewhere and a serious one, too. But we're going now to interview the two guys from Channel 4 who might answer some questions in the producer's absence, Maureen Watson, who hasn't yet turned up.'

'Might she have met a similar fate?'

'I hope not, but there's simply no way we can know until we find her. In the meantime, by 10:00 we should have Bonnie and Ed with us.'

'You're kidding!'

'That's maybe what they're thinking, too. But they're flying to Birmingham at 7:00 where they'll liaise with Marie who'll fly them here.'

Jo and Belinda joined Darcey who had remained outside Room 7, and together the three entered the room.

'We are urgently needing to find Maureen Watson,' began Jo. 'Maybe she spent the night with someone and will turn up. Should she contact either of you, urge her to return. I am sorry to have tell you that you that body of your other colleague, Andie Bolam, has been found on waste ground behind the railway station in Waterbeach.'

Both men seemed genuinely shocked.

'The post-mortem will take place later, but her throat was slit with a knife after what can be assumed to have been a night of drinking. I knew Andie well, and therefore it is not right that I lead the investigation. I have one or two questions not related to the killing which I wish to ask, and then my colleague DI Bussell will take over, until Superintendent Miller arrives.

'So, please tell me what you were doing yesterday in relation to the life and death of Dr Penelope Babworth?'

'Knowing Andie, you will understand she worked intuitively more than logically, based on a hunch for a good story. Sometimes she was spot-on and everyone admired her, and sometimes it ended up as little more than a damp squib. Everyone in journalism knows that happens and you take the rough with the smooth. Andie had more smooth than rough and she often went where angels fear to tread.

'She had a feeling about the two programmes we're here to make. She said that she'd heard, though never said how, that there was something not quite straightforward about the death of Dr Babworth and thought that the Security Service were involved. We had said that if it were so, that would take us into the realm of the Official Secrets Act and that we should leave well alone. She arranged for us to interview someone with face and voice disguised who told us that the post-mortem had been attended by two forensic pathologists, one flown in from Dublin, and they had found that the cause of death was not what it was presumed to be. Andie was very excited about this and hoping to develop this further today. When she went out with Maureen last night she was delighted with what she'd found and looking forward to today.'

'And did she say what it was she was looking forward to?'

'Andie was a drama queen, as you probably knew, so she liked to keep us guessing right up to the last moment what she had in mind. But there was definitely something.'

Darcey asked: 'What do you know about Andie's sexual preferences. I am not asking out of prurience but it may be very important.'

'Andie felt no need to apologise that she was gay and deeply resented the fact that some of those men of whom she had written exposés in *The Observer* some time back hinted that she had slept with them. But I'm far from sure that she had a regular partner, and I heard her say frequently that she was in love with just one person but she was wholly inaccessible.'

'I will leave you with my colleagues in a moment. What about tomorrow's agenda, someone with the name of Alice Watts? Was this part of the same concern with Dr Babworth?'

'I don't think so though as I say she liked to say nothing, other than we would be close to Aldeburgh and the realm of one her favourite composers, Benjamin Britten.'

'Well, I'm sorry you'll miss that. Finally, may I just offer advice that whether the circumstances of Dr Babworth's are in fact being investigated by the Security Service or not, though it seems a little far-fetched, and Andie indeed liked to add spice to things, you might be well advised to act as if it is covered by the Official Secrets Act. Superintendent Miller will need to see your film from yesterday and only when she is satisfied you have nothing more to add, go home, talk about this as little as you can, or even better, not at all. Right, I shall leave you now. Inspector, Sergeant, a word, please.'

Outside, in the corridor, Jo said to Darcey: 'You're in charge, both here and up the road. These two can be allowed some breakfast, as can you. Then get up to the wasteland and see if Socos come up with anything. I shall be in Andie's and Maureen's room awaiting the wanderer's return. Belinda, call Marie and ask what time she expects to land with Bonnie and Ed, and meet them.'

'Ma'am', they said as one.

Jo opened the door of Room 2, removed her shoes and lay down on the bed she assumed was Maureen's. Once again she was overwhelmed by tears and in that condition fell fast asleep.

Shortly after 8:30, just as Bonnie and Ed would be landing in Birmingham, the bedroom door opened, and a woman came in.

'What on you doing in here? That's my bed and who the hell are you?'

Jo emerged from sleep and saw before her a pretty young

woman with short hair wearing entirely inappropriate clothing for a Sunday morning, and not much of it, and assumed (correctly) that is what she had gone out clubbing in on the previous evening.

'In order then: I am here waiting for you, if that is you are Maureen Watson from Channel 4; I am not Goldilocks sleeping in your bed and you don't look like a bear; but I am Detective Chief Superintendent Jo Enright, and I am here to report that something terrible has happened. On your way here this morning you may have noticed a police presence on the wasteland behind Waterbeach railway station. I am sorry to have to tell you that during the night a body was found there, and it was that of your colleague Andie Bolam, a death we are treating as suspicious.'

'You're Jo?'

'Yes.'

'She loved you so much, Jo, until it hurt. She had a few sexual partners, but it was you she adored and wanted more than anything else in the world.'

'Yes, I think I was aware of that.

'But this is so terrible. What happened?'

'There will be a post-mortem this morning and we may know more then. Because I knew her, I have to recuse myself from the investigation, and Superintendent Miller will take over shortly. I suspect she died from exsanguination, a major loss of blood caused by a cut to her neck.'

'Might it have been accidental?'

'No. It was clearly deliberate.

Jo took out her radio.

'Inspector, could you come to Room 2 please and interview Ms Watson.'

'Yes, ma'am.'

Before I leave you in DI Bussell's more than capable hands, I want to ask a couple of questions about how much Andie had told you about what you were coming to in connection with the death of Dr Babworth Even though this matter falls under the aegis of Official Secrets?

'I think that was the clue that galvanised her interest. Today she was hoping to interview a doctor in the place she lived, and the vicar of the Church she habitually attended.'

'Those two are now out of bounds, and unless Superintendent Miller feels you have more to contribute, you can return home. I have also read Andie's file on the matter she wanted you to attend to tomorrow, the question of Alice Watts. Ms Watts left that address some time ago and is apparently now living in Wales, so you would have had a pointless journey.'

'Not that it matters now without the impetus provided by Andie.'

There was a knock on the door and in came Darcey.

'This is Detective Inspector Bussell, and she will have some questions pertaining to the night. I hope to see you a little later and thank you for your bed. Which bear would you have been, by the way?'

'Oh, definitely the mummy bear.'

Jo smiled and left the room.

## 13

Looking at her watch, Jo decided there was time for some breakfast and she went through to the dining area where she was met by a worried-looking manager.

'Must the police cars remain outside the from the of building, Superintendent? It's not good for business.'

'I understand, and I'll see what I can do to put them at the back, though hopefully we shall not be here all that long, but a suspicious death is always a major inconvenience. Mercifully for you, it seems to have taken place behind the railway station and there will be vehicles there for most of the day. Is it possible for me to have some breakfast?'

'Of course it is. Do come and be our guest.'

'That's very kind.'

Jo chose what is usually called a full English breakfast, not least because she couldn't be entirely sure when she would be eating next. Once she had finished she walked outside and made an important phone call.

'Hello?'

'Alice, it's Jo. I hope this isn't too early for you. I wanted you to know that the journalist who indicated that she would be calling on you tomorrow won't be. I was called out during the night into Cambridge to a suspicious death, and it was Andie Bolam. I can't say for certain but maybe like journalists sometimes do, she got herself mixed up with some unpleasant goings on and was killed because of that, but it's too early to speculate. My colleague Superintendent Bonnie Miller will conduct full investigations and although she will become aware from Andie's files that she was due to call and see you tomorrow and might therefore want to speak to you, I will make sure that I handle that, as you, Katia, Kelly and I have another agenda and it is vital nothing impedes that.'

'Jo. How do you know I didn't kill her?'

Jo laughed.

'I would be surprised if you frequented gay clubs, and even more that someone over 35 would be allowed in – that's you and me alike both excluded – then the bus services on a Saturday evening are non-existent and it's too far to jog; you're right-handed and our murderer if left-handed; finally, if you had ever seen Andie you could not have so destroyed her beauty as this person did.'

'You knew her?'

'Yes, which is why I have to recuse myself from the investigation.'

'What does that mean, Jo?'

'If a victim or even the criminal is known to you. It is always possible that your knowledge and relationship might influence and even determine your thinking, so you have to stand down.'

'Is that not frustrating?'

'Sometimes, but if I insist on it with others, I have to observe it myself. Not to declare such an interest is a serious disciplinary matter.'

'What about with cold cases, Chief Superintendent?'

'Oh, I always advise a second jumper and a warm coat.'

'I thought you might have an answer.'

'It makes a change, Alice. Most of the time I only have questions. Now I must go but come and have some tea and cake this afternoon. Josie and Ollie will love that.'

The temporary Senior Investigating Officer, DI Janice (Darcey) Bussell caught up with Jo after she had made her phone call.

'I think you should come and see the film they made yesterday of the "whistleblower" talking about his observation of the post-mortem at Addenbrookes of Dr Babworth. It's primarily concerned with that murder, ma'am, rather than the one from which are recused and I'm content that you can see it without any compromise on my or your part.'

'Thank you, Inspector,' replied Jo with a warm smile. 'Perhaps we should have left Superintendent Miller in Scotland and appointed you SIO permanently.'

Darcey looked back at Jo, who was following her and returned the warm smile with interest. They had worked together for a long time and cared for each other a great deal.

Although the man's face was in the shade, his voice was clear and his spoken words only added later by an actor.

He said he had been present at the first post-mortem which had confirmed the GPs diagnosis of motor neurone disease, but then he was also in the mortuary when the pathologist examining slice of the brain tissue expressed her certainty that this was incorrect and left the room to make a phonecall. Later, and having been brought by a military helicopter, a second Forensic Pathologist arrived, and the two of them spent a considerable time in a whispered huddle. The first pathologist again went to make a phone call, and he clearly heard her report that the patient had definitely not died of motor neurone disease, but from an injection of Etorphine which would have induced a cardiac arrest within one minute.

'But,' said the man, 'I then heard Dr Colville say that they had discovered an unknown drug which she had being taking which had brought about a serious loss in weight and muscle wastage to make it look like MND.'

Jo knew the man well enough as he was the senior mortuary assistant, or at least he was until today. Her radio crackled and Marie reported she was making her final approach into Cambridge. Jo passed this on to Belinda and instructed her to bring Bonnie and Ed to the police station in town for a briefing, and then asked Darcey to join them there after ensuring she was in full possession of the videotape she had just watched, and then letting the two men go home.

'Congratulations on solving the mystery of the missing royal paintings with the minimum of fuss.'

'Thanks, Jo. There were two we didn't trace until just yesterday when Tom was inspired to seek out the one place we hadn't thought of looking, and there, lo and behold! We handed over three men who worked in the castles to the Procurator Fiscal. What have you for us here?'

'I'm not allowed to say as I have recused myself, so I'll ask the temporary SIO to do the briefing. Darcey.'

'Thanks ma'am. We were called at ten minutes after midnight following the discovery of a badly mutilated woman's body on waste ground behind Waterbeach railway station. Both DS Gorham and I recognised the body. It was Andie Bolam.

'We have learned from her colleagues that she was here to do a report for her tv station on a matter covered by the Official Secrets Act of which Chief Superintendent Enright is fully aware and in touch with the Security Service concerning. After what she regarded as a good day yesterday, Andie and the Producer, Maureen Watson decided they wanted a night out and went to the AAA Gay club where Maureen lost sight of Andie in the crowd. Maureen spent the night with someone she met there called Alison Kitchen and returned this morning to the hotel, claiming to know nothing about Andie's whereabouts but commenting that from her first entry into the club she had received a lot of attention which is hardly surprising. The post-mortem is set for this morning although there is a complication. Yesterday the tv team filmed a man breaking just about every aspect of the Official Secrets Act, and that man is Nigel Thompson, the chief mortuary assistant at Addenbrookes. For the rest I must hand back to you, ma'am.'

Jo recounted the episodes leading up to the "suicide" of Dr Penny Babworth by a large dose of Etorphine.

'Jesus,' said Ed. 'That has a potency somewhere between 1,000 and 3,000 times that of morphine.'

'I have already alerted Major Atwood to Andie's death and to the interview given yesterday by Nigel Thompson. She wants me to arrest him immediately, which Belinda and I will do at the mortuary when we leave here but to save him for officers from Special Branch who will come for him in the morning. The post-mortem should go ahead, and there may be no connection with the deliberate sabotage of the work being done by Dr Babworth. No one is to pursue any links between Andie and the person the team was due to call on Monday, and that is by order of the Home Office. I shall be on the periphery of this case which doesn't matter. I'm sorry to throw you in at the deep end.'

'I'm sorry too, Jo. Andie was in love with you and although it was hard for you to know how to respond, you must be hurting. As SIO, I don't want you present at the post-mortem. Go with Belinda by all means to make your arrest, but then leave Ed with Sheila and the obligatory bacon sandwich. I'll collect you later, Ed.

'Thanks, Bonnie,' said Jo.

Arriving at Addenbrookes, Jo, Belinda and Ed went directly to the mortuary office where Sheila was sitting reading The Observer.

'Ah, Chief Inspector Secker, how wonderful to see you – my best assistant.'

'Alas, Sheila,' said Jo, 'before you get to work, I have to make an arrest. It's a very serious matter related to the Official Secrets Act. So DS Gorham will do that and leave you.'

As they approached Thompson, he gave them a broad smile.

'Good morning, sir and lady. The top brass here again. Two murders in one week. Cambridge is getting more and more like the Oxford of Inspector Morse.'

'Nigel Thompson, I am arresting you for offences relating to the Official Secrets Act. You do not have to say anything but it may harm your defence if you do not mention when questioned, something that you later rely on in Court. Anything you do say may be given in evidence.'

His face fell as Belinda moved in and placed handcuffs on his wrists.

'You will be taken to Cambridge Police Station and then interviewed by officers from Special Branch, after which you will be transferred to prison in London awaiting examination by magistrates.'

'All I did was to pass on to that television reporter woman

what I overheard.'

'Make sure you tell the Special Branch officers everything, including how much you were paid. If you conceal anything at all, they will find out and it will be used against you. If you're totally honest you might even be back among the dead before not too long. Please, Nigel, take notice of what I am saying; good mortuary assistants are difficult to find but you need to know that what happens or is said here is confidential.'

'Stupidity and a quick buck and look where it has got me.'

'How many bucks?'

'Fifty.'

'Ok, let's go.'

Belinda directed Nigel towards the car, where Jo waiting, but as Nigel was being put in the back, Jo recognised a passing face and got out It was Judith, the priest who had taken Karen's funeral, the Dame Kelly Holmes lookalike, and just looking at her made Jo's heart skip a beat.

'Sunday morning, Judith. Shouldn't you be working today?'

'It's Jo, right? The Police officer. I've had a terrible shock and perhaps you can tell me if it's true.'

'Hang on, a few seconds. Belinda, my darling, I need to stay here a while. I don't think you'll have any trouble with Mr Thompson, will she, Mr Thompson?' (his head shook), but when you've got him booked in, please come back and collect me. I'll be in the restaurant.'

'Ok, ma'am.

Jo returned to Judith.

'Coffee?'

Judith nodded her head.

Jo got the drinks and sat down opposite Judith.

'What sort of police officer are you?'

'I'm a Detective Chief Superintendent and head of the Sensitive Crime Unit. So tell me.'

On Saturday nights I prepare myself for Sunday morning by going out clubbing, which you will think a contradiction.'

'Oh, I shouldn't worry about what you think I think is a contradiction, as you will almost certainly be wrong.'

'I often go to the AAA Club, which is a lesbian club. It's a great place for being myself and meeting others, and twice that includes having met other clergy there. I went there last night, arriving at about 9:00pm and it was very busy. I couldn't help but notice, and that I think that went for everyone else there, the Channel 4 News Reporter, Andie Bolam. We use the word "beautiful" far too casually, but she is. She had with her a friend, partner or colleague with whom she spoke and laughed a great deal. I would have given a great deal to dance with her.

'I did notice, however, that she had attracted the attention of one person in particular. I think she is called Bev Allwood. I know nothing about her other than her reputation, which is pretty scary. It is said that she is in to heavy BDSM and comes on a Saturday night to find her next victim to feed off. Apparently some girls are happy to be chosen, but it concerned me that seemed to make a beeline for Andie Bolam. I left before midnight in case I turned into a vicar and lost a glass slipper.'

'Alone?'

'Does that matter?'

Only for corroborative purposes.'

'Alison Kitchen is her name.'

Jo nodded.

'It was when I got up to do the early service this morning that I heard on Radio Cambridgeshire that a body had been found, believed to be that of the Channel 4 presenter Andie Bolam. Please tell me it isn't true?'

'I have handed over the investigation to a colleague, recusing myself because I knew Andie very well indeed.'

'Oh, I'm so sorry. Here am I upset and I didn't know her at all.'

'Judith, what I need you to do is to repeat everything you've said to me to the Senior Investigating Officer, Superintendent Bonnie Miller. Maybe you can provide essential information which will help us catch the person who did this terrible thing.'

'I will, of course, but you might help me think ahead if you can tell me that my evidence will have to come out in court. I mean that I was in a lesbian club.'

'I'm sorry Judith, but maybe your evidence will be important and if that is so, I fear that aspects of your life will be in the public domain. And it will be for other members of my team to discover that what you saw may not at all be relevant. But I didn't know that being a lesbian was an obstacle to being a priest.'

'It isn't in theory, but a lesbian who visits clubs will not go down well in certain circles. My bishop, for example, will probably want my fallopian tubes for garters.'

Jo laughed.

'That's a new one on me. But once upon a time in this hospital when my partner was seriously injured in a car crash, I found a man who said he was the Bishop of Ely sitting by her bed, holding her hand, reciting poetry from memory. He was quite wonderful.'

Yes, he was. It was the last Bishop of Ely, Peter Walter, and so different from the cretin who has replaced him, who has all the answers but none of the questions. I hope your partner made a full recovery. Was it Marie with whom you were at the funeral?'

'No, she was called Ellie. Tall, black and extraordinarily beautiful. It was some time later in the course of my work in Norfolk that I met Marie and we now have a shared IVF baby. But let me call Bonnie. In court, a defence barrister would use my conversation with you to get the case thrown out.'

She rose and went outside and called Bonnie, who at that moment was in the AAA Club gathering CCTV pictures in the absence of staff who had been in last night.

'I've come across a priest who was in the AAA last night and saw Andie with someone undesirable. We're in the restaurant of Addenbrookes and she may have seen something important.'

'Thanks, Jo. We'll come immediately. You know you mustn't interview her.'

'Of course I do,' said Jo irritated,'but if we hadn't had some conversation I wouldn't have known to call you.'

'Sorry, Jo.'

Jo went to the car where Belinda was waiting patiently.

'All sorted?' asked Jo.

'Yes. You gave him some hope that he won't be sent to the

Tower.'

'I have to recuse myself because of my relationship with Andie, so could you come with me and stay with Judith until Bonnie arrives and then work with her on the murder?

'Of course.'

They went in to where Judith was sitting, looking terrible.

'That funeral you did, Judith, was outstanding, the best I've ever been to. I'd stopped expecting anything of the Church and you proved me wrong.'

'Ancient texts do that and the real secret is to let them do the speaking. Modern services are dreadful and clergy feel they have to perform to make up for the awful words.'

'Are you in the wrong job?'

'You might very well think that.'

They could hear a police siren approaching, which Jo thought was a little over the top on a Sunday morning. Moments later, Bonnie and Darcey came in and made their way towards Judith, Jo and Belinda. Jo slipped her a card with her home address and phone numbers on.

'Come and see me. It would be a funeral follow up.'

Jo left at once, but taking Darcey with her

'What matters even more than her murder, at least from the point of view of the scientists at MI5, is how Andie got hold of the information about the post-mortem and knew to come to interview him. Bonnie, Ed and Belinda, and the rest of the team when they get back are involved with who killed her, but you and I, my darling, have bigger fish to fry. Who wished to go to the lengths they did, killing Dr Babworth in the bizarre way they chose, in order to sabotage the Zenith Project?'

'But isn't that for the Security Service to find out?'

'No chance. The Security Service investigate something when no answer is likely or even sought as it could be very embarrassing to discover that a supposed ally is responsible, but if it's Russian, then there's nothing to be done, anyway. They go through the motions. To be honest, we don't have access to the scientific resources necessary to finding this out but we should have a go.

'However, I want you to take on a task that you cannot share, even with Belinda, as I cannot tell Marie, just Kelly and me. It is going to require all our skills, and might fail, bringing the force of the gods in Valhalla down upon our heads. I trust you, my darling, but if you don't want to do it, then I'll fully understand and not hold it against you, apart from insisting that you bring the coffee and tea across the road to the office every day for three years.'

'In which case, Jo, what choice do I have? I'm in.'

'Tomorrow morning I'll pick you and Kelly up at the office at 9:00am and we shall go for a ride and I'll tell you all about it on the way.'

Jo drove home, only to find her mum and dad's car outside. She had forgotten to tell her mum her acting skills would not now be needed in the morning. Not that it mattered. She loved her parents and didn't see them anywhere near enough and the children would be over the moon that they had come to stay, as would Marie, as Jo's mum was a better cook that her, something she didn't mind admitting.

## *14*

After supper, whilst bath time was in the hands of grandparents, Jo crossed the road to talk with Alice and Katia.

'Grandma and grandad would like to do the school run in the morning, if that's ok with you.'

'Quite right, too. And have you found yet the person who killed the tv presenter coming to see me tomorrow.

'I don't know. I knew Andie Bolam very well and therefore I have had to rule myself out of any involvement in the case and leave it to other members of the team.'

'Jo, I'm so sorry about that.'

'Thank you, but now we need to turn our thoughts back 36 years. It certainly wouldn't be right to involve either of you in any role that could become public so you will have to learn to be patient. You've already met the wonderful Kelly to whom I have told everything. There is another person whom I need to involve by telling her too, and that is my Detective Inspector, Darcey Bussell.'

'Alice and Katia burst out laughing.'

'Well, she's really called Janice, but never let her know you know that. I recruited her as a cadet and I would trust her with my life, but I cannot tell her anything unless you agree.'

'Of course I agree.'

'Can she dance, Jo?' asked Katia.

'I've never seen her doing so, but there are very few things she can't do, and one day she will have my job.'

Jo, Katia and I have been talking. We want you to know that whatever becomes of this, your belief in me means everything, and more than we can say.'

With Jo working away and potentially late back, and Marie embroiled in the first stages of a Court Martial hearing, Jo's mum and dad decided to stay for a few days, but let Alice do the school runs. They liked Alice very much, but noticed that she was reluctant to say anything about herself.

Both Jo and Marie left very early on the Monday morning. They had lain cuddled up to one another after going to bed on the previous night as Jo described the shock of what had been done to Andie with a knife.

'Do you think it was a deliberate statement of hatred towards such beauty?

'I think it must have been.'

'I only met her once, but I know how much she was in love with you,' said Marie. 'She was quite open about it.'

'It was a fantasy, my darling. She was in love with what she saw as power and influence, which we both know it's not. I was flattered that she thought of me as she did, but for the beautiful woman that everyone talks about, underneath there was a willingness to do anything, however deceitful or underhand, to get a story.'

'Well, going to bed with a Dame every night still turns me on ...'

Recusing herself from the investigation did not mean she could abandon her role as senior officer, to whom Bonnie as SIO had to make a daily report. The PM reported Andie had drank a lot and also swallowed Ecstasy, which she had probably acquired on the premises of the AAA Club. CCTV cameras show she had attracted a great deal of attention including that of Bev Allwood, who had a reputation for rough sex. But Andie seemed to be well in charge and turned away from any who got too close.

'To my surprise, she left unaccompanied. Outside, she seems to have been seeking a cab, but there was no evidence of sexual assault, which is most odd, just the terrible left hand inflicted slashes from a knife, across her face, her breasts and her neck which brought about her death.'

'It will not be easy, Bonnie. Afterwards I fear there'll be a fair amount of paperwork to catch up on from Scotland, but give everyone some time off after that. By the way, how were Steph and Tom in Scotland after I'd had a brief word with them?'

'I never caught them speaking to one another and both worked hard, so whatever you said must have worked. I like them both so I'm glad.'

'You must take some time off too, Bonnie. You work very hard and I think you need a break from crime. However, you need to know that Darcey, Kelly and I are doing something that has to remain utterly confidential, even to the rest of the team. It is not just a cold case but something almost freezing and if we get to the root of the matter, will hit the newspapers and the television. All I can say is that somehow or other Andie Bolam was seeking to involve herself with it too, so if you come across anything resembling a cold case related to her, let me know.'

'Of course.'

Jo, Darcey and Kelly set off north towards Nottingham and Jo recounted the story of a just turned ten-year-old girl, already the subject of extensive sexual abuse, babysitting two small children, and then murdering them by drowning. Darcey said nothing. Then the story turned to her imprisonment and constant hostility and hatred from other inmates and the press who hounded her even though she was given lifelong anonymity.

'But I don't believe it,' said Jo, categorically. 'It's clear to me that what was described in court did not happen and that the babies died at the hands of others, and we three are going to prove that by arresting and bringing to delayed justice those who did.'

'So it's pretty straightforward,' said Kelly mischievously, ' and we should be finished by lunchtime.'

'Can I ask how you have got permission to do this? It's a most odd enquiry,' asked Darcey.

'Not as odd as you might think. These days, desperate post-graduates will try to find anything to research because most other things have already been done, and so police files get trawled in the pursuit of an elusive PhD. Our friend Dani advised me what to write to the Nottingham Chief Constable, using her as a reference helped a great deal. As far as he's concerned we're looking at crime patterns in relation to the use of drugs in that year, which should give us a free hand. However, in those days there weren't any computers so no records were kept other than on paper, which whilst making it a little tedious also makes it potentially more interesting.'

'May I ask how you got involved in this, Jo?'

'Because when we moved into our house in Saxmundham, I discovered that the ten-year-old girl, Ella Epton, as she was known then, though she has had other names too, forced upon her by the hounding of the Press and now called Alice Watts, lives across the road from me. She and I have become good friends, and she takes my children to and from school every day. The nickname she had in the papers was given by police officers: Little Monster.'

'Oh my God, that's horrible.'

'I've met her,' said Kelly, 'and she's a lovely person, even though always on the lookout for that appearance of the Press.'

'Last week she received a letter from none other than Andie Bolam, saying she wished to call on her this morning. I had devised a plot whereby my mum would be in the house and answer the door saying Alice had left eighteen months earlier and was now living in Wales, but it wasn't necessary, given what happened to Andie but what I don't know is if there is a link between Andie's murder and our visit to Nottingham, and because I've placed all contact with Alice off limits, I may have an uncomfortable conversation with Bonnie who doesn't know what we're doing, though will probably have to. But we all know that the more people who know, the greater the capacity of leaking and that must not happen for the sake of Alice and Katia, her delightful daughter.'

'Are the files in some sort of archive at the Central Police Station?'

'No,' said Kelly, 'incongruously they are stored in the basement of the major library at Nottingham-Trent University, but that will be to our advantage as we shall just look like regular researchers.'

'Jo, I'm uneasy about what you've just said about Bonnie. She may well have to know about what Andie was going to do today as part of her investigations and to all intents and purpose you've closed that door off. You can trust Bonnie with anything but to do so she has to know.'

There was silence in the car, and then Jo pulled into a lay-by and for a brief moment Darcey wondered if she would be getting out and making her way back to base.

'Ever since you first came to work with me, Darcey, you've proved yourself a real pain in the neck by pointing out the mistakes I've made and redirecting investigations aright. It's one, but just one, of the reasons I love and respect you. Few people would have dared to say what you did to me, but you did so because you knew you are right, as I know you are. So now, Darcey and Kelly, prepare to hear your senior officer not just eating humble pie but making it is as well.'

She called Bonnie, who listened attentively and then laughed.

'Thank you, boss, for telling me that. Whatever we find relating to Alice Watts and I'm far from sure we will as I still think Andie's death was related to the other major matter but I'll keep you in touch.'

Jo turned towards Darcey.

'Thank you, Darcey my darling.'


In Cambridge, the search was on for a cab that might have picked Andie up at or close to the AAA Club. This was in the hands of Ed. Belinda was trying to find the notorious Bev Allwood, which it turned out was not her actual name. Belinda learned this only herself coming all nasty with the membership secretary of the Club who had two lists of names, the ones members used to preserve privacy, and a second containing the names with which they paid their membership fees. Bev Allwood paid her membership with the rather benign name of Susan Wood. It also gave her address, making it a straightforward matter of visiting, though Belinda realised she would probably be at work.

A man opened the door to Belinda's knock.'

'Good morning, I'm Detective Sergeant Gorham and I'm looking to have a word with Susan Wood.'

'It's for you, Sue,' shouted the man, walking into a room at the front of the house. Down some stairs came a woman that Belinda immediately felt attracted to. She just had something she could almost smell, which drew her.

'I'm Detective Sergeant Gorham and I'm looking to have a word with Susan Wood.'

'How much do you know about the Gorham Judgement?'

'Enough to know that controversy relating to one of my ancestors has put me off religion for ever. The judgements I'm interested in now are those that put guilty people in prison.'

'A far better answer than I might have expected.'

'From a police officer, you mean, on the assumption that we're all basically stupid?'

"Well, you're obviously not. Please come in.'

She led Belinda upstairs into a large room at the back of the building, the walls of which were covered in dark and somewhat bizarre female images, many of them blatantly sexual.

'Interesting choice of wall decoration in a room in which to have to live,' said Belinda.

'Are you offended by any of it?'

'I wouldn't choose it and my sexuality would be differently expressed, but I'm not even slightly offended. It's one with your reputation, or the reputation of your alter ego, Bev Allwood. And it's her I need a word with today. Are you able to summon her?'

'Go on.'

'You read History at Newnham and emerged with a First, but with something of a reputation of dressing bizarrely and being an avid lesbian seducer.'

She laughed.

'Well, at least the college, from whom you must have got this information, got something right about me.'

'An avid lesbian seducer is probably better than being a rabid lesbian seducer.'

Again she laughed.

'But your past is not why I'm here. You might have heard that sometime shortly after midnight on Sunday morning, on her way back to her hotel in Waterbeach, the tv presenter Andie Bolam was murdered.'

'Yes, I did. Was it a sex attack, an attack by a man, I mean?'

'I can't reveal the details of the post-mortem at this stage.'

'I understand.'

'Can I call you Sue?'

'Only if I can call you by your name?'

'Belinda.'

'I like it.'

'I'm not keen, to be honest, but I'm stuck with it, and my partner seems to like it, and if she likes it, I'll put up with it.'

'Did you know you've just told me something I couldn't possibly otherwise know?'

'You really must think all police officers are stupid. Of course I know. But I need to ask you about Saturday night at the AAA Club. We have CCTV which shows you speaking with Andie. We also know that you did not leave with her, but was there anything in your conversation with her that might, however tenuous, that might have some connection with what happened to her later?'

'I told her how good it was to see her with us, not pretending as many in the media do, that they are not gay. She said she'd heard stories about me and that I was into offering lesbian sacrifices in the middle of the night. I told her it was quite true but I didn't want it on Channel 4 News. We both laughed and I said that having a persona can be quite useful, something she agreed with, but that mine only served to conceal the fact that like most people what I want is unconditional love. She then told me, and maybe I shouldn't be telling you this, that for some time she had been in love with just one person, someone she longed for, but who seemingly inaccessible. She didn't mention her name but told me she was a senior police officer, which blew my mind, and perhaps does yours. We kissed briefly, and she was still in the club when I left.'

'Yes, we've seen you on the CCTV. And the lady you were

with?'

'Alison Kitchen.'

'Really? A lady of many parts. Another witness also left with Alison Kitchen.'

'Aah, well, that's the name we give when asked by anyone in an official position. Poor Alison Kitchen doesn't know what she's missing.'

'At the moment Sue, I don't need to know who it was you left with, but were it to matter, I would have to return.'

'I'd be very happy for you to return whenever.'

'I might have to spread the gossip that far from being BDSM Bev, you are in fact a lovely lady and more of a softie than you let on.'

'Oh, that's outrageous police provocation! I will say one thing though before you have to go. I've hardly ever known anyone quite as beautiful as Andie Bolam. One of your senior police officers has been missing out on something special.'

Belinda drove a hundred metres and then turned right and stopped the car, taking out her phone.

'Hi ma'am, it may be nothing but when I was interviewing BDSM Bev, who is not at all what she likes to give the impression she is, she told me she left the club on Saturday night with someone called Alison Kitchen.'

'Can you locate her?'

'No, because she's evidently in more places than one at a time.'

'What do you mean?'

'I mean that Judith the vicar told Jo that she also left the Club with the same lady – Alison Kitchen.'

'I hadn't read Jo's notes, but excellent work, Belinda.'

'Should I call in at the vicarage, boss?'

'Do so.'

Belinda drove to the edge of the city and found the vicarage easily. It was a big old house which must be difficult to heat in winter. She walked up to the impressively large front door and rang the bell. The woman opening the door was not wearing any form of identifiable clerical dress.

'Hello. Can I speak to the Reverend Judith Bartram, please?'

'That's me. And you?'

'Detective Sergeant Belinda Gorham, but please don't ask me anything about the Gorham judgement.'

Judith laughed.

'Come in.'

'They sat in her study, where Judith brought coffee.

'A large number of books.'

'A nightmare when moving house.'

'Tell me about your girlfriend Alison Kitchen, with whom you spent the night on Saturday?'

'Er, well that's not easy.'

'Yes, I thought it might not be, given that she spent the night with quite a few others.'

Judith looked embarrassed.

'You have probably guessed that to preserve a modicum of anonymity, one of the things agreed to when we join the Club is to use real names as little as possible. Alison Kitchen (and don't ask me why that name in particular) is the name of whoever we go home with.'

'Do you go home with a different Alison every time?'

'No. There are one or two girls who mean a great deal to me and they tend to be the ones I prefer to be with.'

'I wonder how they feel waking up on a Sunday morning in a vicarage after a night of passion with the vicar?'

'Are you disapproving?'

'Not at all. I've had my moments in clubs too.'

'I find they're my temporary cure for loneliness, and also enable me to spit in the face of the Church.'

'Didn't women have to fight for their established place in the Church, and now you want to spit in its face?'

'Maybe I had a fantasy church and priesthood in mind, or one that might just have been worth being part of, but not this one, full as it is of moralistic, unintelligent, happy-clappies.'

'From where I stand, which is well outside, that's how it appears, and certainly has nothing to offer me. I can't even get married in a Church. But if you feel as you do, why stay? It might be like stopping banging your head against a brick wall.'

'There was a day not long ago when I was asked to take a funeral at the crem. There were just five of us there, and one of them was attending the wrong funeral. I was asked to use the old service and not to do an address of any kind, which was how it always was in older, wiser times. The principal mourners were a married lesbian couple who clearly loved each other a great deal. What I could do for them has stayed with me, and makes all the total shit of the Church of England worthwhile. Why should I be the one to quit?'

Belinda smiled.

'Yes, you're right. It meant a great deal to both Marie and Jo, who is my boss.

'When you see Jo, please apologise on my behalf that I misled her about Alison Kitchen.'

'She will more than understand. She has gathered a diverse small team and we work on what are called sensitive crimes, so she values working with those who know what sensitivity means in terms of their sexuality.'

'Is she a good boss?'

'She is an outstanding detective who leads from the front and encourages each of us to use our intuition as much as our logic, and that makes her a brilliant boss. She can also be tough dealing with stupidity, especially her own. In our own and different ways, we all love her.'

'That's impressive.'

'But I need to know the real name of your Saturday night partner.'

'She said she was called Mo, but more than that, I don't know. I met her outside the Club as we both had left early at much the same time. Wonderful lover. And what about you, Belinda? Is there an Alison Kitchen in your life?'

'Thankfully, yes, though I was less than delighted when she got up at 5 o'clock this morning because she's involved in an investigation I know nothing about.'

'You must live with confidential matters all the time.'

'Yes, but we get used to not talking about our work when we

are together, the exception being if we've witnessed something awful such as a post-mortem.'

'Isn't that done by a pathologist?'

'If there is a possibility of foul play, a police officer has to be present as a witness.'

'How often does that happen?'

'We have a team member called Ed, who is usually the one in attendance. He is fascinated by the process and how it can help our investigations, though there is an ulterior motive for Ed, because it is an unbreakable rule that after every PM he has a bacon sandwich! And I'm not joking.'

Judith could barely control her laughter.

'I must go. Thank you for the coffee and conversation, Judith. I have really enjoyed being with you. I shouldn't think we shall need to disturb you again.'

'Oh, I rather hope you might.'

*15*

The many hundreds of files in the university archive had been dumped in no particular order, and even by lunchtime they had not found the ones they wanted. They had a break and then plodded on, which Darcey thought appropriate for her and Jo as they were plods after all. Just before Jo felt they should stop for the day and get back to Suffolk, a noise was heard emanating from the direction of Kelly.

'Boss, Darcey, come and see what I've found.'

'It wasn't everything they wanted or, more espcially, needed, but an extra hour's search came up with the complete files on the murders of Peter and Anna Worrall in 1980. Jo picked them up, thinking how best to protect them until their return on the following morning, but then saw a label attached allowing readers to keep them reserved in a cupboard in the main body of the library. That was of little significance, but the name on the list of the last withdrawer was: Andie Bolam. According to the date, she had been here before them less than two weeks earlier.

Once the files had been safely stored and Jo given a key code, she said she needed a cup of tea and they went into the university refectory which at this time of day was almost deserted, and once they had sampled the late afternoon tea from the urn, they could understand why it was so forlorn.

'This is a real turn up for the books and certainly one my famed intuition had not expected. It is vital we find out what is on Andie's computer and on anything else where she may may have made notes about these murders. I'm afraid, ladies, that this means you will have to head south in the morning. You, Kelly, will have to analyse everything on her computers, but you will need Darcey to provide you with a legitimate means of entry. I can't come, remember, as I'm not allowed on her case, so I'll come back here and do some work on the files.'

'I'll miss the refectory tea,' said Darcey in a voice full of irony.

'Nonsense, it will put hairs on your chest.'

'O thanks for that, ma'am, I'll pass your good wishes on to Belinda.'

Earlier that morning, Bonnie had decided that Ed and Belinda needed to pay a visit to Andie's flat in London. It was only over their supper that Darcey mentioned that she and Kelly were London-bound in the morning.

'We've been today, Ed and me.'

'I'll have to call the boss and let her know.'

'By the way, I learned something today. If we were to have a night out at the AAA Club and leave together as I imagine we would, one of us would be Alison Kitchen – apparently everyone agrees to that when they become a member.'

'Yes, I knew that?'

'How? Are you or have you been a member?'

'Of course not. There's only ever been you. But as a constable I once arrested a woman who was a member, and she told me.'

'A likely story,' said Belinda, who rose and came to put her arms around Darcey.

'You have completely changed my life, Inspector.'

'Tell me about it,' she replied, kissing her partner.

'Andie's computer is in the office waiting for Kelly's keen eye and skills. It means that you're back with me and the coffee, Darcey. I'll collect you from home at 7:00.'

Jo's mum and dad were still with them and they had an unexpected extra for supper in the form of Dianne, who wanted to let Marie know that the Intelligence people from the RAF would not need to come and see her, for which she was glad. In the past few days she'd begun setting out the pattern of her work. Jo's dad was extremely interested in what she was doing and once the children were in bed he asked her to set out in simple form for a layman, some of her findings, which she was more than happy to do.

They sat there for almost an hour, intrigued and entranced by her accounts of Egyptian history which mysteriously omitted Joseph and his amazing technicolour dreamcoat, Moses, the terrible plagues, the Passover and the Exodus. Millions of Hebrews are said by the Bible to have crossed the Sea of Reeds (which is the correct translation of the Hebrew) which would have taken at least a fortnight, and then they wandered for 40 years but clearly without eating or shitting, as they've left no remains.

'Religious groups must find all this challenging,' said Marie, who was very interested.

'They do. Jews lose the origins of the Passover and they all lose the Patriarchs which have played so important a part in their belief systems. The Egyptians don't like me, not because of the content of what I say, but because they fear the loss of important revenue from tourists and pilgrims alike.'

'Thank you Dianne, that was fascinating. So these accounts with which I was familiar at school – are they worthless?' asked Jo's dad.

'By no means. They are some of the world's earliest literature. The German Jewish novelist Thomas Mann turned them in the most incredible novel, called "Joseph and his Brothers" which extend to about 1700 pages. To read these stories is to honour those who wrote them well after the events they purport to describe. People get wedded to the stories because they need to; what matters is the evidence.'

This last sentence of Dianne's stung Jo to the quick, and she kept turning it over in her mind as she prepared for bed.

'Has David got some sort of initial hearing?' asked Jo.

Marie looked up from her book and sighed.

'Yes, but it's a closed hearing. No actual evidence will be submitted, but he has to be seen by magistrates, but nothing can be reported given the circumstances.'

'I am sad for David, but even more for you. You have worked

closely together from the day you began his training. What on earth went wrong?'

'I think it may have been gambling and his determination to keep the knowledge of how great his debts were to himself.'

'It has brought many people down.'

'And your own work, now they won't let you near Andie?'

'I'm doing something which takes me into the archives of Nottingham Trent University. Nothing yet, but cold cases are like that. Darcey and Kelly have been with me today, but Bonnie needs Kelly tomorrow to take apart Andie's computer.'

'You must be pretty devastated by her death.'

'She was an extremely complex person who was, I'm sure, capable of terrible deceit, and maybe more. So I was never taken in the alleged beauty everyone speaks of. Yes, she was, but underneath there was a lot far from beautiful, and too often that is what I saw. Besides which, my wife is by far and away the most beautiful woman in the world. Little wonder some Arabian king wanted you for his queen.'

'If you think, Jo Enright, that flattery like that can get me putting down my book, removing my nightie, and then welcoming you into bed with open arms, you're absolutely right!'

By the time Jo arrived at the office it was clear Kelly had already been at work some time. Andie's mac stood between two of Kelly's own and judging from Kelly's expression was clearly offering forth goodies.

'She wrote a great deal about many ideas she had for work projects, but Bonnie will be most interested to know about her contact with a rogue doctor who had been struck off, and the possibility that might be the person responsible for Penny coming to think she was suffering from motor neurone disease. Am I allowed to tell you his name?'

'No, that's for Bonnie. What about our name?'

'There is an email from the Home Office to her thanking her for a "wonderful" night "again" – the sender as someone called Jerry Ironsides: "The name is now Alice Watts" and gives her address, but from what I've read, her only plan was to get a scoop interview with her but it mentions that she wanted to find the original case files and read them so she could know what she was talking about with her, but there is no sign that she was considering some sort of cold case review.'

'Anything else?'

'Some lesbian porn, but nothing including men.'

'I was slow to believe her, but she insisted she was 100% gay, even though she certainly wasn't above giving Jeremy from the Home Office something to trade in for what her journalist's eye needed. I've never understood why so many journalists took the moral high ground over the Martin Bashir and Princess Diana affair. Every journalist I have ever come across would have given their eyeteeth for that scoop. He got it so everybody hates him.

'Bonnie, now knows, thanks to Darcey challenging me, what we're involved with. Please tell her that although I would prefer a free hand with Jeremy Ironsides because he's involved with what we're doing and in which Andie has has little more than an incidental role, but if she needs to haul him in, then I need to know.'

'Ok. And if I find anything else, I'll let you know. That reminds me, what shall I do with the poems addressed to and written about you?'

'Leave them where they are, I doubt they will figure in evidence, other than prove I have been right to recuse myself.'

'They're quite good and her talk of love was real.'

'Yes, I know, but don't overlook the reality of the two Andies, an inner and an outer, but only one was beautiful all the way through. We'll speak later.'

Jo picked up Darcey on time, and soon they were on their way to Nottingham.

Bonnie was delighted with what the computer had produced and she was also relieved that the rest of the team from Scotland would be back today, hopefully by lunchtime. In the short term, however, what she needed more than anything was background on the former doctor, Andrew Harrison, before anyone set about interviewing him. She wasn't sure about the Home Office person,

Jerry Ironsides. Strictly speaking, it was a different case and unless it proved necessary, she would leave it to Jo.

'I had a significant reminder last night of our task in Nottingham. Our new neighbour Dianne, a black Canadian archeologist just deported from Egypt, joined us for supper and my dad persuaded her to offer an introduction to the work she's been engaged in. It was fascinating, but at the end she said: "People get wedded to the stories because they need to; what matters is the evidence".' And that my darling Darcey is what we have to keep firmly in mind in what we are doing in Nottingham.'

'I suppose we might say that it's our constant watchword as detectives. Evidence above feelings even though we both both now that feelings can also be of enormous help at times.'

'I've had good feelings about Alice the time I first met her, and if we can find the evidence to exonerate her, proving the guilt of someone else is less important, not least because they might be dead. I keep seeing in my mind a ten-year-old forced to accept a terrible burden of guilt.'

'Jo, forgive my asking but what if we discover it was as Alice has told us the story, that she was the child who drowned two others? What then?'

'I lay in bed this morning thinking about that, close to 4 o'clock. My answer then is the same now: we look for evidence, and if it was as she remembers, it will not change my feelings for her one whit. She was ten years old and to my mind the guilty trio were her mother, the wretch she lived with and the mother of the children, though the appalling legal system has a great deal to answer for. So the thought is there, and I keep half an eye on it, even though I think the evidence could still be found to refute it.'

They collected the files and returned to their seats in the library. Perhaps students at this University didn't need to study, because throughout most of the day, the place remained considerably less than half-full.

Together they worked through the transcripts of the trial, amazed and appalled by the content of the social reports on Doug, and Alice's mother Beatty Epton, which openly stated that not only was Beatty openly operating as a prostitute, but that to entice more men she and Doug offered Alice as part of the package.

'I hope they suffered in prison,' said Darcey as they read together. Jo nodded her agreement.

Jo looked at the photographs of the tiny victims. It was little wonder that people were more moved by the fate of these two than that of the ten-year-old they were told had done this thing. She was just passing the photographs to Darcey and reading the medical and psychiatric reports when she stopped and looked again at the photographs. The court report said Ellie had held them by the neck and pushed them under. But that couldn't have been so and the more she looked at the photos, the surer she was.'

'Darcey, is your iPad handy?'

'Yes.'

'Drawing no one's attention, can you photograph these originals and send them straight to Sheila? There's something not right about them. Look at the bruising. That's not been done by a ten-year-old girl. I'll email Shiela myself now and I'll also add the comments made by the pathologist at the time because they don't add up.'

Darcey looked at the photographs and knew at once that Jo was correct. How could anyone have missed that, unless there was pressure to impose guilt upon the little girl, then called Ella, and cause her to have a life of almost total unhappiness?

Jo's phone rang, and she had to go outside to answer it. It was Kelly.

'It may be, boss, that Andie was on to more than we imagined. In a file she had deleted, I found a piece about Alice Watts in which he raised the possibility that she had never been guilty in the first place. The name of Worrall, she wrote, is the key. What do you make of that, boss?'

'I'm not sure yet, but if Andie discovered it, then I must follow. But why did she delete it?'

'So no one would find it. Recovering deleted documents is a piece of cake for me and I should think for her too, so she could recover it when needed.'

'Worrall was the surname of the two children who died, and their mother. Thank you Andie, and well done, Kelly. We need you here tomorrow.'

'Great idea, boss, especially now everyone's back from Scotland. They're all very noisy. Anyway, we've tracked down a former doctor who may have had some contact with Dr Babworth, and Bonnie and Ed are going to see him tomorrow – in Bournemouth!'

Jo reported the news to Darcey.

'What do you think she meant by Worrall being the key?'

'At the moment I have no idea but perhaps we can go through all those statements and reports again, something might leap out at us that we missed before. Whatever we need to find had clearly already made an appearance to Andie. We have to try and follow in her footsteps.'

'I tell you what, Jo. I much prefer doing this than facing a drive to Bournemouth! Oh look, we have some visitors.'

Two uniformed police officers, a man and a woman, were approaching and stopped at their table. Jo looked at her watch.

'Good afternoon,' she said with a smile, 'are you wanting something in particular or can I tempt you to spend 15 minutes with Detective Inspector Bussell and myself in one of the worst refectories in the world, and allow us to ask you some questions?'

There was a slight look of horror on their faces.

'Have you got any ID?'

Jo handed over her warrant card. The horror level rose.

'Thank you, ma'am', said the man as he handed back the card.

'Radio through and tell them you're doing some questioning.'

Immediately, the woman officer did, then the four went to the Refectory, Darcey having first put all their papers in the allocated cupboard.

'Don't order the tea,' advised Darcey *sotto voce.*

Armed with drinks, pies and sandwiches, the four sat down and Jo produced from her bag the letter of authorisation from the Nottinghamshire Chief Constable.

'We were called because two women were breaking the rules about photographing documents from the police archives.'

'That's shocking and frankly, I don't care. I'm head of the SCU, the Sensitive Case Unit, based near Cambridge but working anywhere and everywhere, and indeed to prove the point, some of the team have just returned from settling a series of nasty events in the far North of Scotland.'

'We're here for a couple of days, doing some digging into times before computers. We haven't found a great deal, but if we see something then I copy it onto my iPad,' added Darcey.

'DI Bussell and I know each other well, not least because I recruited her as a cadet when I was head of CID in Norfolk.'

'But ma'am,' said the woman officer, 'you're only 21 now.'

They laughed.

'Do you know, that age is going up every time someone says it. It used to be 18 and now 21. Most worrying, but after flattery like that, any time you want a job with SCU, just let me know.'

'You might be able to help us,' said Darcey after a quick glance at Jo, who nodded.

'Does the name Worrall mean anything to you – any context at all?'

They thought for a while.

'I've arrested no one with that name,' said the male officer.

'Nor me,' said his colleague. The only instance I've come across it was a former DS Worrall from here who came to speak to us at Police College on the art of obs. He was pretty useless.'

'Never mind. It was a pretty long shot, but it's great to meet you both.'

'Ma'am, please may I ask something personal.'

'You want me to reveal the name of my deodorant, I imagine!'

They laughed.

'There was a rumour going round, that some years back there was a major terrorist event, rather than incident, of considerable proportions, and that this was halted by a senior woman officer, but that no one is allowed to talk about it because of the Official Secrets Act. This was in Norfolk, perhaps whilst you were there. I just wandered if you knew anything about?'

'If it's an official secret, no one can talk of it and that, my darling, includes you. Nice try though. Now the criminals of

Nottingham are calling out to you. I hope we'll see you again, and remember what I said, Francesca.'

They stood and shook hands and the officers departed.

'Alas, the coffee is no better than the tea,' said Jo, 'but worth it for the name of DS Worrall.'

Outside, the two officers got into their car.

'Impressive pair,' said the man. 'I think she took a shine to you, Franky. How did she know your name?'

'She must have read it on my warrant card when we arrived. And to be honest, I took something of a shine to her. And did you notice how she encouraged the DI to ask important questions. That's called trust. It's different from what we get. Do you know any more of the rumour you mentioned?'

'No, other than that it was serious and involved a lot of people in a conspiracy, but the other thing I heard was that the officer who dealt with it all has been awarded the DBE.

'God, I thought you had to be Cressida Dick or Kelly Holmes to get one of those.'

'Or single-handedly overturn a rebellion.'

'She could overturn me any time she likes,' said Franky to herself.

'Let's go through the statements, looking not at the content this time but at the signatures, looking this time for a Worrall, even if barely legible. I'll go outside and call Kelly and see if she can find him. He could be still alive if he was a DS or even a DC in 1980.

Kelly reported to Jo that Steph had been to see Dr Ventner and asked how much she knew of Harrison, the ex-doctor now some sort of homeopath dispensing unlikely bogus medication to what was a large number of followers, not unlike Andrew Wakefield who had poured scorn on the MMR vaccination for babies, and which according to some, was responsible for outbreaks of measles.

'She knew of him and also knew he had been giving talks and seeing patients in Cambridge in the past month but then moved on to operate elsewhere before the disappointed had chance to catch up with him. Steph asked if she knew whether he dealt in crash diets, but she did not know.'

'Good. We have a name for you. He was a police officer in CID in 1980. The name is Worrall, the same as the surnames of the children who drowned, but it is of course quite possible that it is just a coincidence.'

'First name?'

'No idea.'

'Ok, boss, I'll get on with it now.'

Jo was re-entering the building when her phone rang.

'Hi, mum, are you both ok?'

'Yes. I just wanted you to know that the local vicar called this afternoon.'

'Does it not occur to him that people work in the daytime.'

'He said he was Chairman of Governors at the school Josie is at and to which Ollie will go, and just wanted a chat. I told him to come back at 8:00, as you both might be in from work by then.'

'Thanks, mum, can't wait.'

Jo had no sooner sat down at the desk opposite Darcey than once again her phone begged for attention.

'It's Kelly. I'll take it outside.'

'Joseph Worrall, still alive in Arnold, a posh bit of the city to the North East. His birth certificate has the same parents as Sybil Worrall, given as the parent of the two children but no name of the father is given. By the way, Sybil Worrall died five years ago of cancer.'

His address?'

Kelly gave it and said she would also send it by email.

'Any word from Bournemouth?'

'Just to say they've arrived, and he's at home.'

'Tell them from me that if they want to stay over and return in the morning, that's fine. It's a long way back in the dark.'

'One room or two, boss?'

'I wish.'

## *16*

It would have been too much to expect to find a statement by Worrall himself, and that made some sense if he was involved in some way. Either he would not complete a written statement or someone in a position of authority might well have removed it from the collection that would have gone to the courts, especially if it contained any even remotely ambiguous.

'Alice had to face the terrible reality that everyone both wanted and needed to find her guilty because she was guilty. There was no other possible explanation so she had to be guilty, and if, as I have suspected all along, she was schooled into her admission of guilt, everyone was happy.'

They were on their way back to the office, leaving a visit to Worrall until tomorrow at the earliest. It was still raining hard.

'What have you picked up about Sybil Worrall as you've read?' asked Jo.

'Only what I've been reading between the lines.'

'Say more.'

'As the mother of the victims she got all the sympathy and that's perfectly understandable in the circumstances, but what sort of mother claims to have chosen a ten-year-old daughter of a prostitute and her pimp, from a couple of houses along the street, to babysit two tiny infants. She was said to be going to a job interview, but this was never mentioned again in reports of the proceedings, so what was she doing and who with, and more especially where? What if it was upstairs and there were no babysitters, just screaming children downstairs?'

'But if we can consider this possibility, why didn't they?'

They had every reason not to want to consider other possibilities. Who knows how many officers knew Mrs Worrall, if you take my meaning. Having a ready-made culprit quite unable to speak other than what she had been taught to say would ensure none of that came out.'

'Excellent Darcey, excellent. Thank you.


'There's only one thing worse than Bournemouth when the crowds overwhelm the beaches in summer,' said Ed, 'and that's Bournemouth when they're not there in winter.'

'You're not wrong there, Ed.'

'Here's the road. Number 16. Whatever it is he does must be good for business judging from the house.'

Ed stopped outside the house. Bonnie had insisted on a marked car as it made the sort of statement to the neighbours the former doctor would not wish.

She rang the doorbell and a man in his mid-40s, well put together, and with a smile, opened the door.

'Good afternoon. I'm Detective Superintendent Miller and this is Detective Chief Inspector Secker from the Sensitive Crime Unit. Are you Andrew Harrison?'

'I am. Please come in. Some tea will arrive if we sit here in my study. How can I help you?'

'Do you call the people who consult you patients or clients?'

By force of habit, I suppose, I tend to refer to them as patients.'

'How long is it,' asked Ed, 'since you were struck off?'

'Four years, meaning that I can apply to have my name restored to the medical register in the New Year.'

'Will you?'

The door opened and a youngish woman came with tea and cake, smiled and then departed.

'That was my wife, Elspeth.'

'I was asking whether you will apply to the GMC for restoration,' continued Ed.

'I doubt it. My present practice of medicine, albeit not approved by the GMC, I won't stop and so they would be bound to strike me off again. I use unorthodox methods which have the embarrassing quality that they work, unlike so many of the orthodox which do not.'

'And are they better paid?' asked Bonnie.

'That seems always to be the assumption, so knowing you were coming and that money would be bound to raise its head, I've printed out my accounts for the past year. You will see what I charge for a consultation and medications I provide, though what I have to pay for hotels and travel have to be included in what I charge.'

He reached for a file and handed each of them two stapled papers.

'Are your consultations and treatment of Dr Penelope Babworth included on these accounts?'

'Yes.'

'How often did you see her?'

He reached for a book and opened it.

'Twice.'

'Because we know what the postmortem recorded, I should welcome hearing what you were treating her for,' said Bonnie.

'I am reluctant to do so. Should it become known that I was willing to do this for one of my deceased patients, there would certainly be some who might no longer wish to have me treat them. I'm sure you know only too well the effect of certain contentions in biographies which cannot be defended.'

'At the moment, Mr Harrison, this is not a formal interview, and I cannot imagine you would wish to be taken to the police car outside and to the local police station. So I repeat I should welcome hearing from you what you were treating Dr Babworth for.'

Bonnie watched him thinking.

'I will show you my notes,' he replied, once again standing and bringing from the top drawer of his metal filing cabinet a blue file, which he handed to Bonnie.

'It tells you that when I first saw her, Dr Babworth was seriously unwell. That it was mistaken by her GP and others as motor neurone disease is not surprising. The thought had come to me too when first we met. Or are you suggesting that I induced in her the symptoms of motor neurone disease? Making healthy people manifest the symptoms of something as serious is not possible, Superintendent. If you look at the notes I made at our first appointment (and she asked to see me, not the other way round) she was losing weight and slurring her speech. I considered MND but also MS, and even Parkinson's. My notes for the 2nd appointment show I was still not sure, and I suggested she see her GP and seek a consultant's opinions, but I did not suggest MND. That must have come from either the Internet (and any doctor will tell you the impact of self-diagnosis via the web) or her GP or the neurologist she saw.

'Perhaps it would have been wiser to consult other doctors before coming this far to do what? To charge me with the impossible? Dr Babworth wished to see me because she was not well and not satisfied by the doctors she saw in Cambridge. Don't you think you should have been speaking to them? She was an extremely intelligent woman – I imagine you did not know her – allowing me to make her ill, even if I could, she would see through at once.'

There was little conversation between Ed and Bonnie on the slow journey back to Suffolk.

Jo's mum had a splendid supper waiting for her and Marie though both knew they had to be finished by 8:00 when the vicar was due to call, which he did bang on time. Marie opened the door the door to him.

'Hello, I'm Canon Browne.'

'Do come in. I'm Marie Enright.'

'I'm pleased to meet you and you are Josie's mum, I think.'

'One of them.'

They went into the sitting room.

'And this is Jo, my wife.'

'Hello.'

Sitting down, Marie said, ' I've met no one called Canon before. Was your father in the Royal Engineers?'

He laughed.

'No. It's an honorary Church title, one up from Reverend, I

suppose.'

'And what do you have to do to get it awarded?' asked Jo.

'It's mostly given to those men and women who have been in the diocese the longest.'

'Oh, so not given for any actual accomplishment – numbers of heathen converted, for example?'

'No, nothing like that.'

'That's rather different from how things are in our worlds, but do tell us why you have called, not that we're not pleased to see you,' said Marie.

'Yes, of course. Well, it's slightly delicate. As you will have found, a community such as this is, well, one might almost say, sheltered, and although same sex marriage is now perhaps taken for granted in London, there is a possibility that some people hereabouts will find it more disturbing.'

'Are you talking about church people, because I'm told there are precious few of those?' said Marie.

'Oh, you would be surprised how many we get at Christmas and on Mother's Day.'

'We're not churchgoers,' said Marie, but for us you would need to move the apostrophe to the plural – Mothers' Day.

The vicar tried to laugh and failed.

'I'm not entirely understanding what you are saying, Canon,' said Jo. 'Are you suggesting that the governors will be encouraged by you to turn Ollie down for the school, because that would be against the law and pretty close to being a hate crime against a legally married couple of lesbians, as it would be if we were Moslems.'

'No, no, no. I just feel it might be best if the fact of your liaison were kept quiet around the place.'

'Do you know anything about the work we do?' asked Marie.

'No. It would be interesting to hear.'

'Jo is Detective Chief Superintendent and head of the Sensitive Crime Unit, a special police unit mostly dealing with murders and other serious crimes. She is also Dame Joanne Enright though may not say why she has thus been honoured though I can tell you it wasn't for just hanging around a long time.'

'Marie,' continued Jo, 'is a Flight Lieutenant in the Royal Air Force, pilot of the largest transport planes in the fleet, and principal flight instructor, and has two awards for bravery. That is what we do and we feel only joy in our life together as a family, not least in the way Ollie was born of us both by IVF, Marie's egg fertilised outside the womb, and then implanted into mine. Marie missed out on the huge bump and labour. We are immensely proud of this and the fact that our children have two mums. Saxmundham people know what is going on in the world out there and those who know in the community here are amazed and delighted by what we tell them. I rather suspect the only person with the difficulties is yourself.'

'It's not a problem and thank you for telling me about the world's you inhabit. You earn your titles – that's for certain. Well, I must be going. Perhaps I'll see you in Church at Christmas.'

He stood and Marie showed him out, returning to find Jo and her parents, who had heard everything from the kitchen, in howls of laughter, in which Marie joined. Eventually, Jo said, 'We're right to laugh, but really it's quite pathetic and seriously offensive.'

They had a glass of wine with which to recover when Jo's phone rang. She could see it was Sheila. She went through to the other room to take the call.

'I'm sorry to ring late, Jo, but I think there are some things you need to know. First, the photographs you sent me. If there was a question of a court appearance, I would need to see the originals, as I'm sure you know, but to be honest it's quite obvious from what Darcey sent me that those marks on the neck could only have been made by someone with larger hands than a ten-year-old and how a pathologist could have thought otherwise I just don't know. Who was it?'

'Hang on, I'll get my book. Yes, he was Melvyn Harmer, and he worked as the pathologist at the City Hospital in Nottingham.'

'You mean he wasn't an official Home Office or Forensic pathologist? Did he have a paediatric pathologist with him?'

'I think the answer is no to both.'

'Jo, it is certain that no little girl of ten years could have left those marks. I have shown the photos to a paediatric pathologist I sometimes work with and he says exactly the same. Are you able to send me the transcripts of the trial where the pathologist made his report?'

'Yes. Darcey has them on her iPad. I'll call her straight away and get her to send them.'

'And then, although I shall need to report to Bonnie as she is SIO, I'll tell you. Andie had considerable quantities of cherry meth in her blood – gamma hydroxybutryic acid – GHB to you and me, the most lethal date rape drug, without the new saving grace of Rohypnol which now releases a dye and turns the drink green to warn the drinker. I think it's possible that the amount she had been given, without knives and a slit throat,would have brought about respiratory failure and death, anyway.'

'But I thought there was no indication of an attempted sexual assault.'

'By a man. But she was in a lesbian club when the drug was administered.'

'I imagine that when you are doing your work, the fact that someone could have been extraordinarily beautiful in life disappears with the changes that follow death, but Andie was as beautiful a woman as I have ever known. Might it be someone who felt taunted by that beauty and wanted to destroy it rather than simply wanting sex of a sort, though as lesbian I can't imagine what sort of form that might take having rendered her unconscious with GHB.'

'I can recognise beauty in the mortuary, Jo. Yes, her face was so well-defined and her breasts had superb shape, just as some young men have wonderful muscle tone, As for the rest, I will take your word for how lesbians make love, but I'm pretty sure that didn't happen to Andie..'

By the way, Sheila, anything further from toxicology on Dr Babworth?

'Not toxicology, who continue to maintain the drug used to kill her was Etorphine, but there is from me. This afternoon I have been looking closely at the puncture wound of the injection sight, and comparing it with a whole library of photographs, and I am certain that Dr Babworth was murdered. Someone was there with her, someone who administered the drug, tidied up and left when she was dead, in less than a minute.'

Jo telephoned Darcey, and informed her of what Sheila had said.

'That's significant news.'

'Yes, but Sheila wants you to forward that part of the trial transcript in the which the pathologist gave his evidence to her this evening. Can you do that?'

'I will do so at once.'

'Change of plan tomorrow. I've been pushing you and you need a break, so tomorrow and the weekend are yours, not least because I'm making a link in my mind between what we are doing in Nottingham, what Andie was doing in Nottingham and her terrible fate in Cambridge. If they are linked, we need to go slowly and carefully.'

'No clubbing this weekend, then. Belinda will be disappointed.'

'Tomorrow I want to spend a day working with Belinda. I haven't given her as much time as I should, so can you tell her to be ready at 7:00 and I'll collect her from your home, and we'll have a day out in London or at least we will go the Home Office and interview our friend Jeremy Ironsides and inform him of what sex with a lesbian can lead to. After that the weekend is yours and Belinda's.'

'She'll be really pleased, Jo.'

Finally, she called Bonnie who had just arrived home and admitted that it had mostly been a wild goose chase.'

'They happen, Bonnie, but you end feeling completely knackered.'

She then told her about Sheila's toxicology report on Andie, but then added the caution that she might be mixed up with her own investigation in Nottingham, and gave Sheila's observations about the photographs. Finally she said that Sheila was convinced that Penny Babworth had received the fatal drug at the hands of someone else and no one else.

'All of which will make watching News At Ten a doddle,' said

Bonnie.

'Now Bonnie, an important question. You know that I am Chief Super, and that you are my subordinate, being only a Super?'

'Yes, ma'am.

'Ok, then listen hard and obey. You are off work tomorrow and all the weekend. End of. I shall email everyone and tell them they all are, except Belinda, whom I'm going to visit the Home Office with and see Jeremy Ironsides.'

'She'll enjoy that. I will do as you say, Jo.'

Jo had an automatic group email for the whole team, so it took only seconds to send.

When Jo and Marie were sitting together, Marie said, 'Your mum wondered tonight and whispered it in my ear whether we should begin to recognise that IVF becomes a little less straightforward when I become 36. If it was to happen, it would be my turn to be pregnant.'

'Would you be the first pregnant Flight Lieutenant in the Royal Air Force, I wonder? What would Douglas Bader or Guy Gibson say?

'It would be a lot to go through on your part. I'm sure you remember all those injections and we'd possibly have to go again through the scrutiny we both had to last time.'

'I think it's a wonderful idea, and it gets my vote. Now, my beloved, I need some sleep, so keep your wicked ways until tomorrow night!

Belinda was ready when Jo called.

'Maybe three of us will return, depending on how Mr Ironsides responds to our questions or we may have to hand him over to the Met, which in some ways I would prefer.

'But tell me, my darling, how it has been coming over here, leaving the West Midlands and discovering how much in love you are with my "blue-eyed girl" as someone called her, and being back in the Force?'

'I don't know whether Darcey is specially chosen in the way

described, but if she were, I shouldn't be surprised. She is so sharp and supportive to others, not least to me. I love her so much. I've never been a detective before and it's taking me some to learn about it. Maybe you should have sent me on the National Detective Programme.'

'No chance, Belinda. You're far too good for that bunch of romantic dick-heads. I need you to learn how to handle firearms – everyone in a small team has to have those skills but where do you stand on learning taekwondo?'

'I have no idea.'

'Chris Arthington, now the head of CID in your last posting, was British Champion, and believe you me, she saved my skin a couple of times. If you had lessons, because you're tall and strong, I think you could come in handy, and I'm not joking. I will pay, of course. Think about it, and remember the sight of you in full battle kit might send wonderful shivers up the back of my blue–eyed girl.'

'I think we might manage the shivers without the kit, Jo, and her eyes are green.'

'I've    never    noticed    she    lied,'    said    Jo.

## 17

Jeremy Ironsides was not exactly a great specimen of manhood, but wore the regular suit and tie demanded of his role as civil servant (Higher Executive Officer, as he pointed out when they were in is his office). After directing Jo and Belinda to their seats, he remained standing.

'Please sit down,' said Jo.

'I'm fine standing, thank you.'

'Sit down,' said Belinda with real menace in her voice (which greatly impressed Jo and had the desired effect on Jeremy).

I'm Detective Chief Superintendent Enright and my colleague is Detective Sergeant Gorham. We are both members of the Sensitive Crime Unit. This is a voluntary interview without caution. You can end the interview when you wish but if I or the sergeant feel we must take it further, you will be cautioned and the interview will continue in a police station. Ok?'

'I understand. After all, I work at the Home Office.'

'Please will you tell us of your relationship with the late Andie Bolam, from Channel 4 news?'

He paused before replying.

'Yes, well, I met her in the Clarence, along Whitehall. We were at the bar together ordering and agreed to sit together and chat. I was a little bit amazed because she was so very attractive and drew the eyes of many of the men in there, and I have to say I enjoyed it. She suggested we meet there again, and we did, and she invited me to see her flat in Camden and see what she did for a living. Sadly, we had no chance to meet for a drink again because I heard the news that she had been murdered.'

Belinda took over.

'We have your emails in which you thank her for the two special times you had with her. Can we assume that these occasions involved sexual activity?'

'Ah, well, yes and no.'

'Do you mean one was and one wasn't?'

'No. What I mean is that we engaged in some physical sexual activity, but that it dod not include penetrative sex. We did not have intercourse.'

'Why not?'

'On the first occasion it was because she said she was in the middle of her period and in the second she asked me if I had a condom with me, and of course I didn't, so she did what she could with her hand.'

'Were you disappointed?'

'No, because she said it be would different next time and I looked forward to that.'

'And what was the quid pro quo, Jeremy?' asked Jo. 'What did she want in return?'

'Nothing. I can assure you she was not asking for money in return for sex.'

'Did you tell her where you worked and what you do?'

'I can't remember.'

'Would I be right in assuming that you are not supposed to have relationships with members of the press.'

'Yes, but what is a relationship? We saw each other on two occasions. If it had lasted beyond her death, I would have had to report it to my section head but there seemed no point after she was killed.'

Jo looked across to Belinda.

'Andie was a superb journalist,' said Belinda, 'and didn't need to know anything about you because she already knew all about you. She knew where you drank after work and waited for you. The whole thing went according to her plan. You probably don't want to know, but Andie was a lesbian. Her two reasons: a period and absence of a condom were just so she would avoid intercourse with you.'

Jeremy had turned pale.

'Andie wanted something from the the Home Office,' said Jo, 'and had come to the conclusion that you were the one most likely to be manipulated by her, into getting it, and of course we know you did. It is there on the email you sent her in response to your second session together. It was the name of the supposed child killer in Nottingham in 1980, Ella Epton, now being used by her and her daughter, in contempt not just of the Home Office rules but in contempt of court which had given her lifelong anonymity. You provided her current name and her address. Do you now remember this?'

'She tricked me, totally deceived me. I'm not responsible for what she did.'

'How long have you worked here?'

'Fifteen years.'

'Then you have no excuse. Sergeant, please open the door.'

Belinda rose and opened the door, allowing in a man she had met for a brief moment before they had started the interview.

'Jeremy,' said Jo, 'this is Detective Inspector Allen from Rochester Row police station, and he has heard our whole conversation.'

'Jeremy Ironsides, I am arresting you on suspicion of a breach of the Official Secrets Act and Contempt of Court. You do not have to say anything. But, it may harm your defence if you do not mention when questioned something which you later rely on in court. Anything you do say may be given in evidence. Do you understand?'

Jeremy was utterly dumbstruck at the words of Inspector Allen, and even more when he was handcuffed and led out of the room.

'Thank you, Inspector,' said Jo.

'And you, ma'am.'

Belinda looked at Jo.

'However did you set that up?'

The Civil Service has to be strictly policed because of what it deals with. It is not done heavily which would be self-defeating, but they have a number of rooms available for interviews, in which, without recording, one of their officers can sit and hear everything.'

And what will happen to Ironsides?'

'Horseferry Rd magistrates in the morning. There's no reason he shouldn't get bail – he's no real danger to anyone, but in time he'll be serving time. His thought that Andie might seriously want a relationship with him. Once she had pulled that off, and it wasn't difficult, the rest was easy.'

'The story doing the rounds is that there was just one person she longed for and was in love with, and that was you.'

'Don't think I wasn't tempted, but I also knew and perhaps we've lost sight of it in the light of her death, and that is that Andie also had a streak of darkness in her which sometimes she couldn't control. I saw it and recognised it, and if you remember I locked her up and made her spend some days in prison, perhaps hoping to knock it out of her, but perhaps she needed it to be so good at her job. As for today I want to congratulate you on your interviewing, which I thought was good.'

As Belinda drove them back towards Stowmarket, Jo became quiet, working hard in her mind at all the evidence they had so far. There were still major gaps, but already she had in her mind a scenario about how and why Andie was killed, and after the weekend, she and Darcey would see if, gaps notwithstanding, it still held water.

On arrival at the office, Jo sent Belinda home for the weekend. But knew she could rely on Kelly to be awaiting her return, and she filled her in with all the details of the visit to London.

'You don't think it possible that he killed Andie? You know, spurned in love and aware that he had been used by her? The Beauty and the Beast.'

'Kelly, I'm thinking you don't have enough to do, sitting here dreaming up crime scenarios from fairy tales.'

She giggled.

'But it's not actually impossible.'

'No, but that would technically fall under the remit of Bonnie and as everyone but thee and me are now off for a couple of day's rest, it will have to wait. So what are you doing over the weekend?'

'Going to see my mum and dad in Rugeley, because I will be waited on hand and foot. When I went to prison, they were so proud that I had been trying, albeit illegally, to benefit several charities. They told the newspapers how they thought I was a sort of female Robin Hood and even held several parties to celebrate the deeds of their daughter. It's hard to know whether they are good or mad, but they love me and I love them. But don't worry, Jo, I will still be on duty and have with me what I need communication-wise.'

'Do you wish you were back at MI5 with Aisling and Kim and the others?'

'It was great and maybe one day, but Aisling learned everything in the local station in Belfast and then with you. There's no rush and Jo, I owe everything to you. Who else would have taken me on, an ex-con, to the highly sensitive work you trust me with? I would never repay you by suddenly dropping you in it, in pursuit of personal ambition.'

'Kelly, my darling, it was not a tough decision. I knew at one that you were quality, and we all adore working with you because we know we can trust you and in Major Atwood's words you are "quite outstanding" in your grasp of things. She once asked me how the hell you got caught as you would have been streets ahead of the people checking for fraud. I replied it was deliberate on your part so you could have some concentrated and uninterrupted time learning everything there was to learn about technology, and that prison would provide you with that.'

Kelly laughed.

'That's not a hundred miles from the truth.'

'Wasn't it grim?'

'The first two weeks were – straight out of Dante, but when I clearly wasn't interested in drugs or rough sexual attention, and through observation had learned how the place functioned, it became very much easier. But if I remember right, you wanted Andie to write a report on drugs and sex in women's prisons.'

'Yes. But now Sharon Atwood is beginning that. Her life experience, together with having been a head teacher and Editor of the Times 2 supplement, equips her for the task.'

'When some women inside see her and the way she dresses, their tongues will hang out of their mouths.'

'She's always had that effect on me.'

'I know what you mean,' agreed Kelly.


Shortly before turning into the road where she lived, Jo saw Alice lugging a heavy basket of food from Tesco and stopped the car.'

'Pop it on the back seat.'

Alice got into the passenger seat.

'Can you spare me long enough to look at the sea? I live so near and yet I hardly see it,'

'Of course. Let's go.'

Jo drove to Aldeburgh and, as close as she could get to the beach, and wound her window down.

'In case you think I've forgotten Josie and Ollie, Marie called in to say that grandma and grandad were collecting them today before they go back to Norwich in the morning.'

'You know more than me, then.'

They both smiled.

'You probably would be best knowing nothing about the work I've been doing in Nottingham until we've finished, but I will say we have made significant progress. And this morning another officer and I arrested a civil servant who received sexual favours for breaching the Official Secrets Act and committing contempt of court, in return for providing a journalist with your present name and address.'

'Is this the poor woman murdered in Cambridge due to come and see me last Monday?'

'Yes.'

'And did he do it – the murder, I mean?'

'Oh God, that's the second time someone's suggested that to me this afternoon. All I can say is that don't think so but we're not ruling it out. And one of my colleagues is going to love me when I call him and send him to London this evening. On the other hand if I say he can stay over, he might quite enjoy a night on the town.'

When Ed heard Jo say he could have a night in town on expenses, having missed out on Bournemouth, he was over the moon. It meant he could also stay and watch his team Arsenal play Liverpool at lunchtime and before he set off, he got himself a ticket through a ticket agency he knew for which, knowing his occupation, they did not charge him much over the face value.

As well as the call from Jo, he had received confirmation from Bonnie that he should go. As SIO Bonnie had received from Jo a call saying she had failed completely to explore with Ironsides the possibility that he might have killed Andie.

'Not that I think for one moment this is likely but ...well.'

'You think Ed would be best to go?'

'Your'e completely in charge, Bonnie, but the man will be up before the magistrates in the morning and almost certainly given bail.'

'I could go.'

'No Bonnie. You urgently need sleep, as I do.'

'Yeah, you're right. Ed it is. You've spoken to him?'

'Yes, to see if he was available. But I also told him it isn't my call but yours.'

'Oh God. The thought of Ed by himself in the West End!'

'Do you keep count, honey?'

Fergal looked up from his book.

'Count of what?'

'For example, have counted the number of times we've made love since you ran away from being a priest in Ireland?'

'Well, I imagine it's been once or twice.'

'Actually, my wonderful former priest making up for lost time, it has been every single night and sometimes twice, until I went to Scotland, and since then you've tried to make up for those missed nights. Not that I'm complaining – far from it, though I'm concerned that you've not actually managed a three-in-one-night yet.'

'That's because you start work so early. You're not working

tomorrow or Sunday.'

'Down, boy. The thing is Fergal, lovely man that you are, you spent many years in the Church being called Father, and now you are going to be an actual father. I'm pregnant.'

'How pregnant?'

'100% pregnant. You either are or are not, and I am. I thought I might be so in Scotland but I couldn't get to a chemist to take a test, so when we stopped overnight somewhere, I went out and bought three test kits, and over three days the answer was always the same.'

'Praise be.'

'No, Fergal, it wasn't God, it was you and me.'

'Does that mean no sex until after the birth of the baby?'

'Typical question from a man, and especially one raised in a seminary. However did you advise and counsel parishioners when you knew so little? Sex can happen throughout pregnancy but not usually for six weeks after the baby's birth.'

'Oh, Steph, I feel so happy, above all happy for us as one, because we are one and our baby will be one with us too.'

'Fergal, you must ring your mum and dad, and tell them it's about time they came to stay with us. They will be so excited, but there's no need to tell them you're going for a 3-in-one world record over the weekend!'

There was a DS on duty at the police station in Rochester Row, and at first Ed entered by the wrong door and found himself in the stables with the police horses. Bonnie had warned the officers that Ed was coming and they had Ironsides ready and waiting in the Interview Room. Ed sat and stared at the man.

'You have been charged with two offences but I will remind you that you are still under oath. What did you do last Saturday morning, less than a week ago?'

'The same as I do every Saturday morning: I did my green grocery shopping in Sutton's Ground and then went to my local supermarket.'

'Where they will have CCTV recordings of you?'

'I imagine so.'

'Now, let's consider Saturday afternoon. Where did you go and what did you do?'

'Nowhere and nothing, though I will admit, and no doubt this will get you salivating with excitement, I did, at about 4:00, try to telephone the landline of Andie Bolam, but there was no reply and no answer phone. I imagine you will already know if I tried to call her mobile, and that I didn't.'

'Why not?'

Because I didn't have her number as she had never called me.'

Ed turned and looked over Vincent Square. By now, he had realised that he was flogging a dead horse.

'When did you get your first realisation that she had been using a characteristic journalist's ploy to get information from you?'

'It was on the previous evening. After work I had gone to the pub where we had first met and it dawned upon me that I had been suckered by her. I now realise from what one of the policewomen I saw earlier said, that it was a setup from the beginning.'

'That must have made you feel angry.'

'No. It made feel pathetic and stupid.'

'What did you do on the Saturday night?'

'I spent a fair amount of time considering suicide. I couldn't even phone the Samaritans as there was no way I could yet again breach the Act. I was in bed by 10:30.'

'And what was your reaction when you heard that Andie had been killed?'

'I was stunned and horrified that such a beautiful woman could be harmed in any way'.

Ed, who had been at her post-mortem, knew what he meant. He allowed him to be taken back to his cell and had completely lost the will to throw himself into a London social evening. He called Bonnie and headed for home.

Belinda and Darcey went into Cambridge to see a movie and indulge in some awful junk food they loved. Friday night was busy with students throwing off the shackles of study. What amused them both was that they each stayed in role as police officers, observing and commenting on what people were up to, though, perhaps, later they might have wished that they had not.

After her morning with Jo, Belinda was on a high and indulged herself with popcorn at the movie, even if a large proportion was on the floor when they left. They now went to McDonalds in Rose Crescent, close by their car park. The place was packed but a table soon became available, where Belinda had a Chicken Legend with Hot and Spicy mayo and Fries, and Darcey had a Double Quarter Pounder with Cheese, also with Fries, both washing the nourishing food down with Orange Juice.

It was Darcey who first noticed the exchange of drugs going on across the road. It was not an unfamiliar sight in any city, and when she drew Belinda's attention to it, commented that it was not for them to involve themselves. The Cambridge drug squad was fighting something of a losing battle in a university city.

'I suppose what amazes me,' said Belinda, 'that they are being bought and sold so openly.'

'Yes, I know,' said Darcey, and then suddenly added, 'Oh no. Look.'

Across the road, buying, was their colleague, Tom Bridge. Belinda had already taken a photo on her phone.

'What the hell do we do now?' asked Darcey.

'Literally nothing other than finish our food and drink. There's nothing else to be done, and then we drive home. Ok?'

Little was said as they wound their way through the heavy late evening traffic.

'Sweetheart, ' said Belinda, 'we can ignore what we have seen, which is the easiest way forward, perhaps mentioning it to Tom quietly. Or we remember you are a detective inspector and I'm a detective sergeant and take our responsibilities seriously enough to do what is right. Were it to become known that we had failed to do so, I imagine that both of us would be out.'

'Who do we tell?' asked Darcey.

'That's the straightforward question. We tell the boss and leave it with her.'

Once they were home, the process was that first they had to ring Kelly who was in Rugeley, but who answered the urgent line immediately.

'Kelly, it's Darcey. I have a red call for Jo.'

'She'll call you straight back.'

She did.

'Hi, Darcey.'

'Jo, this is not easy, but Belinda and I knew you had to be called at once. In Cambridge tonight we saw a pusher at work whilst we were inside McDonalds. Then, and this is the awful bit, we saw Tom approach the pusher and buy what I am assuming was cocaine. Belinda got a photo on her camera and there can be no doubt what was going on.'

'That cannot have been easy, you two, so thank you. It's not good news. I'll talk to Bonnie. You must give each other the warmest and best of cuddles you can manage. I'm not sure about kissing after the junk food you've had, but give it a go. Try to sleep well.'

Bonnie picked up her phone.

'You told me to get some sleep, Jo. First Ed rang to say he was coming home, convinced Ironsides had no part in Andie's death, and now you call at half past midnight.'

'Bonnie, I have to make the decision but Tom has been seen and photographed buying what I suspect is coke from a dealer in Cambridge, and I want your counsel.'

'You, and we, have no choice, Jo. Doing nothing means we collude.'

'I know, but I still wanted to discuss it with you first. You know I would never make an important decision without you.'

'Thank you. So what is it to be?'

'It can't be us, so I shall have to ask the drug squad to do an early with dogs. Tom will have to be suspended immediately and if drugs are found, they will arrest him. They will need to keep me informed and then I will see him.'

'I agree.'

Jo called the head of the drugs team and the shout was set for 6:00 am. The dogs found a cache of illegal substances in the bed's mattress in the spare room and one of the drug squad officers found a small clear packet of cocaine in the pocket of the coat Tom had worn on the previous evening. He remained silent throughout the search and was then conducted outside and into a van.

Jo had watched from 800 metres away with binoculars and felt as sick as the proverbial parrot when she saw Tom put into the van. The implications could be far-reaching: she had appointed Tom. When one of the team had fallen by the wayside in the four murders investigation, the team leader was asked to fall on his sword. Was this now bound to happen to her? There was only one person who could answer that question.

## 18

Jo drove down the road and into the office once most of the police vehicles had gone. It was there that she received a call from the Head of the Drug Squad.

'Hello ma'am. Not good, I'm afraid. Besides the packet of coke in his coat pocket, which is probably the one he was seen buying last night, the dogs found a stash of various substances, now being identified, concealed in a mattress in his spare room. I have informed him he is suspended from duty and his Federation Rep has been informed and will attend at 9:00. Do you wish to interview him?'

'No. I will come of course, but drugs are your expertise, not mine.'

'I understand.'

'As you said: not good.'

Jo called Bonnie and informed her of what had been found.

'I'll observe the interview, because the drugs squad will want you as a witness as you've been with him over the past few days, so it's best you don't hear what he has to say.'

'Of course.'

'I'll let you know how it goes.'

This was when Jo was now staring down what she thought was the barrel of the gun of her own employment. She picked up her phone and speed dialled Dani, the person who's love for her knew no bounds and which so nearly brought them together, the woman who rescued her from despair after Ellie's death and to whom she owed everything in her work and, to a degree, her life.

'Hello, my love,' said the Chief Constable for Greater Manchester, 'I am lying here on my bed, looking across the room at my photograph of you, and there you are.'

'Oh Dani, you should have worked in Theatre. You know how to paint the most wonderful pictures.'

'But I know you well enough that on a Saturday morning you are calling about something important.'

'Two things, really. The first is the arrest of one of my sergeants. He was spotted by two others of my team trading on the street in Cambridge and at the bust this morning there was a stash of various substances.'

'The latter is a great pity. He might, but only might, have got away with a warning if he was using for personal consumption only, but a stash like that is going to take some explaining away. I think you are going to lose him. Was he good?'

'Of the team I would say he was the least satisfactory, and I had recently had to give him a warning about his lack of respect for the SIO he worked under.'

'Not you?'

'No. But I recall only too well when we were dealing with the four murders and discovered that one of them had been committed by one of our own team, you pulled Martin Peabody, who was head of the team, and redeployed him. So should I see the Chief Constable of Cambridgeshire and resign?'

'Martin handpicked Robbie Douglas, and it was with a great deal of personal pain and detective brilliance that you got the evidence necessary to prove the murder he committed. Martin knew he had to go and actually got promoted to head up Vice, if that is a promotion, which I very much doubt. Martin admits he screwed up because he didn't want to accept Robbie's guilt and whilst neither did any of the team, including you, that did not stop you. Trust me, my love, your position is not even remotely in question. That cannot be said for the SIO under whom he was serving, and seems to have noticed nothing which is difficult to understand. She will come under scrutiny.'

'Yes, I assumed so. And now for the other matter. Hang on. Is this line secure?'

'It is at my end.'

The door opened and in came Kelly.

'Kelly, is this line secure?'

'Is the Pope a Catholic?'

'Who's with you?' asked Dani.

'Someone who's as infallible as the Pope but even more so, my right-hand person, Kelly, whom you met when we were in the West Midlands with that Police and Crime Commissioner.'

'Yes, I remember her. How does she compare with the lovely Asian-Irish woman you had from MI5?'

'Kim thought she was better, and I agree, even though I thought Aisling was superb. Anyway, Kelly and one other of my team know what we are involved with, plus my deputy though she's not involved in the work.'

She explained to Dani where they had reached in their explorations in Nottingham and the opinion of Sheila.

'I am now firmly of the opinion that there has been a dreadful miscarriage of justice but that I am not the first person to realise this. The first was Andie Bolam and I am now convinced that this was she was silenced by being murdered.'

'It is vital, my dearest Jo, that you go slowly, and you are reaching the stage when you should consider 24-hour armed protection for your neighbour. If Andie has a message for you, Jo, it is that. You have done really well to get this far and though it's a crime committed 36 years ago somebody doesn't want this to come out into the open. Look, is there any chance Marie can fly up here tomorrow? You just don't have the resources to do what I'm suggesting. I have two women members of my PPO team, both arms qualified. They're getting bored here, and it's a pity because they're good. I will lend them to you to take care of your neighbour, and I can make sure they're at the Barton Aerodrome.

'At some stage we need to discuss how you take this forward legally, but to do that we need to meet together here with the best lawyers I have. Finally, tell that wife of yours not to bring a taser with her tomorrow. Ok, my love. We'll be in touch to agree times. Bye.'

'How did you know to come back, Kelly?

'All your work calls are recorded, Jo. Surely you knew that. In terms of the team, Tom's arrest is a serious matter and you need me here.'

Jo smiled at her.

'Thank you. First, I must call home and check that Marie can fly to Manchester tomorrow and I've had a thought about that. I must also ask my mum and dad to stay longer, which the children will welcome. Then I need to see Darcey and Belinda and reassure them they have done the right thing before going into Cambridge to witness the interview.'

'No, you can't do all that. Leave Darcey and Belinda to me.'

'Only if you tell them, I will get to see them sometime today or tomorrow.'

'I will. Now, phone Marie and your mum and dad.'

He knew that there would be no protest from Marie, though the thought of travelling with passengers with guns made her feel a little wobbly. He said he would explain as much as he could when he returned home and explained that her mum and dad could make themselves very useful if they could stay a while longer. Marie said they were still in bed, but with two grandchildren with them, definitely not sleeping.

'If you can have three passengers, might you be able to include Alice in the trip to Manchester? She's never flown.'

'I'd love to. Do you want to tell her yourself or should the pilot let her know?'

'Leave it to me.'

Tom was not saying a great deal. He didn't know Jo was watching and listening in the AV Room, but thought it likely. Getting caught like that had been so very stupid, and he knew Jo was the one person who could save him from prison. There was no way back into the police force – that much he knew. The senior interviewing officer finally lost patience with Tom and informed him he would seek the approval of the CPS to charge him with various offences in relation to his possession of illegal substances contrary to the Misuse of Drugs Act of 1971. He was taken to a cell.

Jo knew Tom was holding back something important, and she sat there thinking about it. The Inspector who had been doing the questioning came into the room and sat alongside Jo.

'I've never arrested and recommended a charge for a copper before. It was most odd, ma'am.'

'Have you had the blood test results back?' asked Jo.

'No, but it's a foregone conclusion.'

'Can we just check before I take it back to the team?'

'Certainly ma'am. Come to my office. If it's through, it'll be on my computer.'

Jo followed the Inspector along a corridor and down some steps and then into an office where several people were working. They stood in front of a computer screen and the Inspector tapped the keyboard. They both looked at the screen and then at each other.

Jo went down to the Custody Suite and asked to see Tom.

'Good morning, Sergeant. You and I are going to have a conversation, though I think you should let me finish before you open your mouth.

'You are not a user and there is no trace of anything in your blood but blood and yet last night you were seen and photographed (it doesn't matter by whom) purchasing a small amount of cocaine, which is still in your coat pocket where you left it when you got home. Dogs discovered a stash of other substances in the mattress of the bed in your spare room. Because you are clean and always have been clean since coming to the team, always passing regular tests we all have to take, storing drugs in your property must therefore be for someone else. Acting as an intermediary for that someone frees you from being a user, but is still idiotic and makes you a supplier, but when I asked Kelly to look into your bank accounts, she saw nothing indicative of drug money being paid in.

'This is where I enter the mixture, for it is my failure to provide better support and more demanding work that plays a part in your sense of isolation here. I apologise, Tom. I've heard that it was excellent detective skill in Scotland that finally enabled the work to be completed, and all I did was to play merry hell with you and Steph for being a nuisance to Bonnie.

'I now know there was a reason for that. If you seemed to be a public nuisance to Bonnie, no one would suspect you spending a lot of nights with her. It was the perfect distraction and credit to you both, for no one saw it happening. There was nothing wrong with it. It was what followed, when Bonnie indicated she had a drug dependency and, although she would not have put it this way, was the price of the continuing shared bed your willingness to help her and protect her by procuring and storing in your "safe" house.'

'Did she tell you this, Jo?'

'No. I'm what's known as a detective, and I piece together evidence and a bit of guesswork.'

'What's going to happen to me, Jo?'

'Women don't have a similar phrase to men, so I can hardly say that "if I work my balls off", but you take my meaning, if I trade in every bit of credit I have with the Chief Constable, I just might convince him, and to be honest he thinks much too highly of me, that losing one Superintendent will be enough bad publicity with the addition of an excellent Sergeant who was possibly misled by her. If all these things happen, and I can't promise, though you know I'll do my best, you just might be back at work on Monday morning, when I shall need you.'

'I'm so sorry, Jo. I have proved so unworthy of your confidence and trust.'

'Shut up, Tom, you sound like a prayer in Church. As punishment I might suggest you spend time listening to Canon Browne.'

'Who's he?'

'Don't worry. I wouldn't be that cruel.

'She's not a bad person,' said Tom.

'I know and it would be so much easier if she were.'

As the cell door was slammed behind her and she signed out of the Suite, Jo knew that this was going to be the most demanding day of her working life. Sitting in her car she called Dani and poured out to her the whole story.

'First, if you recall, it was I who sent Bonnie to you. Second, you have to hand over to Professional Standards. This is no longer your responsibility and I'm afraid they must also take over your Sergeant, which the Drug Squad should have known. I know you want to rescue him but you'll have to accept the fact that he's in it up to his eyes. You might save him from prison – just – but he will be dismissed from the Force. As a Chief Constable there is no way I could or would even try to interfere with Professional Standards, no you my beloved Jo, who should be here in bed with me...'

'You're still in bed?'

'It's Saturday and I'm reading the papers. Neither are you going to interfere. You have enough on your plate, not least in finding replacements quickly, and then in moving in with me.'

'Dani, you mustn't say such things. You know you are and will always be first in love. When you say things like that, which of course I want to hear, I end up all in a tizz. I love you, Dani – far too much.'


Jo drove back to the office and for a day when everyone was supposed to be having time off, it was full. Esther had gone to be with Paul for the weekend, though she would have to be told sometime today that she was now SIO for the murder of Andie, and (possibly) the murder of Penny Babworth. There was no sign of Bonnie.

As Jo had driven back she had spoken to a DI at Professional Standards and ten minutes later the Superintendent had called her.

'Ok, ma'am, with your approval, we shall pick up Superintendent Miller and remove Sergeant Bridge and bring them here. When you spoke with him it wasn't as a statement, I take it?'

'No, I'd worked out what was happening and put it to him, and he accepted it. He has been stupid but manipulated by an older and clever woman.'

'Aren't we all ma'am, even if it's only by our mothers? The

Chief Constable won't want two officers in the courts and the newspapers. I'll do my best, ma'am,with these two, besides which you can't afford to lose heterosexuals from your team!'

They both laughed.

'Thank you Superintendent, I'll pass your love on to my girls.'

'All I know, ma'am, is that your team has a great track record.'

'Until now.'

Ach, it's not as bad as you might think. These two are not corrupt, just silly. The problems come when the circle spreads wider and dealers get involved. Anyway, we'll pick her up soon. Get your secretary to send everything through.'

'Of course, and thank you.'

'And you, ma'am. My joke was risky but I'm pleased you laughed.'

It was lunchtime and people were getting ready to go home when they heard two cars go fast through the centre of town and could see that they had stopped outside Bonnie's house. There was no fuss. Having identified themselves, Bonnie smiled at the officers and went and sat in the back seat of one of the cars.

'Good afternoon, ma'am,' said the officer sitting alongside. 'This will sound strange, but are there any substances or medications that you will need to take with us?'

Bonnie looked at her.

'Are you serious?'

'Those taking heroin may need a dose before the doctor can arrange methadone.'

'No. What I have taken is because I am lonely and overwhelmed by work into which I think I have been over-promoted. I have taken sexual advantage of and used a junior office. I deserve what's coming to me, I suppose, though I have learned that even the temporary high of coke really is only temporary and I'd stopped taking it some weeks ago, which is why I had an unused stash.. The loneliness remains, as does the sense that I'm just not up to what is being asked of me in terms of leadership. I'm a good detective but I'm not cut out for being in charge.'

The officer reached out her hand and took that of Bonnie.

Very quietly, she said, 'Keep saying that, ma'am, do you hear, and you might survive?'

'Listen everyone,' said Jo to the rest of the team, 'you all need to go away for the rest of the weekend and I need to go to bed as I haven't been there since yesterday morning but before you go, I'll give you the official version rather than any gossip. This morning, Tom was arrested for possession but also for hoarding a stash of illegal drugs. The drug squad is wanting to charge him. He insists he does not use, and his drug tests bear that out, but he told me he acquires substances for Bonnie, and that they have developed a sexual relationship as part of the deal. Both Tom and Bonnie are being questioned by Professional Standards. I very much feel that a lot of this may be my fault, of not giving you all that you need in the way of support. When I get hold of her I shall ask Esther if she feels up to being SIO of the Andie Bolam murder, and the death of Penny Babworth. I will try my very best to keep both Tom and Bonnie out of prison. Bonnie won't be coming back, that is certain, but I hope Tom might, with nothing more than a kick up the arse, but first I have some backsides to lick to bring that about. Ok, off you go.'

'No,' said a man's voice, so it had to be Ed. 'Jo, we all have to take responsibility for ourselves. If we need help, we each have a tongue in our mouth. I know that every one of us works for you because we know you are there, and we are learning from you all the time. We're all becoming better detectives because we see you at work, and that includes mistakes you make, which makes it much easier to deal with the ones we make. I made a big mistake once, when I slept with a potential expert witness. That could have been the end of my career, but you and Chris Arthington were superb and I learned from it how to deal with mistakes others make, which is not to make a fuss. I guess what I am saying, boss, is that if you go home today blaming yourself, you're wrong and we all know that. And on Monday we have to get going again and get these people, real criminals locked up.'

Everyone applauded, and Jo went red in the face. The team

began to leave.

'Kelly,' said Jo. 'Are you going back to your mum and dad in Rugeley?'

'Not now.'

'Come and stay in Saxmundham. Tomorrow my neighbour will receive two personal protection officers to give her and Katia 24 hours of safeguarding. They will be armed and I think you and I together will need to convince her it is what she needs.'

'If you've got room for me, I'd love to come.'

## 19

Jo asked Kelly to drive and she fell asleep on the slow Suffolk roads, though it was not just tiredness - Jo had a widespread reputation for being able to fall asleep almost anywhere. Kelly looked across at her and she seemed all done in, yet before her lay a great deal. Arriving back in Saxmundham Jo finally awoke as Kelly parked in the drive. Before they had set off, Kelly had forewarned Marie of the exhausted state of Jo and she was already outside waiting for her.

'My darling,' said Marie, 'you look terrible.'

'Oh thank you my sweet.'

'No. It's only an observation. Bed, now.'

She led her in and Kelly followed. She knew she had one or two enormous decisions to make about things which needed to be acted on only by Jo, even though realistically she was completely *hors de combat*. The person now in charge, though she didn't know it, was Esther, and informing Esther was one of the key things that only Jo should do. Then she had to cross the road and inform Alice that she was going on a flight to Manchester tomorrow. The only team member she could discuss this with was Darcey, as only she knew about Nottingham, so excusing herself, she went outside into the cold November east wind coming from the sea and called Darcey.

'Kelly, is everything ok?'

Kelly laughed.

'I'm in Saxmundham at the home of the Sleeping Beauty. She is utterly exhausted and won't be human again until morning at the earliest. Darcey, someone has to act and Ed is the senior person, but he doesn't know about Nottingham. Esther needs to know what's happened, and that Jo wants her appointed as SIO of the Bolam murder and Babworth killing, but she has to be told about Nottingham. Then, and I think it has to be me, Alice has to be told about her visit to Manchester tomorrow with Marie, and her return with two armed PPOs who will be moving in with her and Katia.'

Speaking to Esther has to be done by a police officer, Kelly, but Alice is a civilian and Jo tells me Alice trusts you totally because you've both been inside.'

'If I ever apply for another job, I'll get her to write me a reference.'

'I'm sure our new acting Super will get in touch. It has not been a good day, and we are now two members short which will exercise Jo's mind when she wakes up.'

'She's in good hands, Darcey, her wife, mum and dad and two doting children.'

'And you, Kelly.'


Darcey called Esther straight away.

'Hi Darcey, we're having a shopping trip in Oxford which one of us is loving and one of is most definitely not.'

Well, one of you might be pleased by what I'm going to tell you and I'm not sure about the other.

'Ooh, that sounds interesting.'

'To cut a long story short, two members of the team have been arrested today by Professional Standards and likely to be charged with possession. It is complicated and Jo remains hopeful that Tom will be back, though the rest of us are not sure. He is not and has never been a user but in return for obtaining and concealing in his house, Bonnie has provided him with sexual favours.'

'Bonnie!'

'Yes.'

'She'll get crucified and Jo will have to work extremely hard to keep her out of jail But what about the regular drug tests we all have?'

'Tom has been completely clear and so has Bonnie, except all her tests have been recorded as negative and then changed on the computer.'

Surely Kelly noticed?'

'No. Once Bonnie was absent at the time of the test which the lab didn't follow up (it wasn't the first time they'd overlooked us or had been told we were done by Cambridge or Norfolk), and maybe the second was the one we do ourselves and she got Tom to do it for her. We don't know yet, but this could have been happening for a while. Kelly hadn't been informed about the regular drug testing programme'

'But why didn't Jo notice?'

'She had handed the task over to Bonnie and Aisling.

'Oh well, whatever is the case will no doubt come back to us with teeth.'

'It's something Bonnie's replacement will have to deal with.'

'Has Jo made an appointment already?'

'Yes, but she missed sleep all last night and Kelly drove her home utterly exhausted, which is why I'm calling you. Technically Ed is senior officer but there are reasons I will come to in a minute why he shouldn't make this call. Jo wants you to take over as Acting Superintendent and SIO of the Bolam murder and death of Babworth.

'You will need also to know about the cold case investigation being undertaken by Jo and myself, in Nottingham, not least because we believe there may be a link with Andie Bolam's murder, but Esther, I cannot tell you about this over an open telephone line, other than to say it is a serious matter affecting some people who from tomorrow will have armed PPO. Tell Paul, I'm sorry, but can you please come back for a full briefing with Kelly and me. She knows all about it too I warn you that it's all somewhat dark.'

'Of course I will. And now that I am the member of the household with the superior rank, he will do the washing up tonight.'

'Clearly every cloud has a silver lining, Esther.

'I hope so because this dark cloud is not good for our team and any who want rid of us, so we need good results soon.'

'I'll tell you what the Super at Professional Standards said to Jo when they were discussing the loss of Bonnie and Jo. He said, "Jo, you need all the heterosexuals you can get". Cheeky sod. Anyway, I'll see you at the office at about 4:00 tomorrow, ma'am'.

Esther was still laughing as Jo rang off, but the laugh was hollow when she thought of that the consequences might be for Jo especially.

Kelly crossed the road and approached the door, opened, as if by miracle, by Katia.

'Hi Kelly, come in. Mum's just made a cake. It tastes great, just don't mention how it looks.'

'I heard that,' said a voice from the kitchen.

'I think you were meant to, Alice,' said Kelly.

'I'll make a cup of tea to help you wash it down.'

Katia led Kelly into the sitting room at the front of the house where they were soon joined by Alice.

'I saw you make a secret phone call,' said Alice.

'Yes, we have a wee trauma in the past 24 hours and Jo missed a complete night's sleep so I thought I would risk the freezing cold weather and disturb her. She is fast asleep. But it's less about the past 24 hours that I want to speak than what will happen tomorrow.

'The journalist who was due to come to see you on Monday, Andie Bolam, was, as you know, murdered in Cambridge on Saturday night. Increasingly, Jo thinks there is a connection between her death and her visit to you, that it may well have been to stop her getting to see you. The civil servant who gave her your name and address has been arrested, but we think it possible that there are those in Nottingham still who know the truth about what happened in 1984 and are determined to protect themselves or those close to them – even to the extent of killing. I can't as yet tell you what evidence we have, because too much knowledge of the state of the investigation might make you even more vulnerable, but I will say we are moving considerably forwards.

'However, Jo acting on instruction from a Chief Constable wants you Alice, and I'm sorry that this time it's not you Katia, to go to Manchester with Marie to collect two Personal Protection Officers who will provide 24-hour protection here. Although Marie has refused to let them be armed on the flight, they will be when they are here, though not in uniform.'

'Fly – me?'

'Yes, mum, you must. Just don't turn round and be sick.'

'There's an aerodrome where the police helicopters are based and you'll land there and pick up the two experienced officers.'

'Men or women?'

'I do not know and whilst it doesn't include the loo or the bath, they'll accompany you everywhere. You can even learn the words of "Me and my Shadow" to annoy them. If Jo were awake and here, the only thing she would tell you is that whatever they tell you to do, do it as your lives might depend on it. They will be here to protect you even putting themselves at risk, if need be, but they must trust you to respond at once.'

'Of course. But flying! That's wonderful.'

'Marie will let you know what time to be ready and although I reckon that after Jo she is the most trustworthy person on the planet, she does not need to know what we are doing in Nottingham, nor anything at all about your past.'

'Nothing at all?'

'No. Both take totally seriously the Official Secrets Act and neither feel they must tell the other anything about their work and that means when they get home they switch off the day completely. Nor will the Protection Officers until they are briefed on arrival by Jo herself. So talk about Ipswich Town though that would very depressing, or anything until you are back.'

'Don't worry, Kelly. Mum can talk for England, if need be.'

Small children are not necessarily the best respecters of the needs of their parents so it was at about 6:30 that first Ollie and Josie clambered in between the sleeping Marie and her wife still desperately longing for more, waking both. Yet, on a Sunday, morning there was no rush to leave bed and what is the point of having two mums if you can't enjoy them both together?

After her shower with both the children joining in, Jo dressed and found Kelly still asleep in the small spare room, and decided to leave her. She knew that she could rely on the fact that Kelly would have taken the initiative and done the necessary yesterday. She now had to decide whether to ignore Dani's advice and risk a call to the Chief Constable of Cambridgeshire. On the other hand she could always have called Canon Browne and talked about Theology. Faced with the ludicrous alternative, she opted for the former. She had his private number, though had never used it. On a Sunday morning, she thought it would be the only way of getting to him. He answered.

'Good morning, sir, I'm sorry to disturb you on a Sunday morning. It's Jo Enright.'

'Jo! How lovely. Can you come and join me for lunch today. My wife's idea of fun is travelling to the Belfry to play a game of golf on a famous course, whereas mine is having lunch with my favourite detective. It will be simple and straightforward but your call has made my day. Get here for about 11-30 and you can tell me what you are up to. See you then.'

Jo laughed, though not sure why. It was like being hit and knocked over by a violent wind. But the option of declining the invitation had not been there. Again she laughed.

'That was a pleasant laugh, boss,' said the voice of Kelly behind her.

Jo turned, smiling.

'It was not unlike being with Alice in Wonderland, whereas it was the Chief Constable.'

'Same thing.'

Jo prepared to drive to the home of the Chief Constable. Marie with Alice were leaving just after noon. The children were having a day out with grandma and grandad, Kelly invited Katia and Dianne to join her for some lunch. Jo was the only one who was nervous, though she wasn't entirely sure why. She knew that

Christopher Biddle liked her very much, not least because she had once resolved a serious problem in the University and the diocese with the minimum of fuss, and he had been the one encouraging her to set up the Unit (ordering her more likely), together with his fellow Chiefs from Norwich, Suffolk and Essex. All had, in important ways, benefited considerably from her work. When they met one another, they sometimes referred to it as "The lesbian team" but whilst laughing did not denigrate the work they did. Chris himself had once been a student at Cambridge and therefore knew its ways and was under no illusions about students. As a police officer he knew he had considerably less actual policing experience than many of his officers, but he had a sharp mind and an exceptional ability to choose the right people for their jobs. Jo had heard he was an astute interviewer and therefore knew she not necessarily in for an easy time.

Over a more than a generous glass of dry sherry (and good sherry it was too) she outlined the issues involved with the death of Dr Babworth and her involvement as a "key holder" in the top secret work with MI5 and two others into decrypting.'

'It's why I wanted you involved.'

'MI5 wanted to take it over, but between you and me, sir, this is the sort of thing they're not at their best doing. I think we shall get a result and I'm not wholly sure they want that, for whatever security reasons. Sheila is encouraging us to work on the basis that it was suicide, but the Security Service want us to decide that it was premeditated murder.'

How do you know what they want?'

'Sometimes, sir, it's best if the circle of information is kept narrow.'

'I think I'll write that down, Jo.'

Jo laughed.

'Come on through to the dining room. It will not be top cuisine and it's all cold, but gazpacho, salmon steaks and autumn berries with tiramisu should not be too bad.'

Sir, you are a genius.'

'Oh, how I wish you were my DCC. He says nothing like that.

They sat and ate the soup.

'What else is on the go?'

The murder of Andie Bolam the Channel 4 journalist, a week ago last night in Waterbeach, someone I knew well.'

'I'm so sorry to hear that.'

'However, I now think is is related to something else I'm involved with, not just a cold case but a freezing case built on mistaken pathology, and I think the pathologist was being leaned on, but it has led to a terrible injustice which has had terrible consequences for a woman and her daughter, who are now greatly at risk. I mentioned this to the Chief Constable from the Dark Lagoon, and she offered to send two of her personal PPO to take care of them. I know I should have cleared it with you first...'

'But you are talking about Dani, I imagine, and if you think I'm going to argue with her, you have another thing coming. I know you won't want to tell me more and I think you are right at this stage, but can I take it you are investigating out of your area.'

'Yes, sir, but the woman in question lives most definitely in my area. I have discovered that Andie Bolam was on to this as well, and that is why she was killed as she was. These are dangerous people, so just three of us are working on it, giving the impression that we are not especially involved.'

'Were they to know that it was you, however, they might have cause to think again. How's the salmon?'

'Delicious, sir. Dare I ask if you cooked it?'

'Believe it or not, Jo, I did.'

'I'm impressed.'

'Now let's talk about these two idiots of yours presently locked up by Professional Standards. The transcripts of their interview I received last night. The drug user, Superintendent Miller, did not cover anything up at all. She said she was lonely and felt that your very real confidence in her was misplaced. Most of the time she felt she was failing and terrified about about being an SIO but didn't want to let you down. She thought drugs might help but had stopped taking them and her blood tests were clear. Using DC Bridge as she did allowed both of them to be less lonely and was for him a source of engagement to do her bidding when it came to buying.

'But we have a problem and it is that Superintendent Miller is black, and a black Super in jail is not good news for us or her. Her record is good and depending on what you have to say, I shall have to be judge and jury.'

'Don't laugh, sir, but she was originally sent to us by Dani.'

'I'm sorry, Jo, but I have to laugh and I shall write it down in my notebook for when I next see her.'

He continued to laugh.

'She has messed up, but at the end of the day the person responsible for putting her into a position she couldn't cope with is me. If anyone has failed her, it's me and I think nothing would gained at all by imprisoning her. If she can be monitored on a drug release course and allowed to drop to being the excellent DI she was when she came, then I believe she will continue to be a very good copper, but not, of course, with us. She would be better used in the city and might make friends.'

'What about DS Bridge?'

'Is there any way we could arrange to cut his balls off, sir?'

'There's a queue, I'm afraid, as, when you're in my seat you will learn.'

'Oh no, I'm happy where I am. As for Tom Bridge, he has the makings of being a good detective but a spell back as a DC wouldn't harm him.'

'You'd have him back?'

'As the Super at Professional Standards said to me yesterday: "You lot need all the heterosexuals you can get".'

The Chief Constable could not keep a straight face.

'Do you mind someone saying that?'

'Not at all. I thought it was funny.'

As they tucked into autumn berries and tiramisu, the Chief Constable said, 'I will admit that the tiramisu came from Waitrose. I will also make the arrangements to release Miller and Bridge. Will you collect them and take them to their homes?'

'You could have made a good tiramisu, sir, and yes, I will do so and talk over with them what you have decided.'

'Miller should begin the drugs rehab course after a three week break. By then I will have found her a new position as a DI. Being weekend, neither has been referred to the CPS so they've not been charged.'

'On their behalf, and that of my team, thank you, sir.'

'You see, Jo, when you are a Chief Constable and despite what you say, you will be, it's not all paperwork and ceremony.'

'Cooking as well, sir!'

'Now, tell me how Marie is after her adventure which I saw on the news.'

'Thank you for asking. Marie is unbelievably courageous and if you were in a tight spot you could take for granted that she would get you out of it. She's successfully crash landed a plane in which the engine failed, she dealt with an armed hijacker and now she's dealt with Egyptian special forces, She is fearless, I think, as well as very beautiful, but we say very little to each other about work. She knows nothing about about the matter I'm dealing with and she has actually told me nothing more about Egypt than appeared on the tv news. And it works, because it means that at home we are there full-time for the children and one another, and we recover by watching rubbish on the tv, which we love doing.'

You must go, Jo, and pick up your miscreants. Promise me this, that in what you are involved in, you will exercise proper caution. I don't want to lose you. Oh, and tell Marie, that the next time I arrange a solo lunch, it is her I want!'

'As Chief Constables go, sir, you remind of Dick Emery, one of whose female characters used to say "Oo, you are awful, but I like you."'

## 20

Jo left and drove straight to the HQ of Professional Standards in Grantchester. The Chief had made his calls and Bonnie and Tom were sitting waiting for her in the Waiting Room.

'Jo', said Bonnie, 'I don't know what to say.'

'In which case, my darling, say nothing. Look out of the window and be glad you're on your way home and not somewhere they might want to lock you up. But tell me first what you both need: a shower, food, sleep – you decide and I'll try to get it.'

'Home said Bonnie.

'Me too,' said Tom.

'That's fine by me, though we can we all got to yours, Bonnie, and let me tell you what the Chief Constable has decided.'

'Have you seen him?' asked Tom.

'He cooked lunch for me.'

Once in Stowmarket Jo stopped at Bonnie's house, and let Bonnie go in first to make sure the drug squad had not left it like it like a tip. They had, but soon she made her lounge a place where the others could join her. She went out to make cups of tea but warned them that the milk was not completely fresh.

'Right,' said Jo, 'welcome back. Had Professional Standards had their way, you might not have seen the place for some time. So I want to begin with a confession of my failures. I have not given enough attention and support to either of you and I want to apologise for that failure. I can't really apologise for asking you to take on the heavy burdens of Super and SIO, because I know you are quite superb as a police officer and detective, but I took you for granted and that is my fault. Nor did I consider the isolation and loneliness that comes from being a single copper out here in the middle of nowhere.

'Anyway, the bottom line, Bonnie, is that you will have to complete the next Force Drug Rehab Course in Sheffield in three weeks' time, until which time, you will take paid leave. The Chief has accepted my recommendation that you will resume duties after that as a DI. You can continue to live here if you wish.

'Tom, you revert to being a DC, but I've kept you out of uniform at least. You can rejoin the Unit if you wish or seek a transfer. It's up to you.'

Bonnie and Tom looked at one another.

'Jo, that's astonishing. Did you get the Chief drunk or something?' asked Bonnie.

'You will I'm sure, recall that Gladstone said of Disraeli that he was "a sophistical rhetorician, inebriated with the exuberance of his own verbosity" but the Chief was sober as a judge and full of compassion and understanding towards you both, and wants to lose neither of you, especially after I lied through my teeth and said how good you both are.'

For the first time, they smiled.

'Tom, I'd like you to take some leave as well. This has been an awful weekend for you both and you need time to sleep. Penny will become SIO and acting-Super and I shall have to begin recruiting. But having failed you both so badly, I want now to make sure you have time to recover as you consider the future. If you want to talk, then contact Kelly and she'll make the arrangements. As you both know we're moving into what I hope is the move towards checkmate in three cases soon so we shall be busy. Tom, do you want me to drive you home?'

'Ah well,' answered Bonnie. 'The fact is that all our nights together have rather driven us closer and closer, and now you have given us a "get out of jail free" card (literally), we're going to give being together all the time a go.'

Jo smiled and then gave each of them a kiss. Overhead, they heard a light aircraft coming into land at nearby Crowfield.

'I must go,' said Jo.

When Jo arrived at the airfield She found Marie doing an external check on the plane – Jo admired the fact that she never failed to do a single pre or post flight check, which must be odd given that tomorrow morning she would be piloting one of the largest transporter planes in the world and doing the same checks with that too though she confessed to Jo that if it was raining, she sent the First Officer to do so. Outside the hangar she could see three women, Alice was one and the other two younger women with bags and, not normally seen at Crowfield, high powered assault rifles across their chests – clearly the PPOs sent by Dani.

Jo parked the car and approached the three.

'Hi Jo,' said Alice.

'Hi, Alice, and welcome to the end of the earth, ladies. I'm the wife of your pilot, and I double up as Detective Chief Superintendent Jo Enright, but save in active operation, you call me Jo.'

'Er, we're not used to that, and I'm DS Caro Barnes.'

'And I'm DS Jodie Lovelock, ma'am'.

'I'll just have a quick word with Marie and then I'll take you two, and Alice can go with Marie, and we can do your briefing at the office.'

She was not away long.

'Alice, how was the flight?'

'Magic.'

'Ok then, guys, bags and guns in the boot, and then let's go.'

Once on their way, Jo said, 'Marie probably won't have told you about her day job, but she's not a copper. In fact, she's a Flight Lieutenant in the Royal Air Force and her normal plane is the one of the largest in the Air Force of which she is the leading pilot. So you were in safe hands.'

'But how does she cope with all those men she must work with looking like she does?' asked Jodie.

'Well, she has never hidden the fact that she's gay and being married to a detective chief super in the police might just help.'

They both laughed.

They stopped outside the police station in Stowmarket.

'This is our base and we'll be meeting here with Esther Hayden, newly appointed acting Superintendent. She has been promoted over her husband, Paul who is still only a DCI, so do congratulate her and, contrary to rumours, is proof that we're not all lesbians. Neither is DS Steph Binks who lives with a former catholic priest, called Fergal, in euphoric and apparently, sexual, bliss.'

They went into the building and met Kelly, who gave them the team briefing and necessary information and equipment, and Esther who was trying to adjust herself into her new role.

'Congratulations, ma'am,' said Jodie, 'on overtaking your husband.'

'Thank you, and you are?'

'Jodie and Caro,' replied Caro.

'Well, as the boss has probably told you, here we reserve ranks and titles for working, so I'm Esther, though we shall be working on different cases.'

'Ok,' said Jo, this is a briefing on the matter we are dealing with in Nottingham. Kelly knows everything already. And Esther needs to know, as do both of you.

'All I'm going to tell you is subject both to the Official Secrets Act and a silencing order of a High Court Judge, and it would better if you don't discuss it even alone and never in the presence of Alice or her daughter, Katia. Alice is at the centre but it's best she knows everything only when it is resolved which I am hoping will be soon.'

Jo told them everything, including her conviction that Alice was innocent of the crimes for which she has been traced so badly over so long a period. She went to speak of the role of Andie and her murder because she was getting too close to the truth of what happened 36 years ago.

'These people give the appearance of being professional and using professional killers, which is why I want two professionals of our own. At all times one of you must be with Alice, but on some days I will want the other to be with us in Nottingham. Kelly runs everything and everything must be run through Kelly.

She is MI5 trained and can work miracles with computers and anything technological, and will be with us in Nottingham, most of the time, though you can have her a couple of days here, Esther.'

'Thank God for that.'

'A word of warning about Kelly, however, don't ask her to engage in fraud on your behalf – she's totally crap at that, and I'll let her explain why, and be ready for a surprise. The other member of the Nottingham team is DI Darcey Bussell.'

The woman laughed.

'Yes, I know, though in fact her name is Janice, but apparently she so hated her name, when she was just three days old she changed it to Darcey – or that's what she says, though I have my doubts. When I was head of CID in Norfolk, I spotted her as a cadet and recruited her. She is such a natural detective, and she lives with DS Gorham though working in different teams just now.'

'You and our Chief Constable get on well, ma'am, er Jo, don't you? 'said Caro. 'You probably know she has a large photo of you in her office.'

'I owe her so much. When, following the awful death of my partner, it was she who brought me out of hell. You know her only as Chief Constable and boss, but I know her as someone I love very much, not least because of the care and understanding she showed when I most needed it. She's also quite capable of being very tough and always bossy.'

Again they laughed.

'We would never have worked that out ma'am, er, Jo,' said Jodie with a laugh, 'especially first thing in the morning.'

'Obviously only concealed hand guns when you're in public. You'll be safe for a quiet night tonight, but it's from tomorrow that we have to be especially attentive. He doesn't know it yet, but my dad who's staying with us, will be on Katia school duty and one of you will do the school run with Alice in the village with my two children who are called Josie and Ollie, and in case you might come to wonder, Josie was born in the normal way in Marie's first marriage; Ollie is a product of the miracle of IVF –

Marie's egg fertilised by anonymous donor, and then implanted in my womb for nine months.'

'That is truly a wonder, Jo. Are you intending to repeat?'

'Possibly, but if we do, Marie will do the pregnancy.

'It's a few years now since I did the school run,' said Caro.

'How many have you got?'

'Three, all now in their late teens, and four if you include my husband! I love them – some of the time.'

'What about you, Jodie?'

'None so far.'

'Are you trying?'

'At the moment there's no one to try with, but then again I'm approximately 30 years younger than Caro.'

'Cheeky sod!'

There were questions and an expression of amazement from Esther about the range of cases so small a team was handling.

'I guess they all count as sensitive, especially as nobody higher than me knows what we doing in Nottingham, except the Chief Constable of Greater Manchester. If it all goes tits-up, it's my head that will be on the line. And you all need to know that we've lost two of the team today. I argued their case with the Chief Constable but both have been demoted and will go elsewhere, but not to prison.'

'May I ask what it was for, Jo?' asked Caro.

'Drugs.'

They were soon on their way.

'Do you know, Jo, I said to Caro as we were preparing today, that at least going deep into the heart of the Suffolk countryside would be quite different inner city Manchester, but all you said in the briefing makes me wonder if I was right.'

'I guess human beings are much the same everywhere, including criminals, and that reminds me, and it's better that I say it now than when we get there. If you feel you are under assault, you are authorised to use your firearms to the extent you judge appropriate. I will always support you in that without fail.'

Thank you, ma'am,' said both as one.

'And now welcome to Saxmundham which on a Sunday afternoon is about as busy as it is on any other day in winter. This is Alice's home where you will be based, and Marie and I and our children, live in the house opposite. Use either or both to keep up the obs but my mother is cooking for us all tonight.'

'We have various bits and pieces of tech-craft we need to set up first. With it getting dark this will provide us with adequate cover,' said Caro.

'Go and say hello to Katia first and establish with Alice what space and rooms you need inside and I've set aside a room for you at the front in our house.'

Coming out of the shower, Jo was surprised to see Marie in her dress uniform.

'Bulford', she replied, the single word telling Jo that the day had come for David's Court Martial, held in the military court on Salisbury Plain.

'He's pleading guilty but I'm hoping my evidence, and that of Dianne, will help protect him a little. On the flight there and back he did nothing wrong and obeyed orders throughout without hesitation.'

'Good luck, my darling. How long will it last?'

'With luck I should be home tomorrow night.'

'God, Marie, you look so totally gorgeous in your dress uniform.'

'Thank you my love. Have you had further thoughts on what we spoke about?'

'Yes and I would love to go ahead and try, but think about it closely. I wasn't working when I was pregnant, and you would be.'

Marie came towards Jo and kissed her.

Alice, Caro, Josie and Ollie did the school run.

'This is much easier than how most of my mornings are spent,' said Caro. Getting three lads and the fourth called husband, out of the house and then getting to the home of the Chief Constable is hard work.'

'That was her at the aerodrome yesterday?'

'Yes. To be fair she's doing a good job in an area of considerable crime.'

'Jo speaks highly of her certainly.'

Caro smiled and decided not to mention the large photograph of Jo in Dani's office.'

Darcey had left home early, ready to collect Jo and Jodie. She and her partner Belinda had endured an uncomfortable weekend following their decision to report Tom, and had only relaxed a little when Kelly had called and told them the result of Jo's lunch with the Chief Constable. Jo thought Jodie was the sort of police officer who could take good care of herself. She didn't ask her if she was armed but assumed she was.

Jo was armed with enhanced and colour copies of the marks on the necks of the two children which had been left for with Kelly by Shiela. Sheila had also produced the name of the pathologist and the information that he was still alive and it was to his house in Arnold, a posh suburb in the North of Nottingham that they were now making.

'Isn't that where Joe Worrall, the uncle of the children still lives?' asked Darcey.

'It is, but we shall see Dr Evan Fulwood first.'

Jo pulled up outside the house.

'I think, Jodie, three of us might be over-egging the pudding. So please stay here.'

'I'm sorry, ma'am. I didn't understand what you said. You used a word I've never heard in a police command before,' she said with a grin.

Darcey and Jo walked up the long drive, Jo carrying the file containing the photographs. Darcey rang the bell and an old man opened the door.

'Hello. We would like to see Dr Evan Fulwood.'

'That is me.'

Hello, sir. I'm Detective Inspector Bussell and this is Detective Chief Superintendent of the Sensitive Case Unit. May we come in?'

'Please do. Up to my retirement I saw police officers regularly, but they never looked like you two.'

'Do you think we should have false beards, sir?' said Jo.

He laughed'

'What can I do for you?'

'Do you know Dr Sheila Colville, who serves as our Forensic Pathologist?'

'I've read her name from time to time, and I think she has done fine work abroad.'

'We are dealing with the death of a child and Sheila suggested we come to see you for a second opinion, given your extensive experience,' said Jo. 'In a way it's typical of Sheila. Her feeling is that only by being exact can she serve justice.'

'She's quite right, of course, though not everyone would bother when they're clear. So what is it?'

'A child was found strangled in woodland a fortnight ago. The local force arrested another child, but Sheila is far from happy and photographed the neck of the victim. She would welcome your opinion and if you wish to confirm this, I can give you her phone number.'

'Well, please come through to my study where I have lights.'

Jo and Darcey followed him, and there Jo pulled out a photograph in a sealed evidence bag, and handed it to the pathologist.

'Your evidence bags are better than they were'.

He looked at the photograph with a magnifying glass from different angles, and then stood up straight.

'There can be no doubt and I wholly support Dr Colville's judgement. These marks were made by an adult.'

'I'm sure Dr Colville will be hugely grateful, as I am, sir.'

'I hope you will stay and have some coffee.'

'That would be very kind.'

They returned to the other room and waited for the doctor to return. Over the next ten minutes Jo engaged in creative fantasy, describing the work of the unit that bore no relation to reality, implying that they worked only in Suffolk. They took their leave, saying nothing to each other as they returned to their car.

'There we are, my darlings, the evidence we need to know we are doing the right thing. We shall be back.' she said.

After Esther's briefing, she sent Ed and Belinda to Cambridge gathering every surviving CCTV recording from the night Andie died. Esther was going to visit the vet, or several vets, living near to Penny Babworth, in a search for Etorphine.

The practice in Linton was the obvious place to start. Esther walked to the Reception desk'

'Name and breed?'

'Detective Superintendent Hayden – sometimes human, to speak to your veterinary team, as a matter of urgency, please.'

Esther sat with cats and dogs, all of which she had for about 10 minutes before returning to the receptionist.'

'Excuse me, do you and your colleagues not know the meaning of the word "urgency"? I am investigating a murder and I don't have the time to sit among such delightful creatures. I need to speak to the team now. It won't take long but it's vitally important.'

The team assembled in the staff room and Esther came in.

'Is this everyone who might have access to drugs?'

They looked round.

'Two nurses are not on duty until later, but otherwise, yes,' said one of the vets.

'Please can you tell me about your use of Etorphine and I already know what it is?'

'We use it as little as possible. On the whole we don't get elephants to treat, but there is the occasional Shire Horse with which we might use it as an anaesthetic, but very little given how powerful it is.'

'So you stock it as a matter of course?'

'Yes, and it's subject to stringent precautions in a locked drug cupboard.'

'To which how many people have access?'

'All of us during work time and at the end of the day, we always do a check. If anything was missing because accidentally left out, we find it and return it. I don't know your timescale but nothing has gone missing in my time here.'

'Nor mine,' said a number of others.

'Could someone in the course of work, and I'm not implying it happened here, use daytime access to draw up into a syringe a drug, replace the container and then place it somewhere for later collection?'

'That's possible, of course, but unlikely. The surgery in which we store drugs is in constant use throughout the day. What you have described just couldn't happen.'

'It might at the end of the day,' said one of the nurses.

'Yes, I suppose so, but who would want to do that anyway?' added another.

'I'm nearly done and I apologise for taking up your time. Do you use Etorphine to euthanise animals?'

'No. Much of the time it would be taking a sledgehammer to crack a nut, but it's there just in case an elephant comes along.'

People laughed.

Ok, thank you everyone, you've been most helpful. If someone could show me the drug cupboard, then I'll be off.'

The senior vet volunteered as he was due in there next.

'You appear to have a good and bright team there,' said Esther.

'We all get on well which is so important. Here we are and I'll open it for you.'

He produced keys from his pocket but found the door unlocked.

'Is that usual?'

'No, but it was my doing. I was working in here before your summons and overlooked locking it.'

'Which is the Etorphine?'

'He reached in and pulled out a bottle of clear and lethal liquid.'

'You can see that the seal is still in place.'

'For a brief moment can I treat you as an expert witness even though you can only guess. If I drew up some Etorphine with the intention of killing myself, and then injected it into my vein, would I have sufficient time to stand up, dispose of the syringe and then return to my seat?'

'It would depend on how much you injected though even so we're talking about powerful stuff even in small quantities, but I would hazard a guess from what I see in animals we have to put to sleep, that there would be no no chance that you could do that.'

'Well, the good news is that I'm not intending to do so.'

'I'm very pleased to hear it.'

'And before I go, can you let me have an up-to-date staff list.'

'I'll get you one and do call in again, Superintendent.'

'I will, Veterinarian.'

They laughed.

## 21

By the time she arrived back at the office, she had heard and seen the insides of all the local vets within a 10 miles radius of Linton and all had told almost exactly the same story. She handed over to Kelly the staff lists she had acquired. Ed was already back from his CCTV hunt and Belinda on her way back.

'Anything so far?' asked Esther.

'Just one car that is circling suspiciously in the area of the AAA Club, but as yet I haven't been to able to see the numbers plate. I'm hoping that if it came into the city from outside, Belinda may have something from the A14 coming from the A1. I doubt we'll find anything coming in from the A10 but I'll check all the same.'

Her phone rang.

'Tell only Esther that we've had a clear positive recognition of the bruising as inflicted by an adult. Can you also please do me a favour, Kelly and find an officer in Nottinghamshire, number 241, called Francesca something. In the meantime we're going to have some lunch.'

'Ok boss.'

'Is that the Francesca we met last week and to whom you took a shine?' said Darcey, when the call had ended.

'What an outrageous thing to suggest, Inspector! Though it's more or less how I recruited you. I looked and intuitively I just knew you were a class act.'

'Ah, ma'am, you say all the right things.'

Jodie in the back thought this conversation hilarious though increasingly she was realising on the basis of less than than 24 hours, this temporary boss was special and despite the humour clearly was a toughie and increasingly could sense why her own Chief Constable in Manchester had her photo on the side table of her office.

Their lunch did not amount to a great deal and during it Kelly rang through.

'Francesca Wawszyczk, PC 241. I have no idea how to pronounce the name, and I imagine it's Polish. Single and unattached. Commendation for single-handedly tackling and disarming a gunman robbing a bookmakers. I'll text you the address and phone number.'

'Thanks Kelly. I'll be in touch.'

Once the address came through, Darcey drove the car towards Beeston in the south west of the city and pulled up outside a house in a terraced street. Jo got out and knocked on the door. The door was opened by someone clearly engaged in painting and who at the sight of Jo burst into laughter.

'Hello Francesca. Three questions. 1. Do you remember me? 2. Can we have a drink with you? And number 3 I'll keep a little longer.'

'Yes, to them all, ma'am. Come in and bring the others. I'll put the kettle on and tidy myself up.'

Jo waved to the others to follow.

'This is Detective Inspector Bussell and Detective Sergeant Lovelock.'

'Ma'am,' she said to Darcey and 'Sarge' to Jodie as they shook hands. 'Please sit down.

'Are all these paintings yours,' asked Darcey.

'They are, ma'am.'

'You're very good,' added Jo.

'It's what I do when I'm not chasing villains or police officers photographing files in a library.'

Jo and Darcey smiled. Francesca went into the kitchen, which doubled as her studio, and returned with cups of tea and cake and sat down.

'Please tell me to what I owe the real pleasure of your visit, and when will you ask me question number 3?'

'First tell us how to pronounce your name?' said Jo.

'I'm almost always known as Frankie but you probably mean my surname. It's Polish and that's where my parents came from. It's never spelled as it sounds if it's Polish. Mine is Wuffcheck. Frankie Wuffcheck.'

'Well, Frankie. We have a rule in the SCU,' said Darcey. When we are active we use the proper titles of rank, and when we are not we call each other by our names, so this is Jodie, this is Jo and I am Darcey. I can tell you for certain that it does not in any way diminish our proper respect. When we are working, Jo is Detective Chief Superintendent and what she says goes without question and the same goes for Jodie who is an authorised firearms officer. When she says something we do as we are told.'

'And that includes me,' said Jo.

'And the third question?'

'If I set up your transfer, will you come and join us, Frankie?'

'As this is a work matter, my answer is "Yes, ma'am".'

'Good. I hoped you would agree. By the way what time are on you on duty?'

'I'm not. I'm on leave.'

'Ok. As you already know we're doing something here in Nottingham but almost as UCOs – working not actually undercover but not doing what we say we are doing. We are striving to resolve a serious matter from a long time ago. It's up to you, Frankie. It will take me some days to bring about your transfer and you can spend the week painting and not bothering yourself in this matter, which might be wise, given that we are dealing with some far from nice people, or you can become part of us from today. It's up to you.'

'I'm sorry to say, Jo, that faced with being part of your unit and I've done some hunting around about you, the attractions of being in uniform in a car and attending complaints about people talking illicit photographs and dealing with drunks is just so very compelling, so I'm afraid my answer is Yes.'

'Good. For your security's sake you need to leave your house until we have sorted the matter in hand. I know you had a commendation for bravery for tackling an armed villain, but I'm not going to let you be at risk. We have a spare house, though it will take a little while to get sorted, so please pack your kit and be ready to move soon. You can come and live with my wife and me, and the two kids, and my parents, for the time being.'

Frankie left and could be heard upstairs opening and shutting drawers.

'I need a wee,' said Jo'

Darcey and Jodie admitted the same.

'I never knew until now that very senior officers did that sort of thing.'

'Yes, but why does she have to take so long?'

Esther, Steph, Ed and Kelly sat looking at the screens.

'It's a bit like watching paint dry,' said Steph, 'only not as exciting.'

They had been doing this for over an hour before Ed saw what they were looking for, the same car they had spotted earlier circling the city in the videos Ed had gathered, but here it was coming into the city from the direction of the A1 on the A14 about an hour earlier. More especially, Kelly was now able to get a clear look at the numberplate. They followed the first camera onto the next. There was one occupant and he or she didn't continue on the A14 or M11 but drove directly into the city on the A1307, on the Huntingdon Rd.

'What have you got, Kelly?'

'Audi A4, expensive and allegedly impossible to break into, but was, and stolen that afternoon in Nottingham. No further trace.'

'Let's work on the basis that this is our man or woman,' said Esther.

'Surely no woman would have done such a thing as was done to Andie,' said Steph.

'When you get home, Steph, ask your gorgeous husband whether women are just as capable as men of doing bad things. He won't be able to tell you any of the details. But I'd be surprised if a former Catholic priest from Ireland doesn't answer yes.'

'Where did he or she park and how did that person know Andie would be in the Club, unless it really was a she and she went in to find out?'

'If that is the case we will have her on the Club CCTV,' said Ed.

'And,' added Esther, 'did she approach Andie and suggest that they might meet outside and give Andie a ride home, with the promise of added information about what she was doing in Nottingham?'

'The reporter might not have been able to resist,' said Steph.

'Let's look yet again at the AAA films,' said Esther.

The real difficulty they faced was that they had already looked at them a number of times and having no idea who they were looking for, found themselves frustrated. All they could see was an endless group of women, some of whom spoke to Andie.

'Perhaps we should set that aside for the moment,' said Esther and focus on a different question. How many clubs are there in Cambridge just for lesbians and how did this woman, if indeed it was a woman, though I still think it's a sensible assumption, know in which to find Andie?'

'In addition to the AAA, there is the Bella Club, more for students, and also a pub, the Blue Lamp,' said Kelly. 'I would say that if she was going clubbing, the AAA would be the most likely.'

'But if I was a would-be assassin, that "most likely" wouldn't be enough. I think, Ed and Belinda, you need to pay a visit to Channel 4 and Maureen Watson. She is the only likely source of information to which club Andie was going. If she won't say, caution her and bring her in as a potential accomplice to murder.'

'Yes, ma'am.'

They set off at once.

'I haven't had chance to tell you, boss,' said Kelly, 'but I ran those names you gave me this morning through the computer and one rang an alarm bell, a vet at the last practice you visited, a Helen Ventner, formerly of the Royal Army Veterinary Corps.'

'That sounds like I need to take you, Steph, to the vet, and then to the doctor.'

'Woof, woof.'

Half an hour later, Jo checked in with Kelly, who recounted the results of their busy morning.

'Ed and Belinda are hoping to appear on the tv later – Channel 4, I believe. Esther and Steph are doing their version of the Yorkshire Vet and then consulting the doctor again.'

Anyone hearing would have had little idea of what she was speaking, but Jo understood that whatever the code meant, it was indicative of Esther's new broom., and Jo liked it.

'We've got a new member of the team, the same of whom we spoke earlier.'

'That is what I call a significant coincidence, boss, as having someone from that address might help us a great deal.'

'I'm intrigued, my darling. See you soon.'

When they arrived at the office, there was only Kelly to be found and she was on the telephone to Aisling, her predecessor, now working with Major Kim Atwood at MI5. Aisling had been trying to trace a leak relating to the murder (her word) of Penny Babworth.

'It's taken me a while,' said Aisling, 'but I've traced it back to someone in the Home Office who also leaked information to Andie Bolam and is on bail at the moment and suspended. His name is Jeremy Ironsides and I suspect he's in a bit of trouble. Special Branch went to pick him up, but he's disappeared.'

'Thanks, Aisling. It all adds to the jigsaw. Jo's just come in, would you like a word?'

'Of course.'

The pair spoke for a few minutes, In the meantime, Jodie took a seat whilst Darcey introduced Frankie to Kelly.

Jodie, meanwhile, announced she was going to the loo before Jo moved in there for hours!

'It may be, Frankie, that you are going to be a great success within a short while of being here,' said Kelly.

Jo had finished her call and hearing these words come to Kelly's desk where she was joined by Darcey, and then a refreshed Jodie.'

'Bonnie worked on the assumption that only a man could have

done what was done to Andie,' began Kelly, 'but Esther questioned this and suggested we should consider the possibility it was a woman. We followed a car from the direction of the A1 which was stolen that afternoon in Nottingham. Esther said that a woman could walk into the the AAA Club with no difficulty, approach Andie with the suggestion that she had something for her and wait for her, before taking her on to Waterbeach, where there was no evidence of sexual assault, and it's hard to think a man would miss that opportunity with such a beautiful woman. The car has not been traced.

'Esther then raised the matter of how any killer, male or female, knew that she would be there. She might have wanted an early night and there are two other lesbian clubs that we know of where she might have gone. The only person who could possibly have known that, unless she arranged it in advance, was the producer Maureen Watson, and we have no sign from her phone or iPad that she had pre-arranged it. So Ed and Belinda have gone to talk to her, which may be a euphemism. Who did she say she spent the night with?'

'Alison Kitchen – though that's the given to anyone you pair up with for the night. Why wasn't that followed up Darcey. You were questioning her?'

Yes, I was, until handing over to Bonnie, but it was my mistake ma'am, I didn't consider the possibility that the name was false.

'Well, you're not alone. Bonnie didn't, and I didn't until I interviewed Judith, the vicar, on the following morning and she explained. You're not spending enough time in gay clubs, Inspector.'

'I'm waiting for the Stowmarket Lesbian Club to open, ma'am.'

'We'll both be in wheelchairs by then, my darling. So, Kelly, let's see the films again and this time with Frankie our cinema critic with us.'

'We'll start shortly after we lost sight of the car.'

Frank sat in the middle giving the screen her full attention. It was at 11:35 that she blurted, "Stop".

'Nikki Hampton – let it run. Yes, without the shadow of a

doubt, that's who it is, and if Andie Bolam came up against her, I'm not at all surprised at what happened to her. I don't suppose there is a gang leader in the Midlands who isn't frightened of her, and the same goes for most male police officers. She is exceptionally violent but also clever. We have always thought she had killed, but getting the evidence is a different matter. She cut the cock and balls off a gang member and left him to die in agony.'

'Kelly, wind back to where she comes in. I know we can't see her face but we now know what she was wearing. Yes, that's, where she's signing in, and behold, she's doing so with her left hand.'

Kelly had moved to one of her other computers.

'Boss, come and see here.'

Jo walked over and looked at the screen.

'Well, well. Frankie did you know she had a record?'

'Minor indiscretions only, ma'am.'

'True, but the record offers other information such as her name before a short-lived marriage: Nikki Worrall.

'I wasn't in CID, ma'am, but her reputation was considerable across the force.'

'Yea, well you're in the CID now, my darling, and we are going to have to face up at some stage to inviting Ms Hampton for a chat, though at the moment the only evidence we have amounts to next to nothing, but as we all know, once we have a specific target at least we can know where to look. Finding that car would be a step forward.'

'There are no reports of a torched Audi,' said Kelly.

'And it wouldn't have been left in Cambridge; if you wanted to conceal a bicycle it would be different, there are hundreds,' added Darcey.

'And the best place to conceal an Audi is amongst hundreds of others. Belinda would have been collecting CCTV of vehicles arriving before midnight, not those leaving after, but I bet that the driver returned that way and then was collected at a large Audi dealership where she might clean the inside of the car and leave it among others. Kelly?'

'I'll look and see what might be there on the way back to Nottingham.'

'May I help, ma'am?' asked Franky.

'Yes, of course. Darcey, if you were Jeremy Ironsides, on bail from the Home Office and hunted by Special Branch, and he won't know they're mostly incompetent imbeciles, do you think it possible he might hide in the woman's flat he thought he was having a relationship with, and for which, possibly, he still had a key?'

'Andie's flat, you mean?'

'Yes. I might just forget to let Special Branch know until we have tried tomorrow.'

Jodie thought this quite wonderful and indicative of an extremely independent mind. The longer she was around Jo, the more she appreciated her.'

Ed had called Channel 4 to make sure Maureen Watson would be available, and some sort of functionary had said she would. Nevertheless, and much to their frustration, she was not there when they arrived.

'I would like to speak to the head of the News Team,' said Ed to someone giving every impression of being a guard at the door of the department.

'I'm afraid that is not possible without an appointment. Just leave your name at the door and we'll get back to you.'

'Really,' said Ed. 'In which case you need to know that I am Detective Chief Inspector Secker and this is Detective Sergeant Gorham, seeking to discover the murderer of your erstwhile colleague Andie Bolam, and if you do not open this door and admit us, I will simply push you out of the way and go in anyway. The person we have come to see is Maureen Watson, who seems to be hiding from us. If she does not appear in ten minutes' time, I will call my friends in Public Health, who will come and shut you down completely for two hours whilst they carry out a full inspection. So pass that message on, and do it now.'

The woman looked somewhat panic-stricken, and at once went

into the newsroom. It took just five minutes for Watson to come to the door.

'I'm sorry to have kept you. No one told me you were here.'

'Do you have a room in which we can speak in private?' asked Belinda.

'Of course,'

She led them along a corridor and opened the door of an office and entered before them. They sat down.

'Do you know when it will be possible to have the funeral?' said Watson.

'When there has been a murder, a body cannot be released until defence counsel is satisfied with the findings of the post-mortem or asked for another,' replied Ed.

'Ms Watson, when asked, on the morning after Andie's death, you said you had left the AAA Club before her,' said Belinda, 'and that you spent the night with someone you had picked up, or picked up you, called Alison Kitchen. Is that correct?'

'It's correct that I said that but ...'

'Yes we know. You lied to a police officer investigating a murder, and that is a serious offence. We need you to tell us who it was spent with.'

'That would be to betray someone who would not necessarily want to be outed.'

'I will echo my sergeant's words: You lied to a police officer investigating a murder, and that is a serious offence. We need you to tell us who it was spent with.'

'I am not going to out a sister, and you can threaten me as much as you wish.'

'Ok. Shortly after 9:00pm, the records of your mobile show a phone call made to a burner phone. Who was that call made to and what was the nature of the call?' asked Ed.

'A news team lives on their mobiles, Inspector. I have to make calls and I have no idea what sort or make of phone I am calling. If you've seen my call lists you will surely know that.'

'By that time, had Andie decided which club she was going to? There was after all, a choice.'

'Not really. Andie was set on the AAA.'

'And you were happy to go along with that?'

'Yes.'

'Even though you are not a lesbian?' said Belinda'

There was silence.

'The CCTV is clear. You're like a fish out of water and whenever a girl approached, you backed off,' said Belinda,' and yes, you left before Andie, in fact almost an hour before Andie.'

'So where did you go and where did you spend the night?' said Ed. 'So far we have had nothing but lies and unless you begin to tell us the truth and we are convinced by you, we shall have no alternative but to arrest you. Do you understand, Ms Watson?'

'Do you understand what you would be doing in a television news studio?'

'I'm not going to let a silly threat stop me doing my duty. So answer my questions. Who did you meet outside the club? Where did you go? You see, Ms Watson, I think you met someone just up the road from the Club and you left Andie to her fate.'

'This is pure speculation on your part, as is the sexual speculations of your Sergeant on the basis of a CCTV camera. What was I expected to do to show I am gay? Pull my knickers down in public. And if I'm not attracted by an approaching girl, am I expected to accept her for the benefit of a camera? Perhaps that's how you behave with men, Sergeant, but gay women are not sluts.'

'Maureen Watson, I am not satisfied that in the investigation into the illegal death of Andrea Bolam, you are answering our questions truthfully. You are therefore asked to accompany us to a police station for further questioning. You do not have to say anything. But, it may harm your defence if you do not mention when questioned something which you later rely on in court. Anything you do say may be given in evidence.' said Ed.

'You must be joking.'

'Please stand, Ms Watson,' said Belinda.

She did so meekly. Perhaps to her astonishment no one rushed out to save her with cameras following. Belinda led her to the car and entered beside her in the back seat. Ed was making a call to Rochester Row asking for the agreement to bring in someone for questioning, and the officer said that Number 2 stable was free! Ed got in and headed for Victoria.

## 22

Once they were in the police station and in a genuine interview room where there were recording facilities (it turned out that all the stables were occupied!), Belinda was obliged to accompany Watson to the loo and keep the door ajar. She was then led into the interview room.

'You may have legal representation if you wish, either of your own choice or a solicitor appointed for you.'

'I'm fine thanks.'

'The interview is being recorded.'

'Alright, I haven't been very co-operative so far but I am ready to be so now. We were pursuing two stories. Both came from leaks from the Home Office.'

'Jeremy Ironsides I assume.'

'As you obviously know, I won't try and conceal my source. Yes.'

'Are you aware how Andie persuaded Jeremy to spill the beans?'

'Yes, she told me.'

'His knowledge of the whereabouts of Alice Watts we understand because it was Home Office business but what about the other matter?'

'Did you ever watch *West Wing*? The Vice-President has to stand down because leaks are traced back to him through various women. "I show off" he says, "I want to look big". So it was with Jeremy. He had a friend working in the Security Service at a pretty low level I would imagine. He had overheard a conversation and in the pub showed off to Jeremy.'

'Are you certain it was a he?'

'That's what Andie reported to me. She had a phenomenal nose for a story, and I must also tell you that Andie was in love with someone in your Unit.'

'Actually, Maureen, we all are, said Belinda'

All three of them laughed.

'We came to Cambridge and interviewed the mortuary assistant, and left the sound and camera crew doing the tourist thing. We went on to Nottingham to meet someone called Joe who was one of the cops who had put away the little girl who murdered two children many years ago. He was in his early 70s and although he had indicated to Andie he was willing to speak, when we got there he had changed his mind and was over-protected by a singularly scary woman called Nikki Hampton. She might once have been pretty but now had scars on her face, which with tattoos, terrified me. Her speech was uncompromising. I saw Joe and her by myself – the Producer's prerogative to see whether or not to go on.

'Hampton said she would come and meet with Andie, and only Andie, on Saturday night in Cambridge. She told me that it would be late and gave me a number to call and let her know where Andie would be, which I did, as you know. On the Saturday night I waited in the AAA just long enough to see her arrive and then I left unaccompanied. I was walking up the road and met a woman I'd seen inside. We chatted and in a short while she invited me to her home, which was, I might add, a vicarage.'

'Her name?'

'Oh how I wish I could confuse you and say it was Alison, but she is called Judith Bartram, and to be honest I'd like to see her again. And you know the rest because I returned to Waterbeach.'

'Conjecture time, Maureen, ' said Ed. 'What did you think the beast from Nottingham wanted with Andie?'

'Oh, it's not conjecture. She told me in Nottingham that she wanted to discuss with Andie what she and her great-uncle would discuss and to make the arrangements.'

'Did that make sense to you? You were the Producer after all. Surely that was your business.'

'People don't see the Producer on the television screen, just the presenter, and it was the presenter she was determined to see.'

Ed looked at Belinda, who shook her head.

'Thank you, Maureen for being so full in your answers. It may be that somewhere down the line you will have to give evidence in court but you have helped us a great deal. We would very happy to take you back to work or home.

'Thank you.'


It was Dr Carol Ventner's afternoon off and Esther and Steph found her engaged in ironing after she let them in.

'Hello, Dr Ventner, I'm Superintendent Esther Heywood and this is Detective Sergeant Stephanie Binks. Just a couple more questions, if we may. I imagine it's not unlike the practice of medicine, putting bits and pieces together, though in the case of Dr Babworth, you and the consultant got it wrong.'

'I mostly get it right.'

'So do we.'

'We remain troubled by the matter of how she was murdered, which two pathologists and toxicology agree was by the administration of Etophine.'

'We have a strict rule at our surgery that we do not accept as patients anything larger than a llama, which rather precludes the possibility that we would store a drug such as that, which would never be used in the treatment of human patients.'

'Do you have many drugs in the surgery?' asked Steph.

We have a locked drug store but there is very little contained it. That's how we differ from pharmacies. For them the security issues are greater.'

'And what about syringes and needles?'

'The nurses have them as they use them a great deal, plus the phlebotomist who comes to take blood for tests.'

'You visited Dr Babworth at home.'

'A couple of times and to give her more time to talk. 8 minutes in a surgery is barely enough time to break wind, and before you ask why we cannot change that, the answer is that we would love to, but that would only be possible if fewer people came to see their doctor, especially when a great many are not that ill and almost certainly would be better, if they left alone, within a day or two.'

'Do you see much of your sister Helen?'

'As I'm sure you know, she is a vet. She's the clever one in the family. She got higher grades than me at school and so I had to settle with being a doctor.'

'I've heard that before. Is it true?'

'It sounds ridiculous but it's true. What we need is an "All Creatures Great and Small" based on doctors in the Yorkshire Dales.'

'Your sister's practice would probably have immediate access to all forms of treatment of larger animals, and might possibly include Etrophine in that.'

'I honestly don't know. When we're with each other it's not the sort of thing we discuss.'

'I understand, but if for whatever reason you needed to obtain some, your sister would have a ready supply.'

'And you're therefore suggesting that I killed Penny with something from my sister's dangerous drugs cabinet?'

'As I said, like a doctor seeking to make a diagnosis, we consider all sorts of possibilities. Because you knew her well and had already visited her at home, you are in pole position. Dr Babworth received an injection in her left inner elbow by someone who knew how and where to do so. There is no indication that she was struggling as this happened. Afterwards, as Dr Babworth became unconscious immediately prior to her death, whoever had administered the drug rolled her sleeve down and left with the equipment she or he used. You will therefore present yourself at the police station in Cambridge at 9:00am tomorrow. You can be supported by a solicitor or someone from the Medical Defence Union.'

'I have a surgery of patients beginning at 8:30.'

'Perhaps they are the ones who will be better in two days' time. That will have to be cancelled.'

'This is outrageous.'

'It's amazing how often that word is used about us and against us. We'll let ourselves out and look forward to seeing you in the morning.'

Leaving Linton, they headed East, towards Sudbury, where the Veterinary Surgery was easily found. Going in through the front door there could be no doubt it was Helen Ventner before them, though in jeans and open-necked shirt she looked somewhat differently attired from her sister.

'Hello, can I help you?' she said.

'Hello, you must be Helen Ventner.'

'Must I?'

Esther smiled.

'I'm Detective Superintendent Esther Heywood and this is Detective Sergeant Binks and having just been talking to your sister, recognition was easy.'

'So how can I help you?'

'Etrophine. Is it is a drug you would normally have access to in your dangerous drug cabinet.'

'Yes. We deal with horses and large bulls. It is a drug of last resort and it has to be managed with great care, but sometimes it is the only way we can work on a large animal. They make it look much easier on the tele than it is. We wouldn't need it at all if we were just a small animal practice but we're mixed – few sheep but an increasing number of llamas which also take an enormous amount of handling, and as I say, a lot of horses and beef cattle.'

'You must be very brave,' said Steph.

'Blimey, so must you, but I love it.'

'Are you married?'

'Yes, to Pete, who's my partner here, and we have two children, one of each. But you haven't said why you're interested in Etrophine.'

'In Linton a top scientist and mathematician, a patient of your sister's, died having believed she was suffering from the onset of Motor Neurone Disease. Her death, presented as if it were suicide, was clearly shown by toxicology and two Forensic Pathologists, to have been caused by an injection of Etrophine, administered to the inside of her left elbow. It was murder, and perhaps done to prevent important government work in which she was engaged to be halted.'

A lady and a dog entered from outside.

'Hello, Mrs Makin. I'll be with you and Roger soon. Do sit.'

The lady did so.

'If you come with me into the treatment room, I can show you the facility we have for keeping dangerous drugs.'

Esther and Steph followed her into a room which immediately struck them as well-equipped. She pointed to what was obviously a wall safe.

'It has two doors, each of which is locked. The keys are held only by Pete, myself, and Vera, our head nurse.'

She produced a key and turned the first lock. A light flashed. She then unlocked the second door.

'A light is now flashing at the Reception desk and if ignored for more than a minute would be accompanied by an alarm. Here inside you can see several glass containers, some of which are used to euthanise animals, others are expensive, and this one here is a bottle of Etrophine, unused as you can see, the llamas of Essex being well at the moment.'

Esther and Steph smiled, as they heard an alarm out in the waiting room.

'Thank you, Helen. Does every vet have a similar system?'

'They should have, but some are more careless than others.'

'Well, you've been very helpful,' said Esther. 'When I get my llamas I'll bring them to you.'

'Alpacas are much easier to handle, though don't be taken in by those pretty faces. Their bite is considerably worse than their bark and they spit.'

'Thanks for the advice. We'll be off.'


The team were drinking tea and eating cakes bought up from the tea shop when Esther and Steph arrived. Everyone but Jo stood.

'Are you lot taking the mickey?' said Esther.

The laughter told her the truth.

Tea was poured as they sat down.

'Esther, please meet Frankie, our new team member from Nottingham.'

'Hello, ma'am.'

'Oh sorry, Frankie, were you talking to me?'

'Sorry, Esther. This is all very new to me?'

'To you? I only got promoted yesterday; I was a Detective Constable at breakfast.'

Everyone laughed again.

'Right,' said Jo. 'We have a lot of catching up to do as everyone has been working hard. I'll begin as it's about time everyone knew what we are doing in Nottingham, especially as we are now convinced that Nottingham holds the key to the murder of Andie.'

Jo told everything she knew, and the team heard her in total silence. Then the information about what actually happened at the AAA Club was shared as was the identity of the Alison Kitchen Maureen spent the night with. Finally, Esther rounded things off with an account of the visit to Dr Ventner, whom she intended seeing again in the morning, and her sister the vet, who advised against buying llamas and alpacas.

'What a shame,' said Darcey,' I was hoping to get some.'

'Ok, everyone, let's leave it for the moment.'

'One thing more,' said Kelly.

'We've found the Audi. It's just come in. A firm called Sytner & Co in Leicester. A lot of used cars kept outside, and the local force found it. It's sealed off and Socos will attend first light tomorrow.'

'That's good news. Now, ladies and Ed, go home and allow your conscious minds to turn off all this completely so your unconscious thoughts can come with you in the morning. Briefing at 8:00.'

As they drove back to Saxmundham, Jodie said to Jo, 'I've really enjoyed today, and not least watching able detectives at work, thinking and imagining and working together. I only had a short time in CID in Manchester, as a DC it wasn't at all like today has been.'

I know what you are saying, Jodie, because I spent almost 10 years as a PC in Boston, mainly because some stupid woman-hating man deliberately blocked my way.'

'Ten?'

'At the time it didn't seem so long, but in retrospect it was time wasted. You and Caro will have to decide how you divide your time, but I shall be happy to have you with us. You've seen what we are going to be up against, thanks to the lady in the back.'

'Frankie's fast asleep.'

'Good. She'll be more than happy to play with my children then. Marie is away on Air Force business for a couple of days.'

'Do you miss each other when that happens?'

'She was in America for six weeks once, learning how to fly an enormous aeroplane. It was during that time that I first met Andie at a Press Conference I was giving.'

'Did you like her?'

'Andie made no bones about what she felt for me and would happily have broken up my marriage and simply in physical terms she was startling to look at, but instinctively I knew there were strands inside her which drove her to be so very successful in her career which also were quite dark and destructive, but I can't deny that the outer Andie tempted me, but before you ask, no, I didn't succumb. My former colleague Bonnie prevented me from attending her post-mortem which I think was wise. That beautiful body cut up was evil, like taking a knife to an outstanding painting.'

Frankie had surfaced and was listening.

'It has all the hallmarks of Nikki Hampton, Jo. If you can get her for this you will serve a number of police forces.'

'Unfortunately, the one thing we have little of is evidence. It is all circumstantial so far. We still have a lot of work to do, but a question for you, Jodie. You have borne a firearm all day. Most of our team are authorised. Do we need, given what we might be up against, someone to join you? Darcey, I mean?'

'If you don't want to make use of full armed back-up, and something makes me think that's not your style, then yes, another armed officer I would judge to be essential.'

'Frankie. Have you done risk assessments?'

'Yes, quite a few.'

'I want you to do a risk assessment at the registered address of Hampton tomorrow. Go with Steph, and learn all about her sex life with a former catholic priest. It will be very entertaining.'

'If you say so, ma'am.'

At home the children were all over Jo until they discovered a new arrival in for the form of Frankie. Jodie crossed the road, and the door was opened by Caro.

'You look knackered. Has the boss been working you hard?'

'You're not kidding, but they are a fabulous team. It's just a handful of mostly women detectives, but they work ever so hard. Jo trusts each one and at the centre of it all is Kelly, who served four years for fraud, but was hand-picked by Jo and was trained by MI5. And what about you? How has your day been?'

'Don't forget I can hear every word,' said a disembodied voice from the kitchen.

'We've had a great day. The school walk and then Alice and I got all the cameras and alarms in place, most of them concealed on Jo's house. They all work. We had a pub lunch and talked and talked. I know you can hear me, Alice, but I have to say that you and Katia are simply adorable people, and I am desperate for all this to be resolved as soon as possible for your sake.'

'Thank you.'

'Some bastards, to spare themselves, have caused these two people to have years and years of misery, and if I wasn't a copper, I would want to be one and do everything I could to bring them to justice.'

Alice came into the room with some for food for Jodie.

'From what I have seen today, that is exactly what Jo's team is doing.'

As Jo was getting into bed, her phone rang. It was Marie. They would have to be careful in their choice of words, given that Marie was staying in Bulford Camp.

'Have you had a nice day?' said Jo.

'Sadly, the forecast for tomorrow is not too good.'

'That's a great shame, even if you're not too surprised. It is November.'

'And you? How has your day been?'

'Very positive on most fronts.'

And the children?'

'Missing you and we have a new friend called Frankie, a new member of the team.'

'A man?'

'Yes, a man called Francesca, with a Polish name, Wawszyczk.'

'But that means your only man is Ed, poor thing.'

'Oh, don't worry about him. He doesn't even blush when we get into a discussion of the merits of sanitary towels over tampons. He just thinks women are ridiculous to talk about such things together and says that men in a pub never discuss the relative merits of underpants.'

'I wish you were here alongside me, though it would be a lottery which of us would fall out of this tiny bed first, and I might yet fall out of even by myself.'

'Back tomorrow?'

'Yes.'

How is Dianne?'

'Fascinated by English military legal process.'

'Say hello from me.'

'I will. Sleep well.'

'And the same to you. Night, night.'


Some time before it was light Jo found herself under serious attack when she was so vulnerable – asleep and unprepared. There were two of them, and they pinned her down.

'Wake up, mummy,' said Ollie, who, though younger than his sister, already had strength greater than hers.

'Ah,' said Jo, 'two ruffians against mummy. I may have to tickle you both to escape,' which she did, amidst great laughter. Then they wanted a story, which she was always glad to offer them before she got up, and they cuddled up, one on either side.

'Your mum is back later today (quite spontaneously the

children had begun to call Marie "mum" but retained "mummy" for herself, which pleased her).

Frankie and Jodie were both ready and waiting when Jo had the car ready. She had Radio 3 on in the car, which Frankie didn't mind but didn't appeal to Jodie, who's tastes were other. On arrival, everyone was in place for the briefing.

'Can I remind everyone,' began Jo, 'that there can be no contact between any of us and our two former colleagues, Bonnie and Tom. I know that's harsh, but it's part of the deal that the Chief Constable and I agreed. I'm not suggesting that anyone here has had contact, by the way, but whilst they're still in the town it's possible we might run in to one or other of them.

'Frankie and Steph are going to Nottingham to do a risk assessment. The Nottinghamshire Chief has approved Frankie's transfer to us in record time. I think he said, "Glad to be rid of her".'

'No,' said Kelly. 'What he said was "Sad to see her go".'

'I hope,' said Frankie, 'it was the latter but I fear it would have been the former.'

Everyone laughed.

'Esther and Ed are going to interview Dr Ventner in Cambridge. Jodie, Darcey and I are going to see if we can find our friend Jeremy Ironsides because we urgently need a conversation. Steph and Frankie, on your way to Nottingham, please call in at the Audi garage in Leicester. Socos should be able to give a report but do some sniffing around just to see if anyone knows anything. Once everything is clear, let Kelly know and she can give the good news to the owner, though they can't collect it just yet. So let's get going.'

## 23

Arriving at Cambridge Police Station , Esther and Ed walked towards the Interview Room where Dr Ventner was already seated with the same Medical Defence Union rep who had been with her when interviewed by Jo.

'This is a formal interview of Dr Helen Ventner in which she is accompanied by her rep Dr Tim Bullock. Also present are Superintendent Heywood and Chief Inspector Secker, both from the Sensitive Crime Unit. This interview is being recorded.'

'Thank you Ed. Dr Ventner, I must remind you that are still under caution.'

She shrugged.

'Dr Aberdeen, the neurologist at Addenbrookes, the consultant you sent Dr Babworth to see, has said in a written statement that he saw Dr Babworth for only a short time before handing her over to a Senior Registrar. Both of them were very much guided by your letter of referral, and as you said, the signs were clear that she was in the early stage of motor neurone disease. Please tell me that is not typical of the experience of seeing a consultant.'

Strictly speaking when a referral is made it is to a named consultant "or a member of the team".

'Do you agree Dr Bullock?'

'Yes, that is normal.'

'So the determining factor in the diagnosis is the GP referring the patient, and in the instance of Dr Babworth, with you misdiagnosing, this may well have led to a Registrar, technically a junior doctor, confirming your misdiagnosis, even though with good intention. Is that right?'

'Superintendent, we are doctors and not even remotely infallible. I don't have access in my surgery to what might have shown I was mistaken, and clearly Dr Babworth had not yet had a brain scan which might have told us a great deal more.'

'When you saw Dr Babworth in the period after MND had been confirmed, or apparently so, did you think that her condition was in keeping with your initial diagnosis?'

'I did, yes.'

'An old friend of mine, Dr Ray Fyfe, now departed, told me that the first death certificate he signed was for motor neurone disease, and that in a long practice thereafter he never saw another case. How many cases previous to Dr Babworth had you seen and treated?'

'None.'

'What a difficult and demanding job you have. Penny Babworth could probably have run rings around the four of us in terms of her intellect, but it has not been easy for us to get a comprehensive picture of her. It maybe, Dr Ventner, that although it was a short time, in that time you came to know her better than anyone. Do you think that may be right?'

'I think the word "reticent" might have been invented for her. She was intensely private and to be honest, I learned very little about her. She wasn't cold but she disclosed very little to me of what was going on inside.'

'Let's just imagine for a moment that suicide was her intention. and I can fully understand why anyone, having been told she had motor neurone disease, was determined to do this before it was too late to do it herself, did she tell you this was what she intended to do?'

'Yes.'

'Please remember you remain under oath. What reply did you make?'

'I cannot recall my exact words but they would have been supportive, to say that I fully understood why she was saying this. I did not try to talk her out of it, not least because had the roles been reversed I would have thought likewise.'

'Dr Bullock, do you think the majority of doctors would have agreed with what Dr Ventner said?'

'All doctors have to be very careful with regard to anything said publicly in relation to end of life matters. Most of us get on with our work and say little, and most are not Harold Shipman.'

'I have no doubt of that.'

'Dr Ventner, it was not your fault that you made a diagnostic error and you might have expected better from Addenbrookes than you received. The coroner might want to address Dr Aberdeen but not you.'

'But now we need to concern ourselves with the end of Dr Babworth's life. To the best of your knowledge, was there any other member of the medical team visiting Dr Babworth?'

'Not from our surgery.'

'And yours is the only practice in Linton?'

'Yes.'

'So to an outsider, such as myself, if an injection were given professionally, with no bruising, in the inner elbow, which almost certainly brought about her immediate death, it would make sense that this injection was administered by the one person, a doctor, who was a friend, and perhaps her only friend, and who wanted to do for her the best as they both conceived it.'

'That makes sense, though it is not as easy as you might think do so without bruising.'

'And if that doctor had collected from someone, perhaps a sister, an almost empty bottle of Etrophine, which has now been replaced and is still sealed, the immediate, non-lingering death would be accomplished with ease.'

'What did Helen tell you?'

'Carol, please just give me a simple answer. Did you administer the fatal injection which took the life of Penny Babworth?'

She looked at her fellow doctor and then at Ed, and finally back at Esther.'

'Yes.'

'Carol, please think carefully how you answer the next question. Did Penny Babworth ask you to do this for her?'

'She asked me three times. I believed I would be failing in my duty, not as a doctor, but as a human being if I did not serve the interests of my friend.'

'How much did Penny talk to you about the Zenith Project?'

'I haven't heard those words until you said them now. It would have been pointless Penny talking to me about anything to do with her work at the university. I am not a mathematician.'

Esther looked at Ed who gently nodded his head.

'The interview is ended,' said Esther, ' and we are stopping the recording.'

Carol Ventner looked confused.

'I have to make my report and recommendation to my Chief, and she can overrule me – so I need to make that clear to you. For reasons that you cannot know, and come to think of it, neither can I, the matter of Dr Babworth's death will be dealt with *in camera* because there are major security implications. I am completely satisfied that there was no assassination involved and that, on the contrary, in the face of a diagnosis of an increasingly debilitating serious illness, for which she received outstanding care from her local medical practice, she chose death. Now doctor, you have patients to see and I apologise for messing up their day and yours, but I thought it best to get this sorted.'

'When might I hear if your Chief decides to overrule your report?'

Esther smiled.

'Chief Inspector?'

'She would never overturn anything you decided, ma'am. She has far too much respect for you, as I do, though as that is such a sycophantic thing to say, I'll shut up.'

The others smiled.

'Thank you, Superintendent, for being so thorough and patient, and in the end so generous in your understanding.'

'As you might say: I am just doing my job. By the way, your sister did not tell me anything. I saw a brand new unopened bottle and being a detective with a suspicious mind, I simply put two and two together. You might advise her not to repeat and to give our love to the llamas.'

The four stood and shook hands, and the two doctors were led to the door.

'But for the special circumstances, things might have been quite different. If it had got to court, even had she avoided a custodial sentence, her life and work would have been ruined,' said Ed.

'I think you are correct, Ed, but are you implying criticism of me?'

'Not at all. Solomon would have been proud of you and so will Jo, and least important of all, so am I.'


The Forensic team were clearing away their equipment amidst Audi cars when Steph and Frankie arrived. They parked their car.

'Hey, Frankie,' said one of the male Socos. 'I'd heard a rumour that you'd gone AWOL. How are you?'

'Pretty good, Geoff. What about you and the family?'

'Impossible, as always, but I still love them. You're not in uniform.'

'No, they've given me the letter D.'

'About time, too. Well, this car received an almost professional cleaning when it was left here using industrial chemicals, the smell of which was powerful when we opened the door, which will need repair, not from what we did, but by those who stole the vehicle. It won't be a simple matter of mechanics either. It's all part of the electronics system but whoever broke in seems to have known what they were doing, and known what they were doing in wiping the car clean. No hairs to be found but you can't rid yourself of all DNA and whoever sat in the front two seats have left traces in the creases in the leather missed by whoever did the cleaning job. There's not a lot to go on but it's the most you're going to get. It will go to the lab later.'

'That's great,' said Frankie. 'Have you finished with the car, Geoff?'

'No, I've arranged for it to be collected and taken to our motor vehicle section garage, who will tell you where it has been using the record of the sat nav, and might also give some hints about the grass caught in the rear bumper which has been removed and bagged.'

'Thank you very much. It's great to meet you.'

'And you sarge, and of course the new Detective Constable Wawszyczk.'

'Detective Sergeant.'

'That's a great thing to hear.'

'As Frankie got into the car, she turned to Steph.

'I didn't know about the Sergeant thing.'

'Jo will have forgotten to mention it, but we have no DCs in the Unit. So congratulations on your promotion.'

'Fancy that, I became a detective sergeant and never even noticed.'

Steph drove out to the East and joined the M1 hiding North towards Nottingham.

They parked three roads away from the house in which it was believed Nikki Hampton lived and walked through chatting together about absolutely nothing like actors mouthing "rhubarb", but keenly using their eyes. It was a detached house with a garden to front and rear, so they completed their walk round the back and again made the appearance of conversation whilst each engaged in the task of risk assessment. Frankie said that little was known about Hampton though an officer had once reported than a steady stream of teenage boys called to see her.

'Perhaps she's a youth football coach,' said Steph.

'And perhaps not,' replied Frankie.

They now drove through the route they had earlier walked, Frankie taking photos with her phone, anything bigger being somewhat conspicuous.

They then went to do the same at the home of Joe Worrall and Jo had mentioned she might begin there and see if Nikki came running to rescue her uncle.

Frankie then asked Steph to call in at her home so she could pick up more of her stuff. So absorbed were they in this that neither were aware that they were being followed until they were on the motorway.

'We have company,' said Steph, and Frankie lowered her

mirror, not turning around.

Whoever was doing the following was skilled. On the motorway they kept at an "invisible" distance and once they realised that the car was heading towards Cambridge, they turned off the A14 into Huntingdon and thereafter to the M1. However there was a moment just before they left the road when their car was visible and picked up by the rear camera of the ANPR system in the police vehicle which they might not have anticipated in an unmarked car.

'It looks like two men in the car and its registered home address is in Nottingham, the registered owner Alan Hubert,' said Kelly when she downloaded the tape from the National Police Computer. 'I'll look him up. Yes, he's done time for GBH and armed robbery. His actions today make sense if he's working with and for Nikki Hampton, but how would she know that was the case as only we knew you were going there today?'

In London, Jo, Darcey and Jodie were trying to find Andie's flat with little success. In the end Jo called on the local station to guide them.

As they approached the door, Jo asked Jodie to be the one knocking, as Ironsides wouldn't recognise her.

She knocked on the door a couple of times without result and decided to try just one more time.

'Who is it?'

'DHL. I have a parcel for Ms Bolam.'

'Hold on', and Jo and Darcey moved closer to the door. When it opened just a little, Jodie pushed with such force that the door flew open and the man on the other side was sent flying. When he looked up, his heart sank.

'Good morning, Jeremy,' said Jo. 'People have been looking for you everywhere. You know who I am. This is Detective Inspector Bussell and the officer at the door is Detective Sergeant Lovelock. We thought we might find you here, and before we hand you over to Special Branch, we would welcome a word with you.

'My dealings with Special Branch have taught me they are

more willing to extend the word "persuasion" in their efforts to gain the information they are seeking. We certainly may not use them but they claim that where national security is concerned it is vital to achieve their aim.

'One breach of the Official Secrets Act is serious, but two, considerably more so, and that is why you are hiding here. We are obliged to call them here and therefore I would advise you to give us the information before they take you, because, believe me Jeremy, they will get it.'

'I'm not at all sure what you're talking about.'

'You were given information about the death of Dr Penny Babworth in Cambridge and its relation to something I'm sure you did not understand, called Zenith Project. Are you willing to admit this to us here and now?'

'I don't know what you mean?'

'Yes, you do. You passed on information to Andie about Penny Babworth as you had passed on the name and address of Alice Watts to her. You are already on bail for the latter offence. That bail will be cancelled because of the former offence against the Official Secrets Act, and by this evening you will be in prison, and my guess is that you will stay there for some time to come. The only thing that can save you is to disclose the name of the person in the Security Service that told you this. That name matters far more to the Security Service than you, and maybe your lifeline.'

Jeremy was clearly thinking hard as he sat there with 6 female eyes upon him.

'I don't think he knew what was meant by by the Zenith Project and it sounded to me, when we met in the pub, that he was trying to talk big, but he said that Dr Babworth had committed suicide and she was a key player in the project.'

'His name, Jeremy.'

'Peter Houldsworth. He works in communication.'

'Thank you.'

Jo stood.

'Darcey, Jodie, please remain here. I need to give a woman from Belfast a ring.'

Jo went outside and called Aisling.

'Aisling, it's Jo. I have the name you are looking for, the one who leaked about Penny Babworth, and I regret to say he works in your section. He's called Peter Houldsworth.'

'Thank you, Chief Superintendent for that information. Do you know the whereabouts of Jeremy Ironsides?'

She gave her the address and said they would remain until he was picked up.

'Thank you, boss, as always.'

'And you, my darling Aisling.'

'You've not met Aisling, have you?' asked Darcey. 'She's of Indian stock and grew up in Ireland and she's so very lovely. Worked for MI5 in Belfast, then came to us before returning to MI5 in London. She and Jo are very close.'

'But I think Jo's close to everyone.'

'You do know I'm back in the room,' said Jo, laughing.

'That's why we all work so well together,' continued Darcey ignoring her boss, 'and, but don't tell anyone, I think it's because we're mostly women.'

'Yes,' said Jo, 'I think that too, Darcey, but even more important is the quality of those we recruit, women like you two – the best.'

'You should have recruited Andie,' said Jeremy. 'She was pretty impressive at finding things out.'

'Andie had extraordinary gifts but couldn't be held back in ways that police officers have to be. I thought so highly of her but I always dreaded hearing of the lengths to which she might go to get a story.'

They heard an approaching siren.

'I think this sounds like your taxi, Jeremy.'

There was a knock on the door and two men entered, in plain clothes.

'This is Mr Ironsides for whom you've been looking and I have passed on the Security Service all the information he has.'

Jeremy stood and walked towards them and then turned to Jo.'

'Thank you, you've been very kind.'

He was led away.

'Let's give the place the once over. The Met should have done so after her death but from what I can see it was perfunctory.'

They split up, each taking a room and scrutinising everything. Jodie was in Andie's bedroom and found by the side of the bed a photograph of Jo! Almost immediately her eyes filled with tears. Jo had already lost Ellie as she has been told, and here she was losing someone very much in love with her again. She had also seen the large photograph of Jo in the office of her own boss, the Chief Constable of Greater Manchester, and was at once filled with alarm. Someone so loved could easily herself be lost to the world. That was how the world was, thought Jodie.

The only thing of interest to them was found by Darcey, stuffed at the back of a drawer, deliberately by the looks of it. It was a piece of paper with an address on it, and the address was that of Nikki Hampton.

'Pop it in a bag,' said Jo, 'it's evidence that Andie was already working on the Nottingham connection some time before her Channel 4 team came with her to Cambridge. I want to know who she saw in Nottingham, whose cage she rattled. I think we're done here. I feel extremely sad being here. I wish you could have known and seen Andie, Jodie, and Darcey will confirm not just as everyone knows how lovely she was, but she energised you all the time, even when that energy of hers was misdirected as it often was. I shall miss her greatly. Look guys, I noticed as we drove along that there was the sort of disgusting lunch place we might enjoy. Are you up for it?

'Might just be,' said Jodie.

'Oh alright, the pair of you have talked me into it,' said Darcey, wholly unconvincingly, with a grin. Once they had ordered and all three had gone to inspect the plumbing, Darcey said, 'Jo, when you were allocating tasks this morning, I couldn't help noticing that you omitted Belinda.'

'Did I? Gosh, how careless of me!'

Darcey knew from her years of working with Jo that if she had left Belinda out, it would be for a reason, but not one she intended sharing even with her, and increasingly she was realising that her darling Belinda might only be a DS and herself a DI, but in terms of being a police officer and detective she was clearly outstanding.

## 24

Tom drove down to the house he had been living in and removed the rest of his stuff which he was taking to his parents' house. Apart from a few things still at Bonnie's he had mostly moved out, and had received a message from Jo that the house was needed for a new member of the team.

It had all happened so quickly and he still wondered who it might have been who had reported him and taken the photo which in the end had condemned. Bonnie and himself. The only consolation was that, as he had known would be the case, Jo would stand up for him, and she had. He missed her for although she had delivered a bollocking like no other to him and Steph before they had left for Scotland, he know too that it was over there and then, and by the time they had returned would be as if it had never been.

But there was no way he was going back to being a Detective Constable, the dogsbodies of CID, and he needed money. It was when he got into debt with the gambling, a debt that was now considerable, that he had been approached by the man calling himself Ben. He said he had noticed that Tom had been having a bad run of luck and he wanted to see if he could help him. For a fleeting instant Tom had wondered whether Ben might be on the side of the angels, looking out for those getting into bother and seeking to rescue them, but it took very little time for him to realise that angels was not the appropriate description for Ben, who said to Tom that they could help him a great deal in the mess he was in, if he could be of use to them – especially given that he was police sergeant. Tom refused, of course, and equally of course, Ben expected him to. That was how the game was played.

Tom returned, and unaware that if the Casino had decided you were going to lose, you would lose, and fall into the trap that been laid for him. He was in debt to the tune of £50,000 and should have declared this to Jo. Ben had bought a drink for Tom and told him that the Casino would pay £50,000 into his account first thing on the following morning. It was much too good an offer to turn down. In return all he had to do was to let Ben know, face-to-face only, everything from the police computer relating to the Serious Crime Teams in Cambridgeshire and Essex. Tom knew that in this way Ben and his friends would always be one step ahead in drugs and vice, including the various gambling outlets.

He knew he could never get past the eagle eyes of Aisling or Kelly, so with help from a colleague in Newcastle, he could use a superior sort of iPad to get into the Police Network using a series of aliases that went undetected for a long time. He made sure his own team was not at risk in any way but clearly provided everything that was wanted. In both Cambridge and Essex there was an awareness of a leak, but even the techies could not track it down, though Tom suspected Kelly would manage it.

Today he was going to visit Ben at the Casino. There had been talk of a bonus for all that he provided, but he feared that might go by the board if he informed them of his suspension and demotion. He was therefore somewhat uneasy as parked the car and saw Ben outside waiting for him. They went in and unsurprisingly, the place was in darkness.

'You know, Tom, you should never go into a Casino. Those working here are genuine experts at relieving you of your hard-earned money, even at the Roulette Table. You've seen television and stage magicians and how clever they are. Well, trust me, the ladies and gentlemen here are no less so. The young woman, Tasmin, who oversees the Roulette table can get the ball to land wherever she is told through her earpiece. Coming here you never stood a chance, nor does anyone else. But now we have to take seriously your sheer stupidity in buying drugs in the street.'

'They weren't for me, Ben.'

'We know. That makes it even more stupid and for obvious reasons we're not pleased. We are gambling on you, Tom, to find a way and a job as soon as possible where you can provide us what we need, and of course, what you need. I rather suspect there'll be no lifeline thrown to you if you fail us. We have kept a full record of all that you have provided, and we know where what you have received is stored. Don't blow it all now, Tom. Look on it as a horserace at Newmarket. You've had a good start out of the stalls but have now fallen behind. It's not a long race, Tom, just a few furlongs and you haven't got much time to get back in front, but I recommend you to do so. Losing horses go to the knacker's yard.'

Ben walked away towards the door they had come in. A young woman outside gave him the eye as she passed by, making her way to the car park. On another day Ben might have shown interest, but today he had to be somewhere else. Pity though.

In her car the woman lay down across the two front seats and waited until she heard another car start and leave. She sneaked a quick look, and then sat up and began her own car.

In the office everyone was present for an afternoon cup of tea, brought from the tea shop opposite by the two Superintendents. This would be unknown elsewhere, and everyone was determined to make the most of it. As they were drinking and getting down to business they heard a single engine place fly over on its way into Crowfield. They all looked at Jo.'

'Yes, I think it will be Marie, and in her dress uniform. She's been attending a formal event on Salisbury Plain and she'll be over the moon tomorrow to put on the normal flying attire. So then good people, let's get up to date. Three of us went to London and found Ironsides where I thought he might be hiding and we handed him over to Special Branch. In all this he is small fry, just a nuisance who was convinced that Andie Bolam fancied him. Now let's hear from Esther and Ed about their discovery of who killed Penny Babworth.

Esther told the story of the interview, and of the wrong

diagnosis and the sense of neglect by the consultant and members of the team. It was the wrong diagnosis and a terrible response to it, leading to begging the doctor to end her life.

Esther's words were greeted with silence.

Eventually Jo spoke.

'As you know, a Chief Super can overturn any decision. If you feel unhappy about the fact that I have no intention of doing so, please express your feelings. No one will think the worse of you.'

'I found what Esther said very moving,' said Darcey, 'and I have no wish that your decision be changed, but I am concerned Dr Aberdeen and members of the team should have behaved so appallingly, and wonder whether a visit should be made to see them. They are the experts in motor neurone disease, not the GP, who had never seen it before.'

The others murmured their agreement.

'I fully understand what you are saying, Darcey, and I agree with you, but I don't want to stir up a nest of hornets in which the results of the post-mortem are demanded from MI5 and the role of Dr Ventner brought into the air again. Esther and I can discuss this again, but arranging an informal meeting with Dr Aberdeen, making it clear we will do nothing further, might be the best way forward.'

'If you want me to do that, Jo, then of course I will, though I think myself that Dame Joanne Enright might be the more appropriate person to do it.'

'I have often wondered what to do with that word, and now I know.'

The team laughed.

'But I'm quite serious about listening to any of you with disquiet about this.'

At that moment Belinda entered the room and handed Kelly a small box.

'Looks like I've missed the tea.'

'You'll survive,' said Darcey, intrigued by what her partner had been doing all day.

'Now we turn to things getting more serious by the day and which is going to require prompt attention. Today Steph and

Frankie attended a car which had been almost industrially cleaned with the faint possibility of DNA traces in the seat. They then did a risk assessment on the house of Nikki Hampton but also of Joe Worrall, but afterwards were followed as far as Huntingdon but used the rear camera effectively. Then later, a car went up and down the road at home focusing clearly on Alice's house. Caro got good photos and sent them. We know who the owners of the two cars are through ANPR. My intention is to move Alice and Katia completely out of the region for their safety, enabling Caro and Jodie to provide backup and protection for us. I am authorising Darcey also to be armed. Ed and I will do the face to face unarmed. Esther will head the op. Steph, Belinda and Frankie – be and do what the op head instructs. We leave here at 5:00am. Unless you have any questions, you can go now.

Frankie and Jodie, who needed Jo to drive them back to Saxmundham, realised there was business not requiring their presence and went outside for a walk up the road.

Kelly was doing something with the box given give her by Belinda and Belinda herself had remained seated as the others departed.

'It's not good news, ma'am (this was work). Tom collected belongings from the house and then drove them to the house of his parents in Kettering. So far – nothing. However, he then drove to Luton and parked outside a Casino, the Genting Casino. It was not yet open, but a man was waiting for him outside. Kelly has my photographs. They went inside. Do you remember when the team came over to us in the West Midlands, Andie had a box with a built-in directional microphone? Well, Kelly took it with her to MI5 and she and Kim refined it.'

'It was mainly Kim, said Kelly. 'She is extraordinary. I just made a couple of suggestions whereas she was a wizard.'

'It's being married to Sharon that does it,' said Jo.

'Anyway it's now even more powerful and can collect sound from quite a distance, so I thought I would try it out and Kelly has the results. Now I know it will almost certainly be inadmissible in evidence, but I think it tells the truth about Tom.

There was nothing at all about Bonnie.'

'What we have on Bonnie may be all there is to have, but I felt all along there was something in Tom that didn't ring true.'

'Oh dear, Jo,' said Kelly, who had earphones on, 'this is bad.'

'Tell me.'

Between them, Belinda and Kelly told all that had been recorded, with Jo sitting impassively.

'This is not for Professional Standards, but Serious Crime, and for Tom could hardly be worse, poor lad. As far as you know, Belinda, is he now back at Bonnie's?'

'Yes.'

'Can you please call and ask Darcey to come back? I shall need you to arrest him and for you both to take him and hand him him over to Serious Crime. I'll call them and ask where. Kelly, can that thing of yours be copied?'

'I've done that and I'll give the copy to Belinda.'

'They will need to find that iPad, and pick up Ben, whoever he is, from the Casino in Luton. Have you checked the photo yet?'

'Arthur Carson, with a record as long as your arm.'

'Hand it over to Serious Crime. This cannot be our case. I'll call them now and join you in the car, if I may.'

It was a not especially bright DI who answered the call at Serious Crime.

'Put me through to Superintendent Clifton, please.'

'Not possible. He's busy in a meeting.'

'Then get him out of the meeting, and tell him he will be glad to have done so, and that is order.'

'Who shall I say wants him?'

'Detective Chief Superintendent Enright.

Silence.

'Of course, ma'am.

Seconds later, Clifton's voice was heard.

'Yes, ma'am.'

'How was the meeting?'

'Is that where the silly twat said I was?'

'Please be careful about using parts of women's anatomy as a term of abuse.'

'Sorry ma'am.'

'Oh stop being such a dickhead. Oh dear, what have I said?'

Now they both laughed.

She now spelled out the story of Tom, what he had done in hindering the work of the police in serious crime, and his involvement with what was going on in the casino.

'Two of my team are bringing him in. Where do you want him?'

'Bring him to the Station and we'll take it from there.'

'I'm also sending you the tape and the photographs my genius of an officer obtained. He has been up before Professional Standards recently for buying drugs in the street though his defence was that they were for another person, and that seems to have some truth in it, but get the doc to check him over.'

'Thanks ma'am, and well done your team – again. And I'll send your best wishes to our friend the dickhead!.

'Superintendent! Such language. I'm shocked.'

Again they laughed.


Darcey was back.

'I'm sorry, Jo, but I had to get armed ready for morning, but it's out of sight.'

'That's ok, we're only arresting Tom.'

'Tom?'

'And then you and Belinda will take him into Cambridge and hand him over at the station to Serious Crime. Don't leave him until you're clear Serious Crime has him. Kelly has a tape and other stuff for you to give them. I fear we'll none of us be seeing him for a while.'

They went down the stairs, Belinda and Darcey in a marked car, Frankie and Jodie with Jo in her own vehicle. They drove up the road and stopped, and then Jo led Darcey and Belinda to the door. It was opened by Bonnie.

'Hello DI Miller,' said Jo, 'is DC Bridge in?'

'Tom,' she shouted.

Tom came to the door.

'Hello Tom,' said Jo. 'You're in a spot of bother though I

expect you already know that with so many trips to Luton.'

She stepped aside, allowing Belinda to come forward.

'Thomas Bridge, I am arresting you on suspicion of betraying confidential police information to organised criminals, taking bribes and concealing financial information from authorised police officials. You do not have to say anything. But, it may harm your defence if you do not mention when questioned something which you later rely on in court. Anything you do say may be given in evidence. Do you understand?'

'You're very good Belinda. I'm really sorry I won't get the chance to work with you and Darcey. Do you want to cuff me?'

'You know the rules, Tom,' said Jo.

'Yes, of course,' and then *sotto voce,* 'Jo, take good care of Bonnie and thank you for what you've already done for her. Thank you, too for giving me the privilege of working with you.'

'If only you had told me about your gambling, Tom.'

'I know. I guess I shall now have some time to think about that "if only".

'One other thing, Tom, Serious Crime will come tomorrow and completely dismantle Bonnie's house and your old house looking for the iPad Pro you did everything on. I hate to say it, but to them you're small fry and it's the organised crime group you serviced they want. It will do you no harm and possibly a great deal of good to provide that.'

Tom thought for a while and then turned towards Bonnie.

'Bonnie, could you get me my iPad from inside the middle pillow on my side of the bed, please?'

'They would have found it there, you know, but this will be the best way forward for you.'

Darcey received it from Bonnie and Belinda led him to the car, putting him in the back and getting in alongside him.

'They're bound to come and see you, Bonnie, though you can handle them. But between you and me, did you know about this?'

'Nothing at all. He has sometimes looked anxious, but I assumed it was because of obtaining drugs.'

Jo stood there in silence.

'They weren't for you, were they? You've thrown away your

career and we've lost your skills because you have defended someone else. That's right, isn't it?'

'Life gets complicated, Jo. You know that, but of course I should have known better than to hide this from you of all people, of all detectives. I knew you would find out before anyone else, and I knew that you of all people had the experience to recognise that I haven't even tried weed, let alone the harder drugs Tom was getting for me.'

'So who were they for, Bonnie?'

'My dad has Primary Progressive Multiple Sclerosis, which is the minority version of the illness and the worst. There are very few periods of remission and he is in a great deal of pain much of the time. The NHS analgesia doesn't help and the only thing that does is diamorphine, heroin to you and me.'

'Bonnie my darling, I want you to feel free as often as you need to be there for and with your dad. I cancel your drugs rehabilitation course and tomorrow you should go to see your mum and dad and stay as long as you need. By the time you get back to work I will have cleared everything with Professional Standards and the Chief Constable, if need be. I would like to have you as a DCI again because I think that's where you've said you were happiest and I think they will insist on some demotion.'

'You will be brilliantly served by Esther. Oh, Jo, if only I was gay, I would give you a big kiss.

Jo grinned.

'Give me a hug instead and keep me informed of your dad's condition.'

'I will.'

They hugged.

Jo said little in the car as they drove back to Saxmundham. She knew she ought to devote most of the evening to Marie, but she had to arrange for Alice and Katia to leave the village for what she hoped would be a short while, so she called her dad as she drove.

'Hi there. Are you on your way?'

'Yes.'

'Good. Marie seems very down and needs some of your TLC.'

'Dad, I need you and mum to do so something for me. I need you to go home, to Norwich, this evening, and to take Alice and Katia with you, and to look after them for a day or two. The next 48 hours are those in which they will be at the greatest risk here.'

'Do they know?'

'Not yet, but I'm going to get Jodie to call Caro and let them know, and to tell them it comes from me.'

'Of course we will, darling. Now get home.'

Jo looked across at Jodie who was already dialling Caro.

By the time they got home, Jo's mum and dad were loading the car with their own stuff and that of Alice and Katia. Frankie said she would move in for the night with Caro and Jodie in Alice's house and go straight to bed, and Caro and Jodie tossed coins to decide who would be on watch first because although Alice and Katia would be gone, their house might still be vulnerable. The three of them knew they would need to leave with Jo at 4:00am.

Jo said to Alice, 'You'll be safe with mum and dad. This might soon be over, all 36 years of it.'

Both Alice and Katia gave Jo a hug.

Marie had been crying and was clearly very low. Jo came to her on the sofa and put her arms around her, allowing more tears to flow. Eventually Marie looked up at Jo.

'Ten years', said Marie. 'David got ten years, Jo. It was terrible and I felt so angry with the court and the silly palaver that goes on in the military, and not least the ridiculous rules and procedures that I have to follow. That's not what I signed up for. I wanted to fly big aeroplanes as my dad did, not put myself into a position where people might want to kill me, or even the people I trusted planning to hand me over to an enemy. Well, I'm done with it all now and the time has come to stop. Tomorrow I've got to complete the training of a man called Bertie, whom I know well and very much like, so he can become the new First Officer. He's due to fly me to Iceland and back and I am to be his examiner.'

'Yes, but it's well known that you are a brilliant trainer. Surely you can ask to concentrate on that and avoid everything else?'

'I've been giving a lot of thought to it, and I want us to have another baby.'

'We know what it's going to involve so let's get in touch with Addenbrookes as soon as possible and meet up with the team there.'

## 25

Odd though it seemed to Caro and Jodie who were completely unused to such things, the briefing took place over breakfast in Leicester Forest Service Station on the M1. The others laughed at them.

'It's just one of Jo's tactics. She likes to leave the briefing until as late as possible and to fool anyone who might want to know what's going on, by just having breakfast,' said Steph.

'Well, it's fooled me,' said Caro. 'Armed police are quite used to getting going at a ridiculously early hour, but group breakfast en route to an op is completely new.'

'Ed and myself, in plain clothes will approach the house and ask to speak to Worrall. He can hardly refuse being an ex cop, but it seems likely that he has a way of alerting Nikki Hampton, who will want to come. Frankie and Steph will watch for any movement from her house and inform the rest of you, all of whom will be in vests. If she and any others come, Jodie, Caro and Darcey will take up their place outside the house. Belinda will be with Esther and co-ordinate the whole. You take instructions only from Esther, and the three armed members will receive any authority to use the firearms from Esther.'

They drove into Nottingham and took their positions. At 8:45 Jo and Ed walked to Worrall's house and rang the bell. The door was opened by an old man.

'Are you former detective Joe Worrall?'

'Who's asking?'

'Detective Chief Superintendent Enright and Detective Chief

Inspector Secker of the Sensitive Case Unit in Suffolk.'

'You're a long way from home. Are you sure you're allowed to be here?'

'May we come in?'

'Alright.'

They followed him into his living room.

'So what do you want?'

'I imagine the name of Andie Bolam will ring a bell with you?'

'Two bells. She came to see me poking her journalist's nose where it wasn't wanted and I sent her packing. I then saw that some dyke must have picked her up at a club and killed her. Is that the one you're referring to?'

'When you say she was poking her nose in where it wasn't wanted, what are you referring to?'

'She was muck-raking, trying to make a name for herself, I imagine.'

'But did she come asking about something specific?'

'I think she didn't know what she was asking about?'

'But coming to see you here in Nottingham was hardly an accident. She must have had some reason to speak to you in particular and I discovered her name in the police archive where she had been looking at papers to do with the murder 36 years ago of your infant nephew and niece. Was that the reason she came, to talk about that notorious case?'

'She didn't stay long enough to tell me as I threw her out.'

'You were uncle to the two children.'

Yes, until that murdering little bastard took them away from us.'

'It must have terrible.'

'Even worse than you could possibly imagine.'

'Nikki is your only surviving niece.'

'She's a good girl even if a bit rough on the edges. She's done well for herself,'

'Didn't want to follow her uncle into the Force?

'Not her style.'

'Let's go back 36 years, Joe.'

'I'd rather not, if you don't mind. It's still very upsetting.'

'Yes, I can imagine, but it is to there that we must go.'

'Then I want Nikki with me.'

He stood and went to pick up his mobile and said little but clearly enough.

'She's coming straight round.'

'It'll be nice to meet her,' said Ed.

'Did your guv'nor back then know you were the uncle of the two children?'

'Yes, of course. But he knew I could still work on the case without favour.'

'Tell me about Dr Melvyn Harmer,' said Jo.

'That's a name I haven't heard in a long while. He was pathologist at the hospital and he, poor soul, had to do the post-mortems on the babies.'

'Why was that?' asked Ed. 'Shouldn't it have been either a Home Office pathologist or a paediatric pathologist?'

'The guv'nor wanted to spare everyone as far as possible by not prolonging, so we got on with it.'

'We now know that Dr Harmer's post-mortem report to the court contained a major error which, if it is so, could not possibly have led to the conviction of murder against the ten-year old Ella Epton,' said Jo.

'That's simply ridiculous,' said a woman's voice coming through the door. It was Nikki. 'She was found guilty because all the evidence was there and she admitted it in court. I was there and I heard her.'

'How old you were you?'

'16'.

'And did you know that in the Audi you left in Leicester, despite the industrial cleaner treatment, DNA was still found in the creases of both front seats?'

'You're lying!'

'Nor am I lying about pictures of you on CCTV on the A14 and coming into Cambridge, parking near and then entering the AAA club where you approached Andie. This came after you had called Maureen Watson and found out from her where Andie could be found.

'You like attention, Nikki, you like to be the centre of everyone's concern, and I'm sure that at one time you were a good-looking girl, but you knew, as I do, and every other woman does, that Andie was in a totally different league in terms of beauty and talent, and you couldn't stand that. But you had something else to protect, didn't you? And it wasn't the good name of your uncle Joe, the poor copper involved in the tragic case of the murder of your two cousins. You had to prevent Andie, who had an amazing capacity for putting two and two together, far more than many in my business, from realising the truth about the murders 36 years ago. So you sent her a message via Maureen saying you had vital information for her and that you'd meet her in the club and pick her up outside afterwards. And that is what you did, and knowing from Maureen that she was staying in Waterbeach you drove her there, or almost there. You stopped just past the railways station and on that piece of waste ground you used a knife to uglify her, twice across each side of her face and then across her breasts, before slitting her throat. Her beauty had taunted you and so you wished to destroy it.'

'You talking absolute crap, bitch.'

'But this was not the first time, was it, that your place as the star of the show, as the centre of attention, was withheld from you. Peter and Anna, as little children do, became the talk of the family, taking from you the attention you believed was yours. Framing Ella was easy because you and everyone else knew she was involved in horrific sexual acts with her parents. To you all, I would suggest, she was little better than scum, best got rid of. So it was, Nikki, that you drowned your cousins and began the conspiracy against Ella, not the least facilitated by you, Joe, working when you should not have been under any circumstances. Paying the pathologist off was the least of your difficulties.'

'Nikki Hampton, I am arresting you for the murders of Anna and Peter Worrall, and Andrea Bolam,' said Ed. 'You do not have to say anything. But it may harm your defence if you do not mention when questioned something which you later rely on in court. Anything you do say may be given in evidence. Do you understand?'

Before she could speak, Ed continued, 'Joseph Worrall, I am arresting you for perversion of the course of justice and complicity in the murders of Anna and Peter Worrall. You do not have to say anything. But it may harm your defence if you do not mention when questioned something which you later rely on in court. Anything you do say may be given in evidence. Do you understand?'

Nikki suddenly standing, produced a knife.

'I can see off cretins like you two and I've done so before, so hand over your radios and mobiles or your pretty faces will end up like that cow when you're in the morgue.'

'Behind her and wholly unknown to her was Darcey. She had followed her in and stayed in the hallway listening, choosing her time.

'C'mon Nikki, let's get going. I've a car waiting and I'll soon get you away.'

Nikki turned, confused, wondering who this woman was.'

'You two stay where you are or I will shoot,' Darcey said, showing them her gun. 'Nikki, c'mon.' Darcey pushed her into the hall and towards the door which she opened and fell into the hands of a number of police officers, two of them armed. In seconds she lost hold of her knife and instead was pushed, handcuffed, into the rear seat of a marked police car. Darcey returned as Ed handcuffed Joe and prepared to take him out.

'I hope that wasn't over the top, ma'am,' said Darcey to Jo.

'Of course it was my darling, but had to be to utterly confuse her, and you succeeded.'

'When did you realise that Nikki had also killed the children?'

'When I saw what the killer had done to Andie it began to dawn on me that it was almost certainly a woman who hated Andie's beauty and the fact that it made her the centre of attention wherever she was. She had that effect on me the very first time I saw her at a Press Conference in Bury St Edmunds I was utterly spell-bound and nearly accepted her invitation to spend the night with her. Part of me still wishes I had, but you needn't feel obliged to mention it to Marie.'

'Only if you don't mention to Belinda that I would give anything to spend lots of nights with you.'

'Darcey, my darling, I hope your radio is turned off. Also, I'm far from sure it's the sort of thing you should say to your senior officer.'

'Isn't is what you must have said to Ellie, your senior officer, when you first got together?'

'Detective Inspector, you are outrageous. How dare you speak the truth to me? Darcey, you know how much I love you and so does Belinda and you her. I can see it when you look in each other's eyes. Never risk that love for what may prove to be an illusion.

'What is not an illusion is the fact that today we have solved a 36 year old murder and will free two lovely people from the living hell in which they have lived. And at last a piece of nastiness will soon be in prison for the rest of life, I hope, and a copper still bent after all this time.'

'What about the pathologist?'

'I'll get Ed to pick him up with Steph. It's his turn to hear all about the sex life of a former catholic priest.'

'You call me outrageous but I almost blushed when she was talking to me.'

'I know, but I'm so happy for them. I can't know what he was like as a priest but Fergal is a truly smashing man, and they are happy together.'

They walked outside and met with Esther.

'I think Caro and Jodie should travel with her – just in case, though we should travel together.'

'Good idea. I want to send Ed and Steph to pick up Melvyn Harmer. He was almost as guilty as the other two in perverting the course of justice. Perhaps he'll tell us the nature of his reward.'

'Jo. Very well done.'

'It was a team effort, but if it was primarily about serving justice, I truly believe that what you did with Dr Ventner is at the top. I only caught nasty criminals; what you did was much more important.

'No, Jo. You have liberated captives. Nothing can be higher.

Ed and Steph went to pick up the retired pathologist. Jo traveled alone. This meant that she could use the car phone to call Norwich.

'Hi dad. Are your holiday making pair awake yet?'

'They're up, but whether awake, I'm not at all sure. However, I will bring Alice.'

'Hi Jo. What a wonderful mum and dad you have.'

'Hey don't let them hear you say that or they'll become unbearable. Anyway my darling, let me tell you something. The whole team is in Nottingham, and this morning we have arrested someone for the murder of Anna and Peter Worrall and someone else with perverting the course of justice for suppressing the knowledge of what happened. We have arrested the pathologist who claimed you had done it when he knew it could not have been so. Independent checking of the photograph of the injuries has revealed that you could not have done it. There was a conspiracy to make out that you were responsible and again and again they went over the formula you were taught to confess to the crime. You are totally innocent though this will have to ratified in the Court of Appeal. But in all my days in the Police Force, this is by far the best.'

'I can't stop crying, Jo, and Katia and I will never be able to thank you enough for what you have done.'

'Unfortunately, the person we have arrested also will stand trial for the murder of Andie, and there may be others. She will have to be assessed by a forensic pathologist. I'm not a psychiatrist, but I suspect she has mental difficulties that precede even her murder of the Worrall children. Anyway, stay in Norwich if you wish in the lap of luxury or return when you're ready. There may some tv and press interest when you get back but this time you won't need to move and they'll be on your side.

'It's nice to see the photo of you and Marie here, but Jo, can there ever have been a photo to match the one of you and Ellie. She was stunning and you look so wonderfully happy together.'

'Thanks, Alice.'

Life, decided Jo, was complicated even when it seemed plain sailing, and although she said nothing to anyone, after all this time she still cried for Ellie and would have given anything to have her back. At one time she had thought there might be ambivalence in her thinking, but now she knew better, and this had been very much worse when not so long ago, Marie had left her for a man, albeit a religious fruit cake, even if a clever doctor. She didn't stick it out and returned, but what if he hadn't been like that, if he had taken her to his bed? What then? It all made Jo feel uneasy, and now Marie was wanting a baby. Jo had gone along with her talking about it but was not all sureif it was what she herself wanted and wondered whether there was sufficient stability in their life. Was Marie simply seeking a way out of the RAF? But having a baby simply to get out of her work was not the right reason for bringing a new life into the world. Besides which, and Jo could hardly bring herself to face it, there was another person, thoughts of whom she kept having to turn away, but constantly returned.

Nikki Hampon was on her way to Cambridge, her uncle and the former pathologist were being taken to Nottingham Police Station, where they would be interviewed by Esther and Belinda, and then hopefully Esther would apply to the CPS and they could be charged and taken to the magistrates, though both, being of no immediate danger to anyone, would most likely be bailed to appear in the Crown Court within a week. The niece was a different matter altogether and would be regarded as a very dangerous prisoner. The magistrates would be advised that she would need to see a Forensic Psychiatrist and that they should remand her not in the women's prison in Peterborough, but in Rampton Secure Hospital.

Word about the DNA found in the seats of the car came to Jo as she followed the van down the motorway.

'It's confirmation, Jo,' said Kelly. The DNA within the passenger seat has a 99.9% probability match with that of Andie, and that in the driver's seat shows a 99.9% probability match with that sample of Nikki Hampton taken when she was arrested last time. But while you've all been out gallivanting, one of us here has been gathering evidence.'

'Go on, my lovely.'

'Mr Eddie Marsh who lives in Waterbeach, has cameras positioned in his garden to spot foxes and deer and anything else. He admits that he's not as assiduous in checking them as he should be and it was only this morning when he checked one of them he noticed it had photographed a car which stopped by the waste ground behind the railway station, a camera he keeps there because he sometimes has seen otters. But this is not an otter, but a car driven by a woman and both are clearly shown, and the dress worn by the woman in the photograph is identical to that worn by Nikki Hampton in the AAA Club.'

'How did he know to get in touch with you?'

'He didn't, but rang the Cambridge Police and they diverted him to us.'

'Did he come to you?'

'No, I went to him. I told him he would be visited by a pretty young lady to make a statement, and he liked that idea.'

'Kelly, what can I say? That's superb.'


Jo also called Marie, just to check that she had collected the children from school, Dianne having taken them in the morning.

'Have you done what you set out to do?' asked Marie.

'Yes. We have shown that Alice was not a child murderer and that now she is free to live any life she chooses without that horrendous crime hanging over her.'

'Was I the only one who didn't know? Didn't you think that with that possibility still in place you might have said something to me before you let Josie and Ollie be in her care so much?'

'Marie, we both inhabit worlds in which the need for confidentiality and secrecy are paramount, are demanded. I have always thought we understood that, and that there are therefore things that we can't talk about, and are often glad not to have to talk about.'

'Risking our children when you didn't and couldn't know the truth of Alice's past is a different matter as far as I'm concerned.'

The phone went dead.

Not for the first time Jo wondered why there seemed to be two Maries. Was it what was called bipolar disorder or even something on the spectrum of schizophrenia? She had always known that Marie could switch between her Jekyll and Hyde personalities in a flash. As an aircraft pilot she was outstanding and had proved herself capable of dealing with any situation however dire. It was on the ground that problems seemed to appear though what would happen if they arose at 40,000 ft?

Unsurprisingly, Hampton knew how to manipulate the system following her arrest. She first demanded her own brief from Nottingham who said he couldn't attend until the day after tomorrow and then she asked for a full medical examination. The custody sergeant assured her that a doctor would come, but that because the solicitor she had requested could nor come for 36 hours, she would be supplied with a duty solicitor after the doctor had been.'

'But PACE says ...' she began.

'... does not allow you to come up with a variety of delaying tactics, and it also allows the Chief Superintendent to extend the time for interview, and the magistrates can extend it even longer. If the interviewing officers decide they wish to begin this evening they can do so unless the doctor says you are not fit, which I can tell you now, you are. By the way, do you wish a male or female solicitor?'

'Piss off.'

She was presented by Jo and Esther with the evidence relating to the murder of Andie, with Esther doing almost all the questioning. For most of the time she replied "No Comment" and she manifested considerable calm.

'Being at the centre here and now of such attention must be quite exhilarating for you, Nikki,' said Jo. 'Everything revolving around you, those of us in the room with you, not to mention those watching and listening from the audio-visual room. It's all about you, which must feel great.'

Nikki was glaring at Jo.

'You won't be as much a star in Rampton for the rest of your life, though all small child killers do receive a measure of special attention, but of the sort you wouldn't necessarily wish. As you have heard from Superintendent Heywood we already have enough for the CPS to allow us to charge you with murder. So, before we finish for the night, and you spend the first of many to come in a locked cell, allow me to offer you some counsel. You were manipulated possibly by outside forces, including your uncle who, by the way has indicated that he is going to plead guilty and the pathologist likewise, both of whom are thereby hoping to escape prison, but also by something worryingly dark inside you. The court will be obliged to ask that you see a forensic psychiatrist. Those interviews whilst on remand could make a deal difference to the outcome of the case and to how long or short your time in jail is. Without that possibility it will be life without the hope of parole. As people state these days: just saying.'

Before leaving, Jo made two phone calls. The first was to her own and Marie's answerphone. The message simply said she would have to stay over in Cambridge because she was too tired to drive home safely, and please could she arrange for Dianne to take the children to school.

The second was a to a Cambridge number.

'Hello. This is Dame Alison Kitchen. May I come?'

## 26

Jo rose early as usual, planted a kiss, washed and got dressed. She had several important phone calls to make or texts to send before returning to Hampton in the Interview Room. Her team answered to four Chief Constables, and she wanted the news of their important breakthroughs communicated to them as soon as possible. Texts might do for three, but the Suffolk CC needed to hear from her lips about the fact that a 36 years old cold case had been solved, and asking permission to apply to the Criminal Cases Review Commission which could take the case to the Appeal Court. Only then could the original sentence be quashed, but with Hampton in custody and the witness of her uncle and the pathologist, that should not take too long, or at least she hoped so. There was also a call to be made to the Nottingham Chief Constable who would no doubt draw the Press to hear how well he had done!

Her other call was to Marie who was on her way to the aerodrome and then on to work.

'I am so sorry about hanging up on you last night, more sorry than I can say, and I didn't congratulate you on what was clearly something quite wonderful. You always have been and will continue to be streets ahead of me in every way. You have given Alice and Katia a chance to live.'

'And are you giving Bertie his flying test today?'

'No, he took me to Iceland yesterday - not the shop by the way, though today he has to do some theory, but not with me.'

'So what are you doing?'

'I'm flying to Durham, to HMP Frankland, to visit Nathan and taking Josie with me. Since his mum died he's had no one to visit him, and he wrote asking me to come.'

Jo knew at once there was no chance this could be true.

'I won't ask you to give him my best wishes, as I put him away.'

'I seem to remember you did that to me as well. Where did you stay the night?'

'With Judith at her vicarage, though I don't think she'll be there much longer. She's looking to leave the Church.'

'Jo, did you sleep with her?'

'No. I know I disappointed her but I was so tired.'

'Poor Judith. She is such a lovely person but please try to persuade her to remain in the Church. That funeral she did for us was wonderful. And what are you doing today?

'Hopefully completing my murders and then coming home for a long sleep. Have a safe journey.'

Mysteriously, the solicitor from Nottingham had managed to get there a day early after all, and when all the formalities prior to the interview had been done, it was he who began.

'I want to say straight away that dragging my client away from Nottingham is unacceptable especially as you claim two of the offences were committed there.'

'Well, in which case, I want to thank you, Mr Abell,' said Esther, 'for dragging yourself all the way from Nottingham, especially as just last night you indicated you couldn't get here until tomorrow. That exhibits a genuine sense of duty.'

'And before we get going,' added Jo, 'I would like to inform Ms Hampton that between seven and eight o'clock this morning two vehicles registered in her name were picked up and the occupants of each arrested, one of which has been filmed regularly outside the home of the person once accused of the murders of little Anna and Peter, your cousins. Three of the four men have made statements admitting that they work for Ms Hampton but denying that they had any part in her murder of Andie Bolam, other than collect her Ms Hampton from the Audi garage where she was leaving the car, and subjecting it to an industrial clean though they failed her by being less than efficient. The fourth man was taken to hospital following an attempt to escape.'

'Last night the Chief Superintendent expressed her thoughts, Nikki. I wonder whether you have considered them?'

'What was that, Nikki?' asked the solicitor.

Jo began to speak, 'Our evidence that you drowned the two children is already considerable and it is our intention to question more of those still alive who, knowing that we know what actually took place, will offer testimony to a jury. I believe we already have enough evidence to convict you as it is, but strangely enough I am concerned not just with finding you guilty, but with trying to understand why it happened and why all that has followed it has happened right up to the barbaric murder of that extraordinarily beautiful woman Andie Bolam. You knew she was on to you for what you did back then and you wished to stop her, but her real offence in your eyes was her beauty and that she was at the centre of everyone's world and not you. You needn't have killed for her attempts at investigation because she lacked the resources we take for granted – it was her beauty you couldn't stand.

'Your hope, as I said last night, lies in a forensic psychiatrist who can demonstrate to the court that all you have done results from forces working in you unconsciously from the distant past. With treatment you may be out long before you would be otherwise.'

'May I consult my client for a little while?'

'You know PACE, Mr Abell, so of course you can,' said Esther. 'Recording terminated. Shall we say ten minutes?'

Esther and Jo left the room and outside in the corridor unexpectedly found Kelly clutching a file of papers.

'These came through this morning, boss,' she said, thrusting them into Jo's hand. 'I think they might be important. They're the medical records of Nikki Hampton, née Worrall.'

Jo opened the file.

'You're quite right, Kelly. They could hardly be more important,' and she passed them to Esther.

'Blimey.'

'Yes, I know. I'm desperate for a wee and then a drink. Keep the file close to yourself and I'll join you in the canteen. Kelly, why don't you go into the AV Room with the others?'

'Ok, boss.'

Fortified with two sips of canteen tea, Jo, together with Esther returned to the Interview Room. As they sat down, Jo said to the constable on duty if he would please remove Ms Hampton's handcuff anchoring her to the desk.

'Are you sure ma'am?'

'Constable, if she makes a run for it, this building is so complicated she'll never find her way out. I have enough difficulty and I come here regularly.'

Mr Abell indicated he wished to speak, but Esther said there had been a major development and that the Chief Superintendent would speak about it first.

'Thank you Superintendent, and thank you Ms Hampton and Mr Abell. Nikki, when you were fourteen you had an abortion, your pregnancy having come about because of rape when you were thirteen. Please will you tell us the perpetrator of this terrible crime against you and for which he was never punished?'

'As you obviously know, there's no point in not telling you. It was Doug Pedley, the man who lived with Beatty Epton, Ella's mother. He was a junkie who sold to others and a pimp, setting up sex parties involving Beatty and the young Ella. He was a horrible man.'

'Yes, he was, but something he did to you in the course of being raped meant that you could never have children. When you drowned the two children and in the course of it blamed it on Ella, no one with an ounce of compassion could not see that these things were related in your traumatised mind. Your uncle Joe could defend you by lie after lie, and you got away with it.

'You might wonder, whether now or in the future, why I, and I think my team, have compassion and understanding for you, even in the face of the terrible murder of Andie and some other things it is claimed you did. The answer is that I feel for that small girl raped by that bastard, your life to come now blighted by him, and what it must have done to your mind. And I would say that everything that has followed goes back to that. A forensic psychiatrist will, I know, agree totally, and he represents your very best hope of a release from prison leaving you at least some of your life left.

'I'm not here to pursue vengeance, but to do my very best, and the more I have come to know about you, the more I've wanted to do my best. The way ahead is going to be hard. I would only say that when you're inside, try and stay completely clear of the sub-culture of drugs, and who knows, one day I might come and spoil your life by visiting you.'

'Have you anything you wish to ask or say, Ms Hampton?'

'Only what I've often said: all coppers are bastards, but I've now met an exception.'

'I now will make application to the CPS', said Esther, ' to charge you with three accounts of murder. This afternoon you will be taken to the magistrates court and they will remand you in custody.'

'As I said: All coppers are bastards.'

They laughed.

After many years of experience, Jo could spot a lie a mile off and she knew that Marie had lied to her, so it wasn't exactly a surprise when Marie called her from Durham after having done her visit to say that she was going to have a little holiday with Josie staying with Paddy and Rachel, the friends they had met in a café in Durham, near the Cathedral, and who had come to their wedding.

'Oh, how lovely,' said Jo, 'please give them my love and am I to assume that Dianne is collecting Ollie.'

Yes, until Alice returns.'

'And how was Nathan?'

'Overjoyed to see Josie, especially when she called him "dad". And they've got him assisting the Medical Officer which is so good for his confidence.'

'Ok, keep me in touch with your movements. I've got a huge amount of paperwork but I can mostly do it from home.'

'Well, make sure you get lots of sleep.'

On the following morning, a letter arrived for Marie from the United States Air Force. Jo did not open it, not least because she thought she knew what it contained. She wasn't surprised. Ever since Marie had left her for the cretinous evangelical doctor, she had known the reconciliation would not last.

Jo was well aware, from many police interviews over the years, that the primary source of lies in our society was adultery. And now she had herself told such a lie, something she would once never have done. She had slept with Judith and made love with her long into the night. At one moment she had cried in Judith's arms, cried for so much – for Ellie, as always, and with no diminishment of feeling, but also for Andie, for Dani, whom she longed for more and more, for her daughter and son, Josie and Ollie, and for herself, and wonderfully, Judith could give her the healing balm every part of her body longed for.

She had lied to Marie, and Marie had lied to her. Perhaps these were small things, part of what can happen in a marriage or relationship after a certain amount of time, but she wasn't convinced – they were not what might be called fibs, but a sign of something more than that, as was the way they both gave themselves wholly to work in the way they did, whereby they saw less and less of each other. Hadn't Alice seen in the two photographs at her parents' house, one of her with Marie, and the other with Ellie, and like everyone else who ever saw them, she saw the world of difference between Jo in the one and Jo in the other. And then Marie was talking about wanting a baby, and how many couples had hoped that something new – a house or a baby – could save a marriage that was in trouble?

When Marie returned from Durham and opened the USAF letter, she told Jo that she had been offered a job as a test pilot based in the 412th Test Wing at Edwards Base in Southern California, with the rank of Major. The RAF were willing to let her go.

'I think we both know that ever since I left and returned, things have been completely different and I won't get this chance again.'

'What about Josie and Ollie? She is yours and Nathan's, and Ollie has all your genes and none of mine?

'What has that to do with anything? They are both yours and mine and I want to ask you if you would be willing to allow them to live with you as devoted brother and sister. To split them would be so cruel, and you might bring them over for a holiday to California.

'And do we get a divorce?'

The Chief Constable of Suffolk had no intention of keeping quiet about a wonder that had taken place in his area and brought about by *his* detectives, which as the team all knew was pushing truth to the edge. Even before the case had made the Court of Appeal he arranged for his Press Team to make it a huge celebration of the work of the Force in Suffolk, though he did allow Jo prominence in the Press Conference. Alice and Katia had more than the fifteen minutes of fame Andy Warhol allowed, but no one begrudged them that. Assuming she must receive huge sums in compensation, Alice received 12 proposals of marriage, all of which went into the winter fire.

In Nottingham, Jo Worrall and the former pathologist Dr Evan Fulwood, both in their mid-70s, expected suspended sentences, and were therefore stunned when the judge sentenced both to eight years in prison. Fulwood admitted that as well as being intimidated he had also also received a considerable bribe to lie about the marks on the necks. No one in Nottingham either wept for them nor complained that the sentences were too long. And the happiest man in the city was Mr Angus Hart, who got his Audi back in one piece and remarkably clean.

Almost four months went by before Nikki Hampton stood trial for the three murders. Key evidence was given by Detective Chief Inspector Ed Secker on the prosecution side, and unremarkably the jury returned three verdicts of murder. The judge ordered her to be held in Rampton Special Hospital until psychiatric reports would allow sentencing.

The report by the Forensic Psychiatrist was detailed and clear, setting out in full Nikki's horror story as a child and the rape by Doug Pedley, the man she mistakenly thought was Ella's father and for which, in revenge, she blamed Ella for the death of the children, at much the same time that she was made to have an abortion. The murder of Andie was done for two reasons. The first to protect the great lie of 36 years ago which Nikki feared was about to be exposed, the second because Nikki could not stand Andie's beauty making her the centre of attention, when she wished that for herself. As Jo listened, she was tempted to ask for a fee, as all the psychiatrist had done was to repeat what Jo had already worked out. There was a moment as Nikki was led away, when she turned to Jo in the court's well, gave a little wave to her and smiled, which Jo returned. At that moment she almost despised herself for liking so much this woman who had done so much damage and caused horrendous hurt to those nearest to her.

Jo and Frankie attended court when Nikki was appearing by video link for sentencing. The judge said all that Jo hoped she would and indicated that the sentence was a life sentence but that parole could be considered when the psychotherapists and psychiatrists working with Nikki were satisfied she would cause no further harm to anyone.

As people left the court, Jo told Frankie to wait outside for her, and remained seated for a while, and then said aloud, 'Andie, dearest darling, I hope you approve, and if not, please forgive me'.

She went out of the court into the car park and set off for home, calling in to drop Frankie at her home and at the police station to give Kelly and anyone else who was in, the details of the sentencing. It was a lovely thought that she would be home in good time, allowing them time to think what they might like to do in the forthcoming Easter school holidays.

She called home on the car phone.

'I've just got back with the children, and we're having cakes and drinks.'

'You know you're a terrible influence on them.'

'I love them and they're beginning to love me a little, I think, but most of all, dear Jo, I love you more than I know how to say.'
'And I love you too.'

Printed in Great Britain
by Amazon